HERBIE BRENNAN

THE
SECRET
PROPHECY

BALZER + BRAY
An Imprint of HarperCollins*Publishers*

With great affection for Sebastian,
who also wrote a book with "secret" in the title

Balzer + Bray is an imprint of HarperCollins Publishers.

The Secret Prophecy
Copyright © 2012 by Herbie Brennan
All rights reserved. Printed in the United States of America.
No part of this book may be used or reproduced in any manner
whatsoever without written permission except in the case of brief
quotations embodied in critical articles and reviews. For information
address HarperCollins Children's Books, a division of
HarperCollins Publishers, 10 East 53rd Street,
New York, NY 10022.
www.harpercollinschildrens.com

Library of Congress Cataloging-in-Publication Data is available.
ISBN 978-0-06-207180-4

Typography by Carla Weise
12 13 14 15 16   LP/RRDH   10 9 8 7 6 5 4 3 2 1
❖
First Edition

Blessed is he that readeth,
and they that hear the words
of this prophecy . . .
for the time is at hand.

REVELATION 1:3

The stairs were narrow, but Em was used to carrying the tray by now, so he managed not to spill the orange juice. He hadn't had his own breakfast yet—Dad came first these days—so the smell of the bacon was driving him nuts. Which made him hurry, but he *still* didn't spill the juice.

At the first landing, he came to the tricky bit. Directly ahead was the door to his parents' bedroom. Inside, his dad lay pale and sickly, but getting better by the day and doubtless ready to savage his breakfast. There were two eggs on the plate, alongside all the bacon. And a sausage. There was also the morning paper, folded so Em couldn't read the main headline. What he could read were a couple of paragraphs about a new strain of flu that had broken out in Nigeria. Scientists said it had mutated from a bird flu only found in vultures. The press loved that. They were calling it Death Flu, even though very few people had actually died and the Nigerian authorities were claiming it was totally contained.

Behind Em were three steps to a second landing where the staircase wound up to the attic that was Em's room, which was to say Edward Michael Goverton's room, aka the Swamp on account of the posters and the clutter and the sea of smelly socks.

Em gripped the tray firmly with both hands and used it to push the door. "Room service!" he called cheerfully. "Good morning, Dad. This morning we can offer bacon, two fried eggs sunny-side up, sausage with pork and apple filling, grilled tomato, mushrooms, and just the merest soupçon of baked beanies." Heart attack on a plate, but there was nothing wrong with his dad's heart: it was pneumonia that got him, a resistant strain until the doctors found the right antibiotic combination. But luckily he was recovering well. The doctors had seemed pleased.

His father was still asleep, which was odd. He was asleep on his back, facing the ceiling.

"Breakfast, Dad," Em said, aiming the words directly at an ear exposed by the duvet. "Wake up before I eat it for you."

But his father did not wake up. Em put the tray down on the bed and reached out to shake him by the shoulder. His father habitually slept in just pajama bottoms, so the shoulder was bare. As Em touched it, he discovered it was cold. Perhaps he'd been sleeping with it outside the covers; perhaps that was the reason the shoulder was cold. All the same, Em felt a little chilly himself.

Professor Ed Goverton was doing so well, Em thought. The doctors said he could get up for a while tonight, watch his favorite show on TV. Next week he could go out for short walks.

Em slid his hand down the shoulder onto his father's chest. The breathing was usually labored, but now he did not appear to be breathing at all. His body felt cold. Like meat.

Like dead meat.

Em jerked his hand away. He ran to the head of the stairs. "Mum!" he shouted wildly. "Muuuuum!!!"

There was no way they could get the coffin down the narrow staircase, so they lowered it from the window to the waiting hearse. It swung on canvas straps, and Em wondered how his father felt in the darkness inside the box, swinging like a pendulum.

Em was dressed in his Sunday suit, the one he hated, with a white shirt, black shoes, black socks, and, most importantly, a black tie. His mother had sewn a black band onto the arm of the jacket, muttering something about two weeks of mourning as if he was going to wear the suit after today. He watched as the undertakers removed the straps and lifted the coffin into the back of the hearse. There were several floral wreaths that had to go on top. The one his mother carried was the first.

Nearly all the lecturers were there, and some of them

were dressed in suits as well, although many wore the academic uniform of tweed jacket and slacks, and all had black ties. There was a large contingent of students, not all of them from history courses. Prof. Ed Goverton was a popular guy.

Em blinked. Prof. Ed Goverton *had been* a popular guy.

The undertakers closed the back of the hearse, and the driver started off at a walking pace. Em and his mother—she was dressed entirely in black and was heavily veiled—led the mourners. She didn't look at him and he didn't look at her, keeping his eyes focused on the back of the hearse. It was a short walk to the graveside— the cemetery lay right next to the campus and had, until a century ago, actually been administered by the university. Today it was the preferred final resting-place of faculty, at least those with tenure and long academic associations. Like his father.

Em should have felt sad. He loved his father. He would miss his father. But all he really felt was numb, and a little scared. What would his mother do now? She was a qualified teacher herself, but not at the university level, so even if she found a job after all these years, they would still have to leave their lodgings. Which was maybe a good thing, although he was certain that it wouldn't happen yet. The board would let them stay on for a while until his mother found her feet. He was certain of that. His own situation probably wouldn't change. He'd still be at school for some time.

He'd never seen a burial before. The open grave seemed terribly deep, as if they were worried about you climbing out. They'd lined it with some sort of fake grass cloth. There were loads of people already waiting. Most of them he didn't even recognize.

The priest said stuff about his father at the graveside, but for Em his voice faded in and out. He couldn't believe his father had known so many people Em didn't know, had never met. Important people, too. There was a black Mercedes with diplomatic plates parked on the main driveway. He couldn't concentrate on what the priest was saying. His mother had taken his hand, drawing him close to her. He could feel her body shaking and knew this was because she was crying. They'd had their troubles, his mother and his dad, mainly because of his mother's problems; but there was no doubt they'd loved each other. Em wanted to comfort her but didn't know how.

He found himself looking from face to face among the mourners standing around the grave. There was Uncle Harold, of course, his mother's brother, and Tom Peterson, his father's closest friend on the university staff. But why did he know so few of the others? There was a pretty girl who couldn't have been more than a year older than Em himself. Who was she? There was an old man in a wheelchair. Who was he? There was a gaunt woman in black, veiled like his mother, who sniffled into a tiny handkerchief. There was a muscular man in a well-tailored suit and dark glasses. Who were they?

Em realized suddenly that the priest had stopped speaking and the undertakers were lowering the coffin into the grave. The canvas straps refused to slide freely so that the coffin went down in little jerks, but nobody seemed to care. It reached the bottom eventually, and the men dragged the straps back up. A sober professional approached Em's mother with an open ornamental box. It took Em a moment to realize that it contained soil. His mother released his hand and took some earth from the box. She stepped forward and tossed it down onto the coffin. The earth must have been a little damp, for it made a dull sound as it struck.

The man with the box was standing in front of Em now. "Go on," Em's mother whispered.

Em took a sprinkling of earth between his thumb and forefingers and tossed it into the grave. He could no longer see properly because his eyes were swimming with tears. He stepped back from the graveside and wiped them clear with the back of his hand. The man in the suit and dark glasses was turning away and pushing through the mourners. As he moved past the gaunt woman, his coat pulled open and Em caught the merest glimpse of a handgun in a shoulder holster tucked beneath his left arm. Then the coat fell back again, and Em's eyes refilled with tears.

It was like watching a scene underwater. The man shouldered his way through the mourners, headed in the direction of the parked Mercedes. The windows were tinted, so it was impossible to see in. As the man reached the car, a back window slid down and he leaned forward to speak briefly to someone inside. Then he stood back, the window closed again, and the car drove off. The man in the dark glasses climbed into a more modest car parked a little way beyond. He sat quite still behind the wheel for a moment, turned briefly to look in Em's direction, and then he too drove off.

Em wondered if he really was carrying a gun. It was so difficult to be sure of anything when your father was dead and you were crying so hard you felt your heart must be breaking.

There was a reception, the way you might hold a reception after a wedding. People came back from the gravesite to stand miserably shoulder to shoulder in the living room of Em's cramped home. Now they were chatting in low tones, drinking tea and eating crustless cucumber sandwiches cut into neat little triangles. Em's mum had made every one of those sandwiches herself and baked the apple tarts and buns laid out to follow them. It occurred to Em to wonder if she might be economizing now that they no longer had Dad's salary coming in, but he suspected it would be more a question of good form. It was probably not the done thing to have a funeral catered professionally. The done thing was very important in England, especially academic England.

Em didn't want to be at the reception, didn't even

want a slice of apple tart; but it was important for him to be there. That was the done thing too.

Oddly enough, he recognized more people here than he had at the gravesite, staff members mainly, who came up to him and said things like "Oh, Em, I'm so sorry . . ." and "He was such a good man. . . ." Em tried to smile and nod and thank them, but all he really wanted was to get away and be alone for a while, maybe go and hide in his room.

There was no alcohol served at the reception, but Em thought his mother might be just a tiny bit drunk. It wasn't that she was a lush or anything, but she did sometimes take a drink to help her cope with stress. Now her eyes were a little too bright, her speech a little too loud. No one else would have noticed, or if they did they would understand it was the shock of the death.

The way the lodgings were laid out, it would be very noticeable if Em tried to sneak off to his room: the staircase led up directly from the crowded living room, and four of the steps squeaked. But there was nobody in his father's study, and the door was firmly shut. There was a neat little sign pinned at eye level. Just one word in Mum's blocky handwriting: PRIVATE. But one word was enough. Nobody would be in there now. Em made his way slowly through the throng until he was standing with his back to the door. In a moment when all heads were turned away, he slipped inside and closed the door quietly behind him.

Mum had transformed Dad's study into a shrine. His

desk, which was typically a heap of papers, journals, and dog-eared reference books, had been tidied within an inch of its life and the leather-covered surface dusted and polished. There was neither computer nor typewriter— Dad had never really joined the twentieth century, let alone the twenty-first. Em knew he had been working on a book, the same book he'd been working on for years—a cultural study of the prophet Nostradamus—but the text was handwritten, with frequent cross outs and side scribbles, in a series of notebooks that were nowhere to be seen. Every so often his dad had been in the habit of carrying the most recent notebook into the university, where some long-suffering secretary would type up more of his scrawl. But nobody ever saw the result. The manuscript had been growing in the dark for five years, like some long-forgotten fungus.

Em realized he was crying again, but now that he was alone he didn't care. He walked to the bookshelves, bulging with his father's collection—mainly academic tomes on late medieval and Renaissance history, but with a hefty segment of books on Nostradamus. Most of these were academic references as well, but there was a scattering of brightly colored paperbacks with titles like *Prophet of Doom* and *Armageddon Now: Our Final Days*. Dad used to say that since academics wouldn't take the Nostradamus prophecies seriously, it was left to the nutcases to write about them. Em had once asked him if this meant he was a nutcase himself, since his book would include the famous prophecies, but Dad only grinned and refused to rise to the bait.

Em was reaching for a book when he heard the door open behind him.

It was the pretty girl he'd noticed at the gravesite, looking even prettier close-up despite the severely formal little black suit she was wearing. She had blond hair, cut short, and wide blue eyes. She stared at him soberly as she closed the door. "I'm sorry," she said at once.

His own eyes were still swimming, a fact that would have embarrassed him at any other time. But there was a numbness inside him that kept all emotions at bay. He looked back at her without saying anything.

"I saw you come in here," she said. "I expect you want to be alone." She sounded English, but with the slight overlay of an American accent.

After a blank moment Em said, "No. No, it's okay." He made a vague, meaningless gesture with one hand. She was right: he did want to be alone. But good manners meant he couldn't say so.

"I just wanted to tell you how sorry I am. I didn't have a chance at the grave, and there were so many people out there"—she nodded back toward the reception room—"I couldn't seem to get near you. But I know how you feel."

"Thank you," Em said blankly.

"No," the girl said, "I *really* know how you feel. My mother died three months ago. She wasn't even ill: she just died. It makes you sick and empty and scared, all at the same time, and nobody appreciates that; nobody knows how you feel. But I just wanted you to know that I do."

"I'm sorry," Em said apologetically. "I don't . . . I'm afraid I don't . . ." He let the sentence trail.

"Oh, I'm sorry," the girl echoed. "Of course you don't. It's Charlotte. Charlotte Peterson." When his blank look failed to shift, she added quietly, "Tom's daughter."

They'd been kids together, but he hadn't seen her in years. No wonder he hadn't recognized her. "I thought you were in California living with your mother." He realized at once what he'd said and flushed. "She's dead— sorry. You just told me. I'm so sorry, I didn't think." The thing was, Charlotte's parents had divorced years ago, and Charlotte went away to live in the States with her mother.

Charlotte said, "After my mother died, I moved in with my aunt for a little while. But I wanted to be with my dad, and I wanted to finish my education in England; and anyway, there was some legal thing about custody until I'm eighteen, so I'm with Dad now. I just got back. He told me what had happened—it was pneumonia, wasn't it?"

"Yes, pneumonia."

"We both thought I should come to the funeral."

"I see," Em said, because he couldn't think of what else to say.

There was a long, awkward silence while he looked at her. Eventually she forced a smile. "Well, maybe we could, you know, meet up sometime, not at . . ."

Not at your father's funeral, he thought. Aloud, he said, "Yes. Yes, that would be nice."

There was another silence, shorter this time, then: "I'll let you talk to your dad." Then she was gone, leaving Em to wonder what she meant; but on some level, he knew she was right, because he *had* come here to talk to his dad and not just to escape from the crowd. Despite all Mum had done to tidy it up, to turn it into a shrine to the dead, the study was still the one place in the house, the only place, where his dad was still around.

The idea was, once he'd helped Mum clear up, he could go to his room, maybe go online, try to chill. But when he reached the Swamp and switched on his computer, somehow the old MMOs had lost their appeal, along with everything else. All he wanted to do was kick off his shoes, stretch out on the bed, stare at the cobweb hanging from the crack in the ceiling. That was when he discovered how tired he was, closed his eyes just for a second. . . .

It was dark when Em woke, sometime in the middle of the night, not sure exactly. The confusion felt good somehow; but then it cleared and he remembered again that Dad was dead, even though, for a minute, he couldn't believe it. His stomach knotted, a familiar feeling.

There were voices coming from outside his window.

He couldn't hear what they were saying, but there definitely seemed to be more than one. He pushed himself off the bed and went to look. This part of the lodgings faced across a campus courtyard, poorly lit at the best of times but now with no lights at all. But there was enough moonlight to show a solitary figure staring upward out of the shadows. For a split second it seemed as if the man was gazing directly at Em or at least at his window. Then he looked away and walked off in the direction of the students' quarters.

The voices were still there, but now Em knew they were coming from inside the lodgings, not outside. It happened sometimes if there was a window left open down below. His attic room was directly above the little sitting room where Mum and Dad had sometimes chatted in the evenings. If the window was open, the sound of voices drifted upward. Usually this didn't disturb him, certainly didn't wake him; but the voices were louder tonight.

And his mother certainly wasn't talking to Dad.

Without bothering to switch on a light, Em padded across the room and opened the door. He was facing a flight of steps down to a tiny landing, then three more stairs to his mum's room and the room where he'd found Dad dead, then the long flight down to the living room. Who was Mum talking to in the little sitting room after midnight?

He hesitated for a moment and then walked down the stairs without switching on lights. There was a single standard lamp lit in the living room at the bottom, leaving it mostly in gloom. But there was light streaming under the door to the sitting room. Em took a cautious few steps forward. He could hear the voices clearly now, hear the conversation. One was his mum. The other was her brother, Uncle Harold.

So Mum had probably asked Harold to stay the night for some additional support.

Em turned to go back upstairs, then heard his mother say, "Harold, I'm afraid."

Uncle Harold's voice sounded loud but steady. "None of this makes any sense, you know? Eddie was a professor of medieval history, for Christ's sake! He couldn't have been any more harmless if he'd worked as an accountant."

"I know," his mother said. It came out as something close to a wail.

Uncle Harold's voice again: "So why would anybody want to harm him?"

Em's ears pricked. Who said anybody wanted to harm Dad? He was one of the most popular professors on campus. Everybody said that. Em couldn't think of a single thing his father might have got up to that could possibly have caused someone to want to harm him.

Except . . .

Em frowned. He was thinking of his mother's comment about the stretched salary. Could Dad have got involved with a loan shark? Those guys turned very nasty if you didn't pay them back. Everybody knew that. The really bad ones sent someone around to break your legs. Only Dad never had his legs broken. The worst that happened to him was he caught pneumonia.

"I don't know," his mother said in answer to her brother's question. "But then wives don't, do they? They don't know what their husbands get up to on their own. Gambling . . . other women . . ."

Dad mixed up with another woman? Get real, Mum!

Uncle Harold must have had the same thought, for he gave a short little laugh. "Come on, Caroline. If Ed ever so much as *sneezed* at another woman, I'll streak naked down the M25. And you know what he thought about gambling. . . ."

Mum's voice suddenly stiffened. "What I know, Harold," she said firmly, "is that my Eddie was murdered."

Em usually slept late during school holidays. Most mornings you couldn't wake him until eleven, maybe eleven thirty. Either way, he seldom climbed out of bed before noon, at which time he'd go down and listen carefully to his mother's complaints about his laziness, then have breakfast, or lunch, or whatever you'd call it. But this morning he was wide-awake at six thirty, downstairs a few minutes after seven, and headed straight for the kitchen.

For some reason he was starving. Yesterday's sorrow, last night's worries were still with him; but they no longer rested in his stomach like a leaden ball. That lump had somehow moved aside, leaving a hollow only food could fill. He started with corn flakes, found that the milk was curdled, and doused them in orange juice instead. When that failed miserably to do the trick, he got out the frying pan.

The pork-and-apple sausages reminded him of his father's last meal, the one he'd never eaten. So did the bacon and eggs. But there was nothing he could do about that. However miserable life was, you still had to eat. He considered opening a tin of baked beans, abandoned the idea because he couldn't see one with a ring-pull, but found two cold boiled potatoes in the fridge. He sliced them thinly so they'd crisp and dropped them into the pan.

Something made him think of Uncle Harold, and he realized he hadn't seen him sleeping on the living-room couch, so Mum must have tucked him into Dad's deathbed after all. Dad murdered—where had that come from? There had been no dagger in the heart, no gunshot to the head. Just some unexpected complication with an antibiotic-resistant bug. Em decided there and then he'd never start to drink alcohol. It was doing his mother no favors, however much it dulled her pain.

He finished his breakfast feeling better and stronger than he had for days. Then he finished the orange juice as well and wandered back into the living room. He was thinking of taking an early-morning walk, maybe down to the river before there were too many people about.

But there was something wrong. For a moment Em couldn't think what it was. Then he realized that the door to Dad's study was ajar.

Em stared at it. He'd closed it tight when he left the

study yesterday afternoon and he hadn't noticed it open when he'd come down in the middle of the night. So Mum or Harold must have gone in there after Em had crept back up to bed. But why? He pushed the door.

Dad's study looked as if a bomb had hit it. Books had been torn down from the shelves and strewn across the floor. The drawers of the desk were all open: one had been pulled out completely and now stood propped against a chair, its contents scattered. The standard lamp Dad used to read by had been overturned. Several ornaments were broken. One portion of the carpet had been torn up and folded back, revealing the floorboards beneath. There were pictures missing from the walls. *So much for making it a shrine, Mum.* But Mum had nothing to do with this. Or Uncle Harold.

They'd been robbed!

Em knew that must have been what happened, but somehow he couldn't get his head around it. Stupidly he kept thinking that it couldn't have happened, that it was somehow *impossible.* The study wasn't just trashed; it was no longer the study at all. And Dad wasn't there anymore.

He fought back a wave of self-pity and forced himself to concentrate. A burglary made no sense. There was a flat-screen television in the living room that hadn't been taken. And his father had a nearly new sound system right here in the study. That hadn't been taken either, although the speakers had been ripped from their brackets and thrown on the floor, so the burglars had certainly noticed them. In fact, looking around, nothing of any obvious value had been taken and nothing at all had been disturbed in the living room or kitchen.

It was as if the thieves had been looking for something.

The way they did it on TV police shows was that they sent out an overeducated detective inspector trailing a dim sergeant and one or two technicians: fingerprint man, forensic expert, that sort of thing. But maybe that was just for murders. Certainly it hadn't happened here.

Em opened the door because his mum had started crying and couldn't stop. With Mum not functioning, Em would have preferred Uncle Harold deal with the police; but Uncle Harold, it turned out, hadn't spent the night in Dad's deathbed after all: he'd left sometime around three a.m. Drove home in his car.

There were two men on the doorstep, both burly, both wearing crumpled suits, one a head shorter than the other. Neither produced a warrant card, just mumbled "Police" before pushing past Em with bored expressions. Not knowing what else to do, he led them into the living room, where the tall one said casually, "Sergeant Jackson. This is Detective Constable Tiblet. Break-in, was it?"

"Yes," Em said a little sourly.

The one called Jackson looked around the living room. "Not much sign of damage. The report slip said there was damage."

"It was mostly in the study," Em said. He heard the

stupid, apologetic tone in his voice but couldn't seem to stop it. "Actually," he amended, "it was *all* in the study."

"Your parents around?"

"Mum's still upstairs," Em told him. "Dad's—" The word caught in his throat. "Dad's dead."

"You're the son?"

Nice detective work, Sergeant Jackson, Em thought. Aloud he said, "Yes."

"Any other family living here?"

"Apart from Mum? No."

Jackson lapsed into silence but continued to look around the living room. Tiblet said, "Better show us where it happened, then."

Em took them to the study. "We haven't touched anything," he said anxiously. Then when Jackson looked at him blankly, he added, "In case you want to take fingerprints or something." He wished Mum would hurry up. It wasn't like she didn't know the police were here—she'd heard the doorbell.

"Oh," Jackson said. You'd have thought he'd never heard of fingerprints.

Tiblet peered past them into the study. "Made a right mess, didn't they?"

Jackson grunted, then turned to Em. "Mind if we ask you a few questions? After that we'll have to get your mum down. Bit upset, is she?"

"You could say that," Em said.

Sergeant Jackson nodded sagely.

"Would you like some tea?" Em asked. "We could

talk in the kitchen."

The atmosphere changed at once. Jackson even smiled. "That would be very nice, ah— What did you say your name was?"

"Edward Michael Goverton," Em told him formally. "Mostly I'm just called Em."

"That would be very nice, Em," Jackson said as if they'd suddenly become best friends. He turned to Tiblet. "Wouldn't it, Stanley?"

"Oh, yes," Stanley said.

They got down to business properly while Em was waiting for the kettle to boil.

"Where did they break in?" Jackson asked.

Em realized he didn't know. "Not sure."

"We'll take a look around with your mother when she comes down. Wasn't anywhere obvious anyway? Didn't smash in the front door?"

"No." Em knew Sergeant Jackson was joking but couldn't crack a smile.

Now that they'd mentioned it, Em noticed that the study window seemed to be intact, and there were no obvious signs of forced entry anywhere else. Not that he'd looked for them particularly. Mostly he'd been focused on trying to comfort his mother. Who really should have been dealing with this anyway. If she didn't turn up soon, he'd have to go and bring her down, or at least find out if she'd stopped crying.

He realized Sergeant Jackson had asked him a question. "Sorry?"

"You didn't hear anything?" Jackson repeated.

"Me? No, I sleep in the attic."

"Wouldn't then, would you? Your mother didn't mention hearing anything, did she?"

Em started to shake his head as Tiblet put in, "Thing is, they really trashed that room. Even broke bits off the furniture. Couldn't do that without making noise. Your mother's room is one floor up, right?"

How did he know that? Em wondered. "Yes, that's right; but she's a heavy sleeper."

"Maybe you'd better go and fetch her," Jackson said. "We won't keep her long, but best for her to get it over and done with." He turned away from Em dismissively and said to Tiblet, "Strange business this, Stanley. Strange business."

"I don't want you to worry about anything," Em's mother told him. They were seated facing each other across the kitchen table with the police now long gone. He noticed that she'd put on makeup; not a lot, but it made a big difference. The crying had stopped, and her eyes didn't even look red. Once she'd finally come down, the way she'd dealt with Sergeant Jackson and Detective Constable Tiblet, you'd have thought she'd invited them around for tea. Hardly believe she'd been up half the night, suffered a bereavement, faced a break-in. *Thought her husband had been murdered,* a memory whispered in Em's head.

"I'm not worrying about anything," he said, even though it wasn't true.

"Well, that's good," his mother said. "Because there's

nothing to worry about. We'll miss your father, we'll *grieve* for your father; but life must go on. Eventually the pain will go away. We'll never forget him—I don't mean that—but the pain will, you know, become manageable."

"Yes, of course, Mum."

"I was talking to your uncle Harold last night, and we don't see why things can't go on exactly as before. Your education . . . going on to university . . ." She made a small gesture with both hands. "No need for any of us to change any plans." She smiled bravely. "So nothing you need concern yourself about."

This is your pilot speaking, Em thought. *We are now entering Cloud Cuckoo airspace.* Aloud he said gently, "We'll have to leave this place, won't we? Now that Dad's—"

"No we won't!" Mum said, suddenly animated. "We won't; not unless you want to. I had a word with Dr. Gauld, and he says it could take them up to a year to replace your father; and they won't even start looking for another six weeks because of the summer holidays. And the thing is, because of the economic slump, they may not want to replace him at all to save money; and even if they *do* replace him, the new person might not find this place suitable." She leaned forward. "Meanwhile, Dr. Gauld says we're welcome to stay. There'll be rent, of course, since the lodgings aren't part of your father's job package anymore; but it will be low because it's subsidized."

Dr. Gauld was chancellor of the university—nothing like going straight to the top. Em looked at his mother admiringly but then felt he needed to ask, "You'll have to get a job, won't you, Mum?"

A confused look flashed across her face. Then she said quickly, "Yes, I will. I mean, I don't have to; but I'd like to. I'd like to go back to teaching. That was always the plan, really, between Eddie and myself."

"You've been away from teaching for a long time, Mum."

She looked at him blankly. "Yes."

"It might not be all that easy to get back in. It could take you months. . . ." He shook his head. He didn't want to say *years,* but he was thinking it.

"Yes, well, I'd certainly expect that." From the expression on her face, she didn't know what he was getting at.

Em couldn't put it off any longer. "What are we going to live on in the meantime?" he asked bluntly. It occurred to him that if he left school he might get a job at McDonald's or somewhere. They were always advertising jobs.

To his surprise, his mother's face lit up. "Oh, you mustn't worry about *money*! That's about the only thing that won't be a problem. I always thought your dad's salary wasn't much. I mean, academic salaries never are; but when I was going through his things, I came across nearly two thousand pounds in cash and a bank draft for another twenty thousand. I don't know how he managed to save it; but he was a very frugal man, of course, apart from all his little trips abroad. And then, on top of that, your uncle Harold sold him an enormous insurance policy just after we got married. I was cross at the time—I thought Harold was taking advantage; but he was absolutely right. All that comes to us now, as well. I know I said I wanted to go back to teaching, but it's not for the money."

Em stared at her. It was a lot to take in. Whatever brave face he put on it, he *had* been worried. To give himself time to gather his thoughts, he said the first thing that came into his mind, which was "Did the police find out how they got in?" He'd left Mum with the police when she eventually came down. She'd looked then as she looked now, brisk and competent, so he'd left them to it and gone to his room.

"Oh," she said vaguely, "they thought it might have been one of the upstairs windows, probably the one in the bathroom."

Em knew at once with absolutely certainty that she was lying. "Probably?" he said. "Aren't they sure?"

His mother shrugged. "Well, the latches are quite old in this building. It's difficult to be sure which one they slipped. But the bathroom is the most likely."

And how would the thieves have known that? Em wondered. But before he could wonder aloud, Mum said brightly, "Actually, your uncle Harold and I had a really cool idea last night." She smiled at him. "About you."

Mum never used a word like *cool*, not in her ordinary conversation. She only ever trotted it out when she wanted to persuade him about something. She had this idea—a lot of adults did—that using teen slang made them more acceptable to their kids, although all it really did was make them sound dorky. "About me?" Em echoed suspiciously.

"Yes, we thought it would be neat"—wow, she must be *really* anxious to get him to do something—"if you went away for a while. You know, like a little holiday. A holiday break. Somewhere nice. So you could, you know, recover."

"From Dad's death?"

"Yes, that and . . . everything else. With the cash I found, I could afford to let you have a decent bit of spending money, so you could . . ." She let the sentence trail.

"You mean . . . by the seaside?"

"Or even out of the country." She pasted on a phony expression of revelation, as if she'd just thought of something. "Actually, I think Tom Peterson's going off somewhere. You could go with him. You like Tom. And his daughter's home from the States—remember little Charlotte? She's grown up now, so you'd have somebody to talk to. I'm sure they'd be delighted for you to come along." She looked at him, eyes suddenly wide with anticipation.

As surely as he'd known she was lying before, Em knew now there was something she was covering up. "Where's Tom going to?" he asked.

"France," his mother said brightly. "It's lovely at this time of year. Beautiful scenery . . . lovely food . . . You'd see a bit of Paris and then I think Tom's planning some time in the South of France. Millionaire's playground, eh? You might even see a movie star. Or a pop star, better yet. What do you think?"

Em thought there was something going on. But he knew better than to ask Mum about it directly. She was an expert at denying stuff—and making you feel guilty that you'd even asked. "Tom mightn't want me tagging along," he said.

"Oh, I'm sure he'd be *delighted*!" Mum exclaimed. "The two of you get on so well—he's like another uncle to you."

She's asked him already, Em thought. She must have asked him at the funeral; there just wasn't any other time. How creepy was that? And Tom had said yes. What else *could* he say? Mum dripping all over him, grieving widow, Ed's best friend. Mum had set it all up and was now pretending it was an idea that had just occurred to her so he wouldn't feel pushed around.

All the same, she was right. He *did* get on well with Tom. Any time Tom called to see Dad, he treated Em like a grown-up, which was more than a lot of people did. And they talked about stuff together—interesting stuff, not the usual adult *How are things at school, then?* They both had an interest in Gothic cathedrals, for example, and the mystery of how they got built. Tom liked mysteries generally—rains of frogs, sea monsters, the Egyptian pyramids, lost civilizations—and so did Em. A bit of time together with Tom would be no hardship.

Especially with his daughter there.

Em pushed the thought aside. The other thing was that he'd never been to France before. Actually, that wasn't strictly true. His geography class had once gone on a day trip to Calais, but that wasn't seeing France. Paris would be very different. The South of France would be very, very different. Besides, Mum might need some time to herself.

Em licked his lips. "Well, if you think Tom wouldn't mind . . ."

The look on his mum's face was relief. She just couldn't hide it, although she tried very hard. But after a second it faded. "There's one other thing . . . ," she said hesitantly. Em waited. "Your father"—she swallowed—"just before he got sick, he bought you something. For your birthday."

"My birthday isn't until October," Em said blankly.

"Yes, I know. I don't know why he got it so early. Maybe it was on special offer or something. And then he wanted to get it engraved, and he may have thought that would take longer than it did. But anyway, when he was at the worst of his fever, when it was looking touch and go before he started to"—she swallowed again, and he saw to his horror that her eyes were brimming with tears—"before we thought he was getting better, he gave it to me to give to you on your birthday. But I think maybe since you're going away, I should give it to you now. I don't know much about these things, but seems to me you'd have more use for it on holiday. And it would be a little memento of your father. . . ."

Like he needed one. Em wondered what it was. If his father had it engraved, it was probably a watch. As a hint. Dad had always been fussy about punctuality. He never seemed to figure out it didn't mean much to a teenager.

But it wasn't a watch. It was a brand-new iPod touch. The engraving on the back said:

GOOD LISTENING. HAPPY BIRTHDAY, EDWARD, FROM YOUR LOVING FATHER

Em felt the tightness in his chest and turned away quickly so his mother would not see his reaction. He slipped the iPod into his jacket pocket, scarcely able to hold back the tears. He'd dropped hints about an iPod; but it would be a long, long time before he could bring himself to use this one.

They were traveling first class. The railway carriage had really neat beige seats with bright orange head-rests and new carpet on the floor. A pretty girl in a trim blue Eurostar uniform swooped in with a tray as they were in the process of sitting down. "A glass of cham-pagne, sir?" she asked, smiling. "Compliments of the management." She was talking to Tom, of course.

"Thank you," Tom said gravely. He gave the two of them a grin that said *Aren't you jealous that you're not grown-up?*

"I'll have a Coke. Lots of ice," Charlotte told the hostess without being asked.

That's what came of living in California, Em thought. American confidence rubbed off on you, like picking up the accent. He wished some of it would rub off on him.

He realized the hostess was looking at him now, dropped his eyes, and muttered, "Me too."

As the train pulled out of St. Pancras station, Tom Peterson stood to retrieve his laptop from the luggage rack. "Do you think you two could stay quiet for the next couple of hours?" he asked. "I need to finish my symposium paper."

Em groaned inwardly—he'd been looking forward to a real chat with Charlotte—but Charlotte herself said firmly, "Oh, don't be such a *bore*, Dad. You know we can't possibly keep quiet for two hours." She glanced around the carriage with its light sprinkling of fellow passengers. "Em and I will go and sit somewhere else. Then we can talk and you can get on with your rotten paper."

"I'm not sure they let you do that," Tom said uncertainly. "We have reserved seats. I expect everyone else does too."

"The cabin is half empty!" Charlotte exclaimed. "And if they don't like us sitting somewhere else, what are they going to do: spank us? Honestly, Daddy, we'll just come back and irritate you if they move us."

It was obvious that she had him twisted around her little finger despite the years with her mother. *Or* maybe because of them, Em thought. Either way, Tom was grinning as she wriggled out of her seat and scurried down the aisle to take another vacant place as far distant as she could get. Em glanced at Tom helplessly, then got up and followed her.

After making all the fuss, Charlotte lapsed into

silence and gazed out the window as the rolling cityscape gradually gave way to countryside. Em, who'd always been a bit shy around girls—especially the pretty ones—couldn't think of anything to say, so he stared woodenly ahead, feeling stupid.

Eventually he coughed and asked casually, "Where are we? Do you know?"

"Somewhere in Kent probably," Charlotte said. "I looked at the map yesterday, and we go through Kent before we reach the Chunnel."

The Chunnel was the Channel Tunnel, and Em was frankly just a little freaked out about it. What worried him was the thought of traveling through a shaft that carried the weight of the entire English Channel, not to mention several hundred thousand tons of rock. What would happen if it all just . . . collapsed? Actually he knew perfectly well what would happen if it all just collapsed.

He coughed again. "Have you ever traveled this route before?"

"I've never even been to France. I might as well have been an American since Mum and Dad divorced. Californians never go anywhere, except to other parts of America."

"So you don't know when we go into the tunnel?"

"They tell you," Charlotte said. "According to Dad. They announce it, like the pilot telling you to fasten your seat belts. But anyway, you'll know in daylight. You can't see the scenery, and they put the lights on."

"Does it take long? Like, inside the tunnel?"

"About fifteen minutes, I think. Maybe twenty."

"Is that *all*?" Em asked, suddenly relieved. Fifteen minutes was nothing. Even twenty wasn't much.

Charlotte turned to look at him. "You aren't worrying, are you? About going through the tunnel?"

"What, me?" Em spluttered. He gave a bright, loud laugh. "No, of course not."

"Oh good," Charlotte said, and turned back to the window.

It was exactly as she predicted. A male voice came over the intercom. "Ladies and gentlemen, I hope you are enjoying your journey with Eurostar. We shall soon be entering the Channel Tunnel, and interior illumination will be switched on for your convenience. I'd like to take this opportunity . . ." And so on, just like an airline pilot. The lights did go on shortly thereafter, and the outside world disappeared, leaving Em to stare at his reflection in the window.

"Know what?" one of the pasengers said to his wife. "If there was ever a good time for a terrorist attack, this would be it. Couple of well-placed bombs, and the whole place would come down."

"Let's hope there won't be a terrorist attack then," his wife said calmly.

Ten minutes later, while they were still in the tunnel, all the lights went out.

Em barely mastered an impulse to grab Charlotte's hand. His stomach was suddenly tight.

"They'll sort it out in a minute," Charlotte said.

"Ladies and gentlemen," said a cheerful female voice over the intercom. "A slight technical hitch with the lights as you may have noticed, but the engineer tells me he'll have it corrected before you"—the lights came back on—"ah, there we are! Our apologies about that, but we're almost back to daylight in any case."

Em looked around. The worried husband and wife were gone. There was no sign of a terrorist attack, no sign of anything unusual. At least he didn't think so. There was a man in a well-cut suit seated near the back of the carriage behind a group of Japanese businessmen. Em didn't think he'd been sitting there before, although his face did look vaguely familiar. But probably Em was wrong. Probably the man had been sitting there all the time.

"Have you been to France before?" Charlotte asked. She seemed completely unfazed by the whole lights business.

"School trip," Em said. "It was awful." He glanced back toward the end of the carriage. The man behind the Japanese businessmen was gone. It wasn't until the train was pulling into the Paris Gare Du Nord that Em realized why his face looked familiar.

It was the same man who'd been carrying the gun at his father's funeral.

There was a full-color brochure that featured a chorus line of showgirls on the reception desk of the hotel. Em turned his head away while trying surreptitiously to get a better look. He'd decided that the man on the train couldn't possibly be the same man who'd been at the funeral; but all the same he was feeling a bit emotional, reminded of his father's death, and a bit nervy, probably from being in an unfamiliar city. And the showgirl brochure underlined how unfamiliar Paris really was. The girls were only wearing feathers, which didn't cover very much. You'd never see a brochure like that in a London hotel.

"Freshen up," Tom said as he handed them their key cards. "Have a rest or a bit of a nose around, practice your French. I've got a couple of things to do in my room, so don't disturb me unless you absolutely have to. Don't get into trouble. Don't leave the hotel. Don't charge up anything more than a Coke—"

"How big a bottle, Dad?" Charlotte asked deadpan.

"Very droll, darling. Now, all three of us will meet up here, in the lobby, at quarter to seven for an early supper. We're off first thing for my big day, so you need to get a good night's sleep. I don't want to have to drag either of you out of bed in the morning."

Tom's big day was the symposium on something where he was delivering his paper. Em would have avoided it if he could, and so, he suspected, would Charlotte; but there was no way Tom was going to let them loose in Paris on their own, so attendance was compulsory. As was guaranteed death by boredom. It was the only bit of the whole holiday that Em was actually dreading. He realized his father's old friend was looking at him. "Right," he said.

He was in his room trying to figure out how the shower worked when there was a quiet knock at the door. Charlotte slipped in without invitation when he opened it. "Fancy a walk?" she asked.

"Where to?" What he actually fancied was a long, cool shower, but he didn't want to say no. He wasn't sure how he felt about Charlotte. She was terribly pretty and very friendly, but he was wary of her. She seemed a lot older than he was, although he knew she couldn't be. Maybe living in America had made her more sophisticated or something. Her confidence felt alien.

"Just explore a bit," Charlotte said easily. "See the artists in the Latin Quarter or visit Notre Dame or stare at the Seine or whatever we can do from here and still get back in time for supper."

"Your father said we weren't to go outside."

She gave him a withering glance. "Do you always do what you're told?"

"Well, no," Em said uncertainly, "but . . ."

"Then come on!" Charlotte urged. "This is my first time in Paris. Tomorrow we'll be cooped up in Daddy's miserable symposium, and the day after that we're on the road again. This is our only chance. The City of Light! Gay Paree! Do you have cab money?"

"A bit," Em admitted, "but . . ."

"Then we can go absolutely anywhere." She gave him a huge grin. "Wouldn't you like to look at the posters outside the Folies Bergère?"

He realized suddenly he was being a total wimp. "Okay," he said. "Let's explore."

He felt nervous passing the door of Tom's room, but they reached the foyer without incident. The hotel entrance faced onto a quiet side street. "I don't suppose you have a street map?" he asked.

Charlotte glanced up at him. "I do, as a matter of fact. There was a brochure thing in my room at the hotel. It has a map of the city center." She pulled it from her pocket. "Is there somewhere you specially want to go?"

There was a hint of excited enjoyment rising from his stomach. He was beginning to realize he actually was in Paris, with money in his pocket (not a lot, but enough) and could go anywhere he wanted. "I've always fancied seeing the Louvre ever since I read *The Da Vinci Code*."

"There's a coincidence." Charlotte grinned. "Me too. I think we can walk from here. We need to get onto the main streets though."

"Okay," Em said. "I'm game if you are."

They found their way onto a main road; but as they were crossing the river, Charlotte suddenly hesitated. "I keep getting the feeling we're being watched. You know, like when somebody stares at the back of your neck."

Em glanced around him. Traffic on the bridge was heavy, but none of the hurrying pedestrians seemed to be paying them any particular attention. "I don't think so," he said uncertainly. "What's given you the feeling?"

Charlotte smiled. "Oh, you know—woman's intuition." The smile became apologetic. "It's probably just my imagination."

"Yes, probably," Em said.

As Charlotte promised, the museum was not far, but as the pyramid came into view, they realized that the queue to the ticket desk stretched across the square and down one of the surrounding streets. Em stared at it for a moment. "I don't fancy standing in line for hours," he said.

"Neither do I," Charlotte said at once. "Let's find somewhere and have a cup of coffee."

They discovered tables set out in a colonnade to one side of the square, most taken by chattering couples and groups drinking wine. A scurrying waiter pointed to a small table for two beside one of the pillars and said cheerfully, *"Ici!"* As they sat down, he asked, "You do not require a full meal?" Em shook his head quickly. "In that case, this menu." The waiter handed them a printed card. "I shall return when you have time to consider."

"How did he know we were English?" Em asked, frowning.

Charlotte shrugged. "Perhaps we look English. When he comes back, I'll order us *citron pressés* in French; that'll confuse him."

From their vantage point they could still see the queue for the Louvre. A coach had pulled up in the square, disgorging an enormous party of very young schoolchildren who milled about noisily, quickly filling much of the free space. Em was watching them, and pitying their poor teachers, as their *citron pressés* arrived. The drink proved chilled and very sour, much like lightly watered lemon juice. He fought down the instinctive reaction of his mouth to purse violently, managed something resembling a smile, and gasped, "Delicious!" *Citron pressés* were for sophisticated people with sophisticated tastes. He didn't want Charlotte to think he was a bumpkin.

Charlotte smiled back, then leaned across the table until her lips were an intimate distance from his ear and asked quietly, "You know that feeling I had?"

"On the bridge?"

Charlotte nodded. "We should have paid attention to it. Someone has been following us."

Charlotte said, "I want you to look back into the square as if you're still watching the schoolchildren. Then I'll say something to you; and when you turn to look at me, check out the man sitting at the table at the far end of the colonnade just beyond the door. Linen suit, dark glasses—he's actually the only person in the whole place sitting alone."

Em set down his drink and glanced quickly back to the square. Two harassed adults, presumably teachers, had somehow managed to herd most of the children into ragged lines and were currently trying to round up the stragglers. The coach driver was slowly backing up his empty vehicle, obviously preparing to leave his passengers to their fate. The queue for the pyramid looked changed, but undiminished, and was now largely composed of what Em took to be Japanese and American tourists. *Followed?* Em thought as Charlotte said something to him.

As he turned toward her, everything seemed to go into slow motion. He stared along the colonnade past family groups and couples, past two gaggles of brightly dressed girls at adjacent tables clearly celebrating something, past the busy waiters in their white aprons, past a cluster of businessmen who had shed their jackets because of the heat, and beyond the restaurant doorway to a solitary table squeezed in right at the very end.

The linen suit Charlotte had mentioned looked Italian in cut and made of lightweight, cream-colored cloth ideal for a sunny summer's afternoon. The man wore it with a white, open-necked shirt stretched over a muscular chest. There was a Panama hat on the table in front of him; and like maybe 80 percent of the other patrons he was wearing dark glasses—no surprise in this weather. As his gaze swept past, Em had the uneasy feeling that their eyes met briefly, but it was probably imagination: there was no way to see past those shades.

Em recognized him at once and felt his chest tighten. "I think we should get out of here."

"I haven't paid for the *citron pressés*," Charlotte said. "I'll call a waiter."

"Don't do that," Em told her quickly. He leaned forward. "How do you know he was following us?"

"I saw him in the street earlier. He—"

"Outside the hotel?" Em interrupted.

Charlotte shook her head. "No—later. When we were crossing the bridge. And then when we turned down the boulevard, he pretended to look in a shop window. You know, the way they do in detective movies."

"Why didn't you tell me?"

"I wasn't sure," Charlotte said. "It might just have been a coincidence. Then when I saw him at the table . . ." She hesitated. "You don't think it's a coincidence, do you?"

Em shook his head. "I've seen him before."

She was quick off the mark: "So he's not following us, he's following you?"

"I suppose," Em said.

"Why?" Charlotte asked.

Em had just been asking himself that question. Why had he pretended it never happened? Why had he pretended the man wasn't really carrying a gun at his father's funeral? Or that he hadn't seen the same man on the train? "I don't know," he said truthfully.

"I'll call the waiter," Charlotte volunteered again.

"We don't have time!" Em hissed urgently. His mind was racing at top speed. "It's me he's following, but he knows we're together now. I want you to stand up and walk directly toward him, then go into the main restaurant as if you're looking for a loo. He's bound to focus on you since you're moving; and when he does, I'll slip away. If you go straight through the restaurant, there's bound to be another way out. It'll be easy to throw him off since he's not following you anyway. We can meet back at the hotel."

"He may know where we're staying."

"You saw him on the bridge, not outside the hotel."

Charlotte shrugged. "That doesn't mean anything; maybe I just didn't notice him before. I think we should meet up somewhere else. How about the main entrance to the Musée d'Orsay? You remember—we passed it on the way."

"Yes, all right," Em muttered. Although he was working hard to control it, there was more than a hint of panic rising from his stomach. "Now will—?"

But Charlotte hadn't finished. "It'll never be enough for me just to wander off looking for a restroom. You leave this to me. Once I have his attention, you slip away." She stood up abruptly. "See you at the museum."

"No, wait a—" But it was too late. She was already weaving her way through the tables, headed toward the man in the linen suit. For a moment he thought she was going to follow the plan he'd suggested, but she walked past the door to the main part of the restaurant and directly up to the man's table. Em's view was blocked for a second, then he heard a sudden shout, part anger, part pain. The man in the suit was on his feet, gesticulating. Charlotte seemed to be talking to him urgently, her words lost in the general buzz of conversation in the colonnade.

Em moved without thinking. He ran along one of the lines of schoolchildren, cut across the square, then dived behind the empty coach, which was crawling forward at a snail's pace because of the milling tourists. With no trouble keeping up, he looked around wildly, trying to work out an escape route. It occurred to him that if he could keep the bus between him and the man for another fifty yards, he could take one of the side streets without being seen. Then, if he made it to a corner—or even another side street—he would be free and clear without the man having the slightest idea where he'd gone.

The bus stopped suddenly and so did Em. They were too far from the side street for him to reach it unseen. But if he stayed where he was, he might be discovered. He crept toward the front, hoping to find out why the driver had stopped. If it was simply because of the press of pedestrians, he would move on again in a moment. But if he was preparing to park, Em was in real trouble.

He slowed as he neared the bus's entrance door so the driver wouldn't see him. He still had no idea why the vehicle had stopped and began to debate the wisdom of moving away from it a little to get a clearer view. Then a better idea occurred to him and he dropped down to look between the wheels. So far as he could tell, they were nowhere near a parking bay, but there was a steady stream of people ahead. He was climbing back to his feet when a heavy hand fell on his shoulder.

"Yipes!" Em started in shock, then spun around, bit the hand, and jerked himself free. He was poised to run for his life when he realized he was facing the waiter who had served them in the colonnade.

"Six euros cinquante, s'il vous plaît!" the waiter hissed. He'd obviously abandoned his English for he added,

"Pour les deux boissons."

Three euros twenty-five seemed a lot for a glass of stuff that turned your mouth inside out. But that was beside the point. The focus of Em's mind was that he had two euro coins in his pocket—not enough to pay for the drinks—and a twenty euro note in his wallet that would certainly pay for both drinks but leave him waiting for change, and he hadn't time to do that. So unless the waiter kept the change, which Em didn't want either—it was all the money he had, for Pete's sake!—his only option, his *only* option . . .

Em ran. He ran for the side street. Which meant he ran out from behind the cover of the coach.

He'd scarcely covered fifteen yards when he heard Charlotte scream.

Em spun around, almost losing his balance. He was right out in the open now, completely exposed. But the man in the linen suit was otherwise engaged. Four waiters were gathered around him, gesticulating furiously. Every patron in the colonnade was looking in his direction. Charlotte seemed to be weeping, comforted by an elderly woman with blue-rinse hair. She looked over the woman's shoulder directly at Em. And winked.

Em twisted around again and ran for the side street. Minutes later, he'd left the Louvre far behind.

It took Em nearly an hour to find his way to the Musée d'Orsay. Although it wasn't far from the Louvre, he'd forgotten he had to cross the river again and wasted time wandering along various mysterious *rues* before he plucked up the courage to ask directions in French. By contrast with the Louvre, there were no queues at any of the four entrances; but to his dismay there was no sign of Charlotte waiting outside either.

He hung around for a few minutes wondering what to do. He'd taken the wink to mean she was all right; and the man in the linen suit had certainly seemed to have his hands full. But suppose Em had misread the scene? Suppose Charlotte had been in trouble and he'd simply run away, leaving her to it?

A more likely, but only slightly less disturbing

thought occurred to him. Suppose she was waiting for him *inside* the museum?

This whole little adventure, which was just supposed to be an hour or so exploring Paris, had turned into a bit of a nightmare. He'd run away from a café without paying. There was a strange man following him. (A strange man known to carry a *gun,* a voice in his mind reminded him.) He had only twenty-two euros in his pocket, and he had no idea how much admission to the Musée d'Orsay might be. Why couldn't girls just do what they said they'd do and wait outside the entrance?

He walked hesitantly inside and then took his courage in his hands and marched up to the ticket desk. *"Combien?"* he asked.

The ticket clerk was a matronly woman who looked at him benignly. *"Quel âge avez vous, jeune homme?"*

What age? Em licked his lips. *"J'ai . . . ,"* he said hesitantly. That was right, wasn't it? The French said "I *have* so many years" not "I *am* so many years." He watched the woman's face for signs of confusion. *"J'ai moins de dix-huit ans."*

The woman smiled. *"Ensuite, l'entrée est gratuite."*

Em stared at her for a moment, then smiled back.

He found Charlotte on a bench outside the library room. She jumped to her feet the moment she saw him. "Where have you *been?* I've been sitting here for *hours!*"

"Are you all right?" Em asked. Then, without waiting for her to answer, "What happened?"

Charlotte grinned. "I spilled coffee on his lap, then

when he got cross, I told the waiters he was threatening me." She pursed her lips mischievously. "It was all a big misunderstanding."

"And you're sure he didn't follow you here?"

"Absolutely," Charlotte said. "I was long gone before the waiters were finished with him. By the way, you owe me three euros twenty-five—I paid for your drink." She reached for his hand and drew him down beside her on the bench. "Now you must tell me what this is all about. Tell me everything."

She looked at him expectantly; and Em, with a sudden flooding of relief, told her everything.

"Your mother thinks your Dad was *murdered*?" Charlotte asked incredulously when he finally ground to a halt.

Em nodded miserably.

"Was he?"

Em shook his head vigorously. "No, of course not. He just caught some sort of superbug."

"Then why would your mum think he was?"

That was the thing Em hadn't mentioned. He took a deep breath. "Mum hasn't really been the same since Dad died."

To his surprise she didn't even pursue it. Instead she said soberly, "That man was carrying a gun at your father's funeral. Even if your dad wasn't murdered, there's *something* going on."

Of course there was something going on! His father had died when he was supposed to be getting better.

There were strangers at the funeral—not just the man with the gun, but lots of other people he didn't know. His father's study was ransacked—not their whole home, the way you'd expect from burglars, but just the study. And now Em was being followed . . . all the way to France. Why? He could only nod helplessly.

Charlotte took charge at once. "Well, the first thing obviously is to find out what's going on. Until you do that, there's not much else you can do. You need to *mount an investigation.*" She made it sound as if he was a government department with all the resources of the nation behind him. He opened his mouth to protest, but she cut him short. "We can do it together, if you like."

Em closed his mouth again. He was an only child; his mother had her own worries; and his father, when he was alive, had been a very busy academic. Em had become so used to doing things on his own that he scarcely noticed it. Now he felt an entirely unexpected emotion: a flooding warmth, combined with gratitude and something that could only be surprise. "Would you really?" he asked.

"Would I really what?"

"Help me."

"I've already helped you," Charlotte said. "Who do you think poured the coffee on the rude man's lap?"

The *rude* man? That was how Charlotte thought of a threatening figure with dark glasses and a gun? Despite everything, Em felt the ghost of a smile begin to crawl across his face. He pushed it away in case she misunderstood and said seriously, "You know this could be dangerous."

"I suppose you're right," Charlotte said, and continued to look at him.

"All right," Em said. "Yes, sorry, thank you. Yes, I'd like your help, thank you, if that's all right." He hesitated. "Where do we start?"

"With *Whistler's Mother*," Charlotte said.

He stared at her.

"I've always wanted to see the original," Charlotte told him. "They have it here somewhere."

They walked between the two stone lions and up a short flight of steps into the main body of the museum. "What did your father do?" Charlotte asked.

"You know what he did. Taught late medieval and Renaissance history at the university."

"No, when he wasn't teaching. Did he have any strange hobbies or interests . . . ?"

"You think this has something to do with my father?"

"It was his funeral the strange people turned up at," Charlotte said, "including the one who followed us today. You may not have known them, but you can be sure he did. Or rather, you can be sure they knew him. Was he working with other people on some project, maybe outside the university?"

Em shook his head, frowning. "Not that I know of. All he seemed to think about was Nostradamus. He was writing a book about him."

"The prophet Nostradamus? The one who predicted

the Twin Towers?"

Em shook his head again. "That was a fake—just something that went around the internet."

"So he was no good?"

"No, I don't mean Nostradamus was a fake. The Twin Towers thing was a fake; somebody wrote the prophecy after it happened and put Nostradamus's name on it to make it look good. Actually, Nostradamus seems to have been okay. He definitely made some prophecies that came true."

"Did he think he ever made an accurate prophecy about the present day?" Charlotte asked. "I mean, like who's going to be the next president of the United States, or whether there'll be another war in the Middle East or something?"

"Dad was very wary about stuff like that," Em said seriously. "He used to say it was easy to find a prediction *after* the event. I mean, you could take something crazy like Sarah Palin winning the Nobel Prize for logic, then go through all the prophecies—Nostradamus wrote hundreds of them—and find one you could make fit. But it's another thing to find a prophecy that tells you clearly *in advance* that Sarah Palin is going to do something or other. Know what I mean?"

"I think so," Charlotte said doubtfully.

"What Dad was getting at—" Em began, then stopped, frowning. "You don't think whatever's going on has something to do with Nostradamus, do you?"

"I think it has something to do with your father,"

Charlotte said. "And since you say his only interest was Nostradamus, then maybe it does have something to do with him."

"I don't see how . . . ," Em told her honestly.

"Neither do I," Charlotte said, "but just suppose this book your father was writing was, like, bestseller material, the most popular book about Nostradamus *ever*; and some publisher was going to buy it for millions. Maybe the man with the coffee stain wants to steal the manuscript and pass it off as his own so he makes the millions."

"Not very likely." The most any of his dad's books had ever sold was just short of two thousand copies. None of them made even thousands of pounds, let alone millions.

"It would fit in with the robbery. Or rather the not-robbery. They only went into your father's study, and they were obviously searching for something. You say there was nothing missing, but did you actually check on the manuscript?"

Em hadn't actually checked on anything. That was something else he'd left to his mother. "Not as such," Em said uncertainly.

"Doesn't matter," Charlotte told him. "I doubt they have it anyway."

"How do you know?"

"If they got what they wanted, they wouldn't still be following us." Charlotte stopped suddenly. "Oh look," she said. "There's *Whistler's Mother*."

Tom Peterson wasn't a particularly good-looking man, but he had one of those fresh, plump, open faces that people instinctively liked and trusted. At the moment it was frowning slightly. "Why the sudden interest in Nostradamus?" he asked as he negotiated a forkful of mussels into his mouth.

Charlotte shrugged casually. They'd decided, after a long discussion, not to tell him the whole story, not to tell him anything about being followed; but he'd still been Em's father's best friend and might know something useful. "No reason," she said. "Just wondering what you thought of Nostradamus. Like, could he have made predictions about the present day? Could he have made real predictions at all?" She glanced briefly at Em.

"Actually, there is a reason," Em put in. He felt

uncomfortable cutting Tom out of the loop, but both he and Charlotte were worried that Tom might not believe the story about men with guns and being followed. Somehow it all seemed too much like a paperback thriller. Em licked his lips. "My dad was writing a book about him before he died. I wondered if he ever showed it to you?"

"Oh, his famous *Life of Nostradamus*? He used to bore us all silly about it on the faculty. He showed me an early draft of the first few chapters, but that was years ago. Are you interested in the subject, Em?"

"Sort of," Em said vaguely.

They were together in the dining hall of their hotel, a smallish room with highly polished tables and flocked wallpaper. The only other people in the place were an elderly couple seated near the window and a family group of four by the door who chatted loudly in French.

"Did he ever talk to you about the secret prophecy?" Tom asked him.

Em looked at him blankly. "What secret prophecy?"

Tom took a sip of his Pouilly-Fuissé—he'd ordered a half bottle for himself and a liter of Coca-Cola for Charlotte and Em—and wiped his mouth with his napkin. "He mentioned something to me once about finding a secret prophecy by Nostradamus. One that didn't appear in any of his published works. I thought he might have said something to you about it, but obviously he didn't."

"No . . . ," Em said thoughtfully. A secret prophecy

sounded intriguing. "What did he tell you?"

A mildly pained look crossed Tom's face. "I don't remember exactly. I think he said he'd come across some sixteenth-century documents that referred to an unpublished prophecy. They couldn't have been Nostradamus originals—otherwise it would have been all over the newspapers—but he was still pretty excited. I suppose he thought he might be on the track of something."

"What was the prophecy about?"

"Didn't say. May not have known himself; the documents could just have referred to the fact that one existed. Not that it matters; if the documents were sixteenth century, they were contemporary with Nostradamus. That has to be a bit of an academic coup."

"Where did he find them? The documents?"

"I don't know that either. He'd just come back from a trip to France when he told me about them, so I'd imagine it was somewhere in this country." Tom hesitated. "He never mentioned any of it to you?"

"Not a word."

"And there's nothing in his manuscript about it? You must have seen a much more up-to-date version than I did."

Em's starter had arrived, a curious concoction of leeks in a cream sauce. He poked at it listlessly. Dad would have been delighted if Em had read his manuscript; but the awful thing was, neither Em nor his mum was all that interested. Not really. It was cool to have a father who wrote books, of course, even academic books; but that didn't mean you actually had to like them. It would have been different if he'd written something really interesting, like science fiction or vampire stories; but a biography of some creepy old prophet? Give me a break. Both Em and his mum had humored him, listened when he'd read them bits aloud, even encouraged him to read them more sometimes; but the bottom line was, Tom had probably seen more of the manuscript than Em and his mum put together. Em racked his brain trying to remember if there had been any mention of a secret prophecy in the bits Dad had read aloud and decided there hadn't. "I don't think so," he said uncertainly to Tom. "But he never showed me the whole book."

Tom said, "He must have kept research notes somewhere. Maybe the documents he found are with them. Copies of them anyway."

Em tried the leeks, which tasted better than they looked. The silence suddenly impinged, and he realized Tom was looking at him questioningly. "Notes?" Em echoed. "Yes, I suppose so."

"But you don't know where they are?"

"No," Em admitted.

"Of course you had that break-in," Tom said. "The thieves may have taken them."

Em couldn't think why. What thief would be interested in a bunch of academic notes? "We don't think anything was taken," Em said. "At least nothing obvious." But he and his mum had been thinking about valuables, not papers. And besides, papers could be in his father's desk at the university. A wave of black depression washed over him. None of this would be tackled until the reading of his father's will. And that wouldn't happen before Em got back home, because his mum and Uncle Harold—the two named executors—hadn't yet sorted out the estate. There were, they said, a lot of bits and pieces. You could bet your bottom dollar any papers would be among them.

Tom finished his mussels and sat back. "Know what? We could make a little project, Em—a sort of commemoration of your father. If you're interested . . ."

"Daddy, his father's only just died!"

"Let Em speak for himself, darling," Tom said softly.

"What sort of project?" Em asked.

"Well, you know I want you both to come to my symposium tomorrow? I realize it's going to bore the socks off you—"

"Then why insist we come?" Charlotte put in quickly.

"Because there's no way I'm prepared to let two teenagers run loose in Paris without supervision," Tom told her bluntly. "At least I can keep an eye on you at the symposium. But we're driving south the day after; and to make up, I thought you might enjoy seeing Salon-de-Provence. Especially you, Em."

Em looked at him blankly. "Yes, sure. I mean, cool."

"You don't know what I'm talking about, do you?"

"Sure. Well . . . actually . . . no, not really." The name Salon rang a bell somewhere, but he couldn't get a fix on it.

"Salon was where Nostradamus lived and wrote his prophecies. The house is still there, Em. I thought you might like to visit it."

"Cool," Em said again; and this time he meant it.

He was in his room after supper, preparing for bed, when there was a soft knocking at his door. Em hastily pulled on the hotel dressing gown and opened the door. Charlotte was standing outside.

"Aren't you going to ask me in?" she demanded after a moment's silence.

For some reason Em found himself blushing. "I was going to bed."

"I just thought it would be a good idea to talk about the Nostradamus thing," Charlotte told him. "We mightn't get a chance tomorrow." She went across and sat on the edge of his bed, effectively stopping him from going near it. Em pulled the bedside chair a safe distance from her and sat down on it. He crossed his legs carefully, trying to look casual.

"Go on then," he urged. "Talk."

"Aren't you excited?" Charlotte asked.

"Why? I mean, why particularly?"

"Weren't you listening to my dad over dinner? This is the reason you're being followed. This explains the whole thing!"

"Does it?"

"Well, it might!" she snapped impatiently. "It's like we were saying about somebody trying to get his book because it's worth millions, only it's not his *manuscript* that's valuable; it's this secret prophecy he discovered. Somebody found out about it—well, he talked to people, didn't he?—and they wanted to steal it." She gave him a sorrowful look. "Maybe somebody really did murder your father. It's the only thing that makes sense."

"It's not the only thing that makes sense."

"Why not?"

Em sighed again. "First of all, my dad *didn't* find a secret prophecy by Nostradamus. He only found some documents that referred to one—that's all he told your dad. And like your dad says, he probably didn't even have the documents himself; he probably found them in some dusty old library and copied them: Xerox or something. And even if he did have the original documents, they wouldn't be worth millions. They might cause a bit of a stir in academic circles, but academics don't have that sort of money. They might be worth a few hundred at most, not worth killing somebody for."

But Charlotte wouldn't let it go. "Yes, but suppose your dad found the actual prophecy. In Nostradamus's own handwriting. That would be like finding a new play by Shakespeare. That's bound to be worth millions."

It was an exaggeration, but she had a point. A new prophecy in Nostradamus's own handwriting could be worth a lot of money. Had his dad found one? Whatever Charlotte said, Em couldn't quite believe he'd been killed for it. That really didn't make much sense.

Charlotte was speaking again. "Here's how I see it.

Your father is researching his book on Nostradamus. He takes a trip to France and comes across a book that mentions a prophecy he doesn't recognize. It's an exciting find, but not all that exciting. He tells my dad about it and probably a few others. Why shouldn't he? All he's talking about is a reference in some old French library. But then he gets to thinking. Suppose he could find the *actual* prophecy, the original parchment? Now that would be something really cool. That would make him rich and famous. He could probably sell it to a museum, and it would make his book a bestseller. So he goes off looking for it. *And he finds it!* At least he finds out where it is. He doesn't tell anybody—not my dad, not your mother. He wants to have the original parchment in his hands before he makes the big announcement. But there's somebody else after the prophecy as well, and he kills your father to stop him from finding it first. What do you think?"

"I think you'd make a good thriller writer," Em said sourly. "What you're really saying is, my dad's a thief. If he found the original prophecy, he had to find it *somewhere*: in a library or somebody's collection of papers. Either way, he'd have had to steal it if he wanted to sell it and get rich the way you said. But if he stole it, he *couldn't* sell it because he'd need to establish provenance before any museum would touch it. It would be like trying to sell the *Mona Lisa*: it's just too well-known for anybody to want to buy it. Besides which, Dad wasn't murdered. He got sick."

"Maybe, maybe not."

"Oh, Charlotte—"

Charlotte held up her hands. "All right, all right, maybe he just died. By coincidence. But I'll tell you one thing. Somebody thinks he found the original of the Nostradamus prophecy."

"Why do you say that?"

"Because they broke into his study looking for it. I'm absolutely sure of it. Your dad wasn't a thief—I know that. I shouldn't have said that stuff about him selling it and getting rich: I didn't think it through. But somebody else might not have been so ethical: maybe a collector or somebody who knows a collector who would buy it. So they broke in looking for it. They didn't find it then, and now they think you might have it. Or at least know where it is. That's why they're following you. They probably think you'll lead them straight to it."

"This is ridiculous," Em said.

Charlotte sniffed. "You'll see. Day after tomorrow you're heading for Nostradamus's hometown. Think how *that's* going to look to them."

12

Tom had somehow managed to retune the radio in their rental car to the BBC, where a newsreader was relaying British government assurances that the country was well placed to meet the threat of Nigerian Death Flu thanks to the impending purchase of a newly developed vaccine that would be used in a mass vaccination program to be introduced over the next few weeks.

"Must make sure you have your shot when we get home," Tom murmured, glancing at Charlotte, who was in the passenger seat beside him. "You should have one too," he said over his shoulder to Em. "Get your mum to arrange it."

Em grunted. Personally, he thought the Nigerian Death Flu business was a load of fuss about nothing, since it didn't seem to be any more serious than the seasonal flu that hit Britain every winter. But the name frightened people, he supposed, and his mum might well insist he get a shot. He wasn't about to remind her though. Em hated needles. To change the subject, he asked, "Where are we now?"

"Just south of Avignon," Tom said. "I considered taking you in to see the famous *pont*, although there's not much of it left; but I thought if we were going to detour at all, you might prefer to see Saint-Rémy, to judge from our conversation the other evening."

"Why Saint-Rémy?" Em asked, wondering what conversation Tom was referring to. The previous night, after a mind-numbingly boring day at Tom's rotten symposium, they'd talked mostly about soccer.

"It's the town where Nostradamus was born; don't you remember? The actual house is still there."

Saint-Rémy-de-Provence proved to be a village rather than a town—and a picturesque one at that. They passed beyond the remnants of an ancient wall before reaching the interior, which somehow managed to look more Italian than French and might just possibly have been Roman. Tom found parking, then led them to a narrow back street overlooked by crumbling, dirty, slumlike houses. "What do you think?" he asked as they stopped beside a green gate.

"What do we think about what, Daddy?"

Tom nodded toward a square building with plaster so cracked that it revealed the brickwork beneath. "The house where Nostradamus was born."

How did Tom know where to find it? Em said, "Not exactly a palace, is it?"

"Don't knock it," Tom told him. "That must have been a reasonable middle-class residence in 1503. They may not have had all our mod cons, but they probably lived well by the standards of their day." He stared at the house a moment longer, then shrugged his shoulders. "Nostradamus's own home in Salon is a bit more impressive. As you'll see."

Salon-de-Provence proved to be larger than Saint-Rémy, a medieval town surrounded by an outgrowth of comparatively modern buildings. They abandoned the car in favor of feet and walked through an archway in the original city wall to enter the Old Town. In less than half an hour, they were standing outside a tall terraced house with an imposing entrance door.

"This is it," Tom said. "This is where he lived and wrote his prophecies."

"It looks new," Em said, a little disappointed.

Charlotte peered at the plaque beside the door:

DANS CETTE MAISON

VECVT ET MOVRVT

MICHEL NOSTRADAMUS

ASTROPHILE

MÉDECIN ORDINAIRE DV ROI

AVTEVR DES "ALMANACHS" ET

DES IMMORTELLES "CENTURIES"

MD III MDLXVI

"In this house lived and died Michel Nostradamus," Charlotte read aloud, translating the wording. "Astrologer, physician ordinary to the King, author of the 'almanacs' and the immortal 'centuries.' 1503 to . . ." She hesitated, then turned to Em. "What's LXVI?"

"Sixty something," Em said. "Sixty-six, I think."

"1503 to 1566," Charlotte said triumphantly. She frowned suddenly. "I think they've turned it into a museum!"

Nostradamus proved not to be much of a tourist attraction, for apart from themselves, the museum was almost empty of customers. A bored girl behind a small reception desk issued them with tickets that Tom paid for in euros, then surprised them by breaking into excellent English. "You may go anywhere within the house that you wish. These brochures in your native language"—she handed them out with a flourish—"contain a plan and explain a little about each room."

"*Merci,*" Tom said, looking dazed.

For Em, the house was frankly disappointing. It consisted of narrow staircases and sparsely furnished rooms with wooden floors, small doorways, and low ceilings. When they eventually reached the attic, one of the smallest rooms of all, Em started violently at the unexpected appearance of a fierce, black-bearded and black-robed man wielding a quill pen behind a smallish desk. Then he realized that it was a mannequin, presumably meant to represent Nostradamus himself. Tom said soberly, "This is where he made his prophecies.

This is where he called up spirits."

Em blinked. "This is where he called up *what*?"

Tom looked momentarily discomfited. "Apparently that's how he made his prophecies. He'd come in here with a brass tripod, a small lamp or candle that would have been his only light, a laurel wand, and a bowl of water. He probably had an incense burner as well and maybe some narcotic herbs—he studied herbs, after all. Then he used an ancient Greek ritual to call up a spirit that helped him prophesy."

"You mean he was . . . like . . . some sort of magician?" Em asked hesitantly.

"I suppose you could call him that. He certainly tried to practice magic to call spirits into his water bowl. It could all have been hallucinations, of course, especially if he was using narcotic herbs."

Em stared into the empty room imagining the bearded, dark-eyed figure of the prophet as he crouched over his great brass bowl. He could almost hear the mutterings of the approaching spirits as they swirled stealthily from the depths of the water. He could almost see a luminous figure that towered above Nostradamus, then bend nearly double to whisper in his ear.

It was a vision that remained with him, on and off, throughout the remainder of his trip to southern France. He was even thinking about it vaguely as he opened the door of his home, having waved good-bye to Tom and Charlotte on the doorstep.

"Mum!" he called. "I'm back!!" He hefted his suitcase to the foot of the stairs but decided to take it up a little later. He was tired and excited from the trip, still undecided about whether to tell his mother about the man who'd followed him. "Mum," he called again, "Tom's coming over later with Charlotte—is that all right? We had a great time. We saw the house where Nostradamus lived and Tom got big applause at his symposium and Charlotte bought a top that cost over sixty quid. Tom paid—she has him wrapped around her little finger. Any chance of a cup of tea? I'm parched. I have a little present for you in my case. All the way from Paris. Mum?"

But it wasn't his mother who came out of the kitchen. It was his mother's brother, and he looked serious.

13

"Hello, Uncle Harold," Em said. "Where's Mum?" He glanced around vaguely, as if she might be hiding under the stairs.

Harold said, "Come into the kitchen, Em. I've something to tell you."

"What's happened?" Em asked at once. But Harold only turned and walked back into the kitchen. After a moment, Em followed him.

Harold Beasley looked nothing like Em's mother. He was fat and colorless and wore round, rimless granny glasses to correct his short sight. But that was only on the outside. Inside his head, Uncle Harold looked heroic. He'd once been a fairly useless policeman, but that hadn't stopped him from writing to his sister: "Last week we had seven robberies, two murders, and eighteen assaults in the precinct AND SOMEHOW WE HAVE TO STOP THIS!" Now he sold life insurance but retained the urge toward self-dramatization. "Sit down, Em," he said in something close to a sepulchral tone. "I have something very serious to tell you."

"What?" Em demanded. "What's happened?" A feeling of pure dread was crawling up his spine, made all the more unpleasant for having nothing to focus on. Something had happened to his mum—it had to be that. Maybe she was ill. Maybe she'd fallen, broken a bone of something. "Is it Mum?" Em added.

But Uncle Harold insisted on his little games. He gave Em a sorrowful, pitying look. "I think it best you sit down," he said again.

You could sometimes stop Uncle Harold's nonsense if you tried hard enough, but it was far quicker just to give in. Em sat down on a kitchen chair, suppressed the urge to ask questions, and looked at him expectantly.

"Your mother is in the hospital," Uncle Harold said.

She'd fallen down. Em was certain of it. She'd had one drink too many and fallen down.

"They took her into Saint Brendan's while you were in France," Harold said.

Their local hospital was the Costa General. Em had never heard of Saint Brendan's.

"They sectioned her," Uncle Harold said. He hesitated, then added guiltily, "There was nothing I could do about it. I did try."

Sectioned? Some sort of operation? They were

opening up sections of his mother? Sounded horrible, but if it was for her own good, why would Uncle Harold try to stop—?

The memory fell on him like some terrible cascade. *Sectioned* wasn't any kind of surgery. It was the name for the legal procedure that committed you to a lunatic asylum! The person who made a sectioning application had to be your nearest relative—he was sure of that. But with Dad gone, Mum's nearest relative was Em himself, and he certainly hadn't made an application. Unless . . .

Harold was his mother's brother. He was legally Mum's closest relative while Em was underage. "You sectioned her?" Em gasped.

Harold dropped his posturing and waved one hand irritably. "No, of course not. Why would I section her? I told you; I tried everything I could to stop it."

"Who sectioned her? It has to be a relative."

"No it doesn't," Harold said. "It was a social worker."

"A *social worker*?" Em exploded. Social workers called on people in council houses who were mistreating their children. Em had never even *seen* a social worker. Social workers simply didn't have any business with people like his mother and himself. "What social worker?"

Harold pulled a chair across and sat down. Now that he'd stopped puffing himself up, he looked defeated. "A Mrs. Harlingford," he said.

Em cut him off. "What had she got to do with Mum, this Mrs. Harlingford?"

Harold shook his head. "I don't know. She just

turned up at the university, demanding to be let into the apartment. Caroline was out somewhere at the time shopping, I think, and you were away in France, so the provost sent for me. When I got here they were arguing on the doorstep; but your mum came back from shopping a few minutes afterward, and the Harlingford woman served her with a commitment order under the Mental Health Act."

"They can't do that!" Em protested. "I mean, a social worker can't just walk up to you and have you committed just like that. You have to get a medical examination or something."

"She had two forms signed by doctors."

Em just stared at him. This was unbelievable. Eventually he asked angrily, "What doctors? Who were they?"

"One was Alex Hollis. I don't know the other one, but there was the stamp of some clinic; I can't remember the name."

"Dr. Hollis?" Em almost felt like yelling. "That's our own GP. Dad and he went golfing sometimes." Dr. Hollis's surgery was only about twenty minutes from the university. He was the GP to most of the faculty. Why would he do a thing like this?

Harold looked down at his feet. "I know; I didn't understand it either. I tried to see him for an explanation, but there was a different doctor at the office, and the secretary said Dr. Hollis had to leave the country for a few days."

"What happened next?" Em asked. "After the Harlingford person served the papers?"

"Well, Caroline protested, of course, and so did I; but Harlingford stoned it: I threatened to call our lawyer, but she just said to go ahead. Meanwhile, she had to put your mother in the hospital. Then she called these two goons she had with her in the car—bouncer types: all dark glasses and bulging muscles—and said she had to go to the hospital right away. Harlingford didn't want to give me the name of the hospital, but I insisted; and finally she said it was Saint Brendan's."

"Where is that?" Em interrupted.

"Other side of town. Highgrove."

"When did this happen?"

"Three days ago."

"Why didn't you let me know?" Em demanded.

"Your mobile must have been out," Harold said. "Tom's too. Somebody told me the French network's pretty shaky." He glanced away.

It was a lie. Em knew it at once. Harold was useless in a crisis. Carefully, he said, "How is Mum? You've visited her, haven't you?"

Harold shook his head. "They wouldn't let me."

"Who wouldn't let you?"

"The hospital. They said no visitors for four days. They were doing an initial evaluation or something. I sent her a suitcase of clothes, though, and I phoned every day to see how she was."

Em glared at him. "So how was she?"

"Fine. At least they told me she was fine. They wouldn't let me talk to her."

"I don't understand this!" Em protested. "Why would some social worker we've never seen want to section Mum?" Behind the question other questions were lining up. Why did their family doctor sign the section papers? And who was the second doctor involved whom Uncle Harold had never heard of?

Harold shook his head again. "Didn't have any idea. All our lawyer could say was that she was acting within the law. He did have the idea that she might not be a bona fide social worker; but when he checked, she was kosher. Working for some government department, too, quite high up."

"How long are they going to keep her there?"

"I don't know," Harold said, "but Mr. Greeve said that under Section Two of the Mental Health Act, you can be detained for twenty-eight days."

"*Twenty-eight?* That's nearly a month!"

"They can extend that to six months if they make another application; and they can make further applications after that, more or less indefinitely."

Em continued to stare at him, his mind working overtime. Eventually he said, "This all happened Tuesday? Three days ago? So this is the fourth day?" Harold nodded without saying anything and managed somehow to look vaguely guilty. "So we could visit her today?" Em suggested.

"Bit late in the day now. Besides, I have stuff to

do . . ." Uncle Harold protested.

"It's all right, Uncle Harold. I'll go to see her on my own," Em said carefully. He had a sudden, surprising surge of sympathy for his uncle. The man was weak, silly, and disorganized; but that was probably just the way he'd been born. Shouting at him now wouldn't help. Em needed the exact address of the hospital, a quick shower, and a change of clothes, then he could go see his mother and find out properly what was going on. He was fairly sure he'd extracted as much information from his uncle as he was likely to get.

"There's something else," Harold said.

Em sat down again and waited.

"The house was broken into again," Harold said.

Saint Brendan's wasn't at all what Em had expected. It wasn't a lunatic asylum for one thing—no high walls, no muscular orderlies carrying straitjackets—but a massive, redbrick general hospital . . . and a busy one to judge by the jam-packed car park and the high volume of traffic.

Em walked through the main gates with a feeling of trepidation. He'd said nothing to Uncle Harold, but behind his shock and outrage there was a niggling part of his mind that wondered if his mother hadn't brought this on herself.

Except she didn't seem to be in a mental institution. She seemed to be in a hospital, the sort of hospital where you got bones set and bleeding stopped and had operations.

Em started moving again, walking slowly toward the main doors.

The feeling of trepidation still hadn't gone away by the time he reached the reception desk. A pretty girl in white gave him a tired smile and asked, "Can I help you?"

"I'm here to see my mother," Em said. "Mrs. Caroline Goverton."

"What ward is she in?"

He should have asked Uncle Harold, but he hadn't thought of it. "I don't know. I'm sorry."

"Doesn't matter." The girl tapped keys on the computer beside her. After a moment she said, frowning, "When was she admitted?"

"Four days ago, I think." For some reason Em felt impelled to add, "I was in France."

"Lucky you," the girl said. She turned back to the screen, and the frown returned. "Was it an emergency admission?"

Em took a deep breath. "She was sectioned under the Mental Health Act."

To his surprise, the girl's face brightened. "Oh, she'll be in our Lydon Clinic; it has a separate reception and records." She gestured. "Back the way you came, turn left outside the front door, follow the signs to A and E: Accident and Emergency; but when you get there, go around the side of the building and stay on the path until you see the sign Lydon Clinic." She smiled. "It's a bit small, so keep your eyes peeled."

It *was* a bit small, so small he nearly missed it: a

labeled arrow high up on a wall to his right. He took the narrow avenue indicated and eventually discovered a group of single-story buildings surrounded by a grove of trees. There were no nameplates, no indication whether or not this was the clinic he was looking for. He was still hesitating, wondering if he should just knock on a door and ask, when a young man in a dark blue pin-striped suit emerged from somewhere, walking briskly away from the buildings.

"Excuse me," Em called. "Is this the Lydon Clinic?"

"Yes." The man pointed. "Main entrance is at the side—bit confusing. You'll have to ring the bell. Reception will let you in."

As the young man had suggested, the main entrance doors were locked, and their darkened glass panels meant that Em could not see inside. He found the bell and pushed. The intercom panel clicked at once, and a female voice said, "Yes?"

"Is this the Lydon Clinic?"

"Yes."

"I've come to visit one of your patients," Em said. For some reason he felt it might be important not to mention names at this stage. Best wait until he was safely inside; although he half expected the receptionist to refuse him entry.

But the receptionist only said, "Yes, of course. Please push the right-hand door when you hear the buzzer." And the sound of the buzzer came at once.

The reception area of the Lydon Clinic was very

different from the massive foyer of Saint Brendan's hospital. Em took less than a dozen steps inside the door before he reached the counter. To one side stood a uniformed security guard who watched his approach unsmilingly. The counter itself was in the charge of a slim, middle-aged woman wearing a severe tailored suit. She favored Em with a polished, professional smile. "May I help you?"

"I'd like to see Mrs. Caroline Goverton," Em said.

"Are you a relative?"

"I'm her son."

The woman's reaction could not have been in greater contrast to that of the hospital receptionist. Her smile vanished at once, and her eyes flicked briefly sideways to the security guard. She made no attempt to consult a computer or any other form of record. Instead she murmured, "Excuse me a moment," and picked up a white telephone, carrying it as far away from him as the cord permitted.

The woman whispered so quietly he could only hear a few scattered words—"son" was repeated several times—before she returned to hang up the phone. "Dr. Marlow will be with you in a moment."

Anger rose up in Em, pushing aside his usual mild-mannered exterior. "I don't want to see Dr. Marlow. I want to see my mother!"

The receptionist eyed him coolly. "I'll ring her and tell her you're here," she said. "But Dr. Marlow thinks it would be wise for him to have a word or two with you before you actually see her."

"Why?" Em demanded belligerently. There was something terribly wrong here, something terribly wrong about the whole situation since he arrived home from France.

The security guard shifted his position. Not exactly a threatening movement, more a preparation for possible trouble. The receptionist said, "I'm sure Dr. Marlow will explain when he arrives."

The security guard moved again, but before Em could react, the entrance door behind him opened to admit a tall man in a white coat. He walked directly across. "You must be Edward Michael," he said, and extended a well-manicured hand. "Julian Marlow. I'm the psychiatrist in charge of your mother's case. Perhaps we could have a word before you see her?" He favored Em with a look that oozed professional sincerity.

So his mother was a case now? "Look—" Em began.

Dr. Marlow took him gently by the arm and led him a pace or two away from the receptionist and her guard. "I know this is hard for you, Edward, but I promise you your mother is getting the best possible treatment available. She—"

"Treatment for *what*?" Em demanded furiously. He hadn't wanted to talk in front of the receptionist and security guard, but now he didn't care. "I don't know what she's in here for. Nobody's told me anything."

If the sudden outburst fazed Dr. Marlow, he didn't show it. "I'm afraid," he said kindly, "your mother has had a breakdown. She's been under a great deal of strain. I understand your father died quite recently, and there seem to have been various other pressures. But the good news is that her condition is treatable. In a few weeks, a month or two at most, I'm certain she will be quite her old self again."

"A month or two?" Em echoed, appalled.

"I understand Social Services is currently making arrangements to look after you while she's here. They may not have contacted you yet since I believe you've been away; but I do know there are provisions within the act for dependent minors, so you need have no worries about how you'll cope while she's away, and I believe the modern facilities are excellent." He gave a tight, benign little smile.

Em felt himself go chill. His mother had been sectioned under the Mental Health Act, and now somebody was making arrangements to take him into some sort of care home. "I can stay with my uncle Harold," he said quickly. There was no way he was going into care in some sort of children's home.

"Yes, possibly," Dr. Marlow told him easily. "I'm afraid those arrangements have nothing to do with us here, but you can take the matter up with Social Services when they make contact with you. I'm sure something can be worked out. In any case, whether you're in a home or with your uncle, you'll be able to visit your mother whenever you want to. Which brings me to your visit today . . ." His face took on an expression of concern.

He was going to refuse to let Em see his mum: Em was sure of it. "I want to see her," he said firmly. He wanted to see her now, try to find out what was going on, then make his escape. He was going to find somewhere to hide until he figured out what he could do. There was no way they were going to lock him up the way they'd locked up his mother.

"Yes, of course."

"I want to see her alone."

"Yes, of course," Dr. Marlow repeated. "I merely wanted to warn you in advance that you may be a little . . . shocked by your mother's condition."

"What do you mean?" Em asked, alarmed.

"I'm afraid she's no longer the woman she was when you last saw her. She's currently on medication; we were forced to sedate her quite heavily to calm her and prevent self-harm. So you mustn't be concerned if she slurs her words or seems a little . . . detached from reality. This is purely temporary, I assure you. You will see a massive improvement within the next few weeks or so; but in the meantime you mustn't allow her condition to upset you, or pay too much attention to the wilder things she might say to you." The professional smile again. "Well," Marlow said briskly, "that's all I really wanted to tell you. Ms. Playfair"—he nodded toward the receptionist, who was trying to look as if she wasn't listening to the conversation—"will give you a floor plan of the clinic and directions on how to find your mother."

Em said quietly, "Dr. Marlow, why was my mother

officially sectioned?"

And Dr. Marlow said, "I'm afraid you'll have to take that up with Social Services, Edward. We only look after the patients when they're sent to us. The legalities of the situation are another department."

Em felt nervous and confused. He'd fully expected to have been escorted to see his mother. He was in a mental clinic, for cripe's sake; and while his mother certainly shouldn't be here, the other patients were probably bona fide lunatics. What happened if one of them tried to talk to him? Or attack him? But he wasn't escorted. Miss Playfair, as Dr. Marlow had said, had given him a floor plan with the clinic's logo on it—a merry little eye inside a triangle—then lost interest in him altogether. Ms. Playfair had told him his mother was in the conservatory, resting, and had marked the area with an X. So far he'd seen no other patients, thank heavens. Perhaps they were all out for a walk or watching television or having supper or something. With luck he might be able to see his mother without even . . .

Em turned a corner. An old woman with unruly, graying hair was staggering drunkenly along the corridor toward him, holding onto the wall for support. Her eyes were wild and staring, her face locked into a contorted expression of manic determination. She gave a strangled call when she saw him and increased her pace.

For a moment Em considered running. He didn't know how to deal with lunatics, and this was clearly a card-carrying escapee from the funny farm.

He should never have hesitated. The mad woman put on a surprising burst of speed and was almost upon him now. "Em," she gasped. "Oh, Em . . ."

Em went cold. If he'd still had time to run, he knew his legs would never have worked. He felt totally paralyzed, except for a jaw that dropped of its own accord to register astonishment. "Mum . . . ?"

Then she was holding him, clinging to him, using him as support while he held her and nearly burst into tears, then did burst into tears as he murmured, "Oh, Mum. Oh, Mum. Oh, Mum."

"They told me you'd arrived," his mother whispered. "That Playfair woman phoned and said you were coming to meet me in the conservatory." She stroked his hair and stared into his eyes. "They have cameras in the conservatory. They spy on everything you do here. I don't want to talk to you while they're spying on us, so I came to meet you. Oh, Em, I'm so glad you've come." She was having trouble with her balance, but he knew she wasn't drunk. There was no smell on her breath, no thickening of her speech, although she *was* talking slowly.

"What have they done to you, Mum?" Em asked.

"Tranquilizers. Heavy-duty. Two capsules the size of a horse pill three times a day, and they force you to take them. Makes you floppy all the time, affects your balance. Bloody buzzing in the ears as well, but think they care about that? They just want you sedated so you're no trouble and don't try to escape. You don't either: I couldn't climb onto a bus in this state, let alone find a bus stop." She kissed him lightly on the cheek. "But you're here now."

"Your hair's gone gray," Em said inconsequently.

His mother actually managed a small smile. "Didn't have my rinse with me, and they don't let you buy in stuff. It'll be fine when I get to a hairdresser."

You've only been here for four days, Em thought. *A rinse wouldn't wear out in four days.* The gray had to have something to do with the drugs she was on. Or the stress of what had happened to her. He opened his mouth to say something else, but she beat him to it. "Don't talk here, Em. There are cameras in the corridors: I don't know how well they pick up sound, but they're monitored, and the staff can lip-read."

In different circumstances it would have sounded paranoid, but he was feeling pretty paranoid himself these days. "Okay, Mum," he murmured.

"We'll go to my room," his mother said. "No cameras there, and I can't find any bugs."

Her room was small, but tastefully furnished with a bed, a couch, two chairs, a built-in wardrobe, and a compact writing desk. There was even a bathroom en suite, shower, and loo. He was about to say something as they walked in, but his mother put a finger to her lips and led him straight through into the bathroom. She turned on every tap and the shower, then leaned forward until her lips were close to his ear so he could hear her above the sound of gushing water. "I couldn't find bugs, but that doesn't mean there aren't any. I think we should be okay now so long as we keep our voices down."

"Mum," Em said, "what's going on here?" Before she could answer, he added, "Do you know this Mrs. Harlingford person? The one who had you sectioned?"

She shook her head. "No, not at all. But she's obviously one of *them*." She spat the final word fiercely.

He wanted to ask who *them* was, but more than that he wanted to make sure Mum hadn't brought this on herself somehow. All his old suspicions came flooding back as he said, "Mum, you didn't make a scene, did you? In a shop or somewhere? You weren't drinking and this woman happened to come past?"

She gave him a withering look. "Look, I never saw her in my life before, not until she turned up at the university. She was trying to get into our home, Em. And she had the committal papers with her. Signed by a doctor I've never seen in my life either. And by Alexander Hollis, who didn't examine me for anything since I picked up that foot fungus eighteen months ago. He never *examined* me! That man was a friend of your father. I swear, Em, I'll never forgive him for what he's done."

Em took a deep breath. "And he wasn't concerned about . . . how you've been lately?"

He expected her to go off the deep end, but she only shook her head. "This has nothing to do with my drinking or a nervous breakdown or any of the things they're saying." She stopped. "Look, I can't keep standing up. These drugs . . ." She flipped down the cover of the toilet seat and sat down. Suddenly she looked very small and very lonely.

"What's going on, Mum?" Em asked again.

"They killed your father!" his mother blurted. "I know I should have told you before, but you're only a child, Em. I know you think you're grown up, but you're really just a boy, and I wanted to protect you. I thought I could handle it—or maybe handle it along with your uncle Harold; but I'm not sure he really believes me, and anyway, he's useless when it comes to anything practical. But I can't hide it any longer. You need to know, Em. And you need to believe me. For your own safety, you need to believe me."

"I believe you, Mum," Em said to reassure her, then discovered it was true. After everything that had happened, what had seemed incredible before suddenly seemed reasonable. Or at least possible. "But I want you to tell me everything."

"I wish I knew everything," his mother murmured.

"All right," Em said. "Start with Dad. Why do you think he was murdered, and how?"

She looked up at him. "There's so much I don't know. Your dad was a harmless soul. A bit dull even, to tell the truth, but I loved him. He never got mixed up in anything bad; he just wasn't the type. All he was really interested in was history. Sometimes I think he *lived* in the past. He was very steady, stuck to his routines. But about a month before he died, all that changed. He got excited about something."

"What's this got to do with his death?"

"It's very difficult to think straight with the drugs they've been giving me, hard to order my thoughts; but I'll be as clear as I can. You'll just have to be patient with me."

"Take your time, Mum," Em said, even though his impatience was clawing inside him.

His mother closed her eyes, then rubbed her face briskly with both hands as if trying to clear away the effects of her drugs. She looked back at Em soberly. "He had a visitor. A well-dressed, middle-aged man, graying hair, quite distinguished. He said he was from Oxford—a visiting scholar who wanted to discuss the Renaissance. Edward saw him in the study. But I've never seen a scholar as well-dressed as that. And if he were a scholar, why didn't he meet your father at the university? The thing is, after the visit your father was frightened."

"What about?"

"He wouldn't tell me. Actually, he denied being frightened at all; but after eighteen years of marriage, I can tell. Any woman could."

"What was the man called, the one who came to see him?"

"Kardos. Stefan Kardos. It sounds Hungarian to me, but he didn't have a foreign accent. I thought he was English. Very well-spoken. He could easily have come from Oxford. Anyway, I never found out what the visit was really about or why it frightened your father, and quite soon after that he became ill."

"We're still a long way from murder," Em said. He

caught his mother's expression and added hurriedly, "Sorry."

"You remember that in the first few days, he ran that very high temperature? He got very delirious in the night when I was sitting up with him. Talked a lot, though I don't think he even knew I was there. Very confused, of course, not making much sense; and I only caught parts of it. At first it was about Nostradamus and some prophecy, then he kept saying they were coming to get him. At one point he kept repeating 'Themis' again and again."

"That's Greek, isn't it? What's it mean?"

"She was a Greek goddess. I looked it up."

"Bit outside Dad's speciality," Em remarked.

"I told you he wasn't making much sense. Your father was very ill at that point and very confused; but the one thing that came through loud and clear was that he was terrified, and he believed there was somebody out to get him. This happened over a couple of nights, maybe three; but then his temperature started to drop and he stopped raving, and after that we all thought he was getting better. Even the doctor said he was over the worst of it."

A sudden thought occurred to Em. "That was Dr. Hollis."

"Yes, that was Dr. Hollis."

"One of the doctors who signed the papers that got you in here. You don't think he harmed Dad . . . ?"

"No, I don't. I couldn't believe that. I still can't, even

after what he did. But anyway, your father had another visitor."

"He had lots of visitors," Em said. "Once he started getting better. Most of the faculty came to see him at one time or another. It cheered him up."

"This was a stranger like Mr. Kardos. I assumed he was another scholar. He called in with a packet of papers he wanted your father to look at. And some grapes."

"Oh," Em said. He had no idea what this was adding up to, but it was certainly adding up to *something.* "What was his name?"

"I can't remember. I had something in the oven, and I was distracted. He told me his name all right, but . . ." She shrugged. "Anyway, I don't know. The thing is, he was alone with your father for fifteen, twenty minutes."

"But he couldn't have killed him," Em protested. "He was still alive after!"

"The grapes were poisoned," his mother said flatly. "He was getting better, and that bastard gave him poisoned grapes. He was eating them the night before you found him. I asked him where he got them, and he said this man Grannell brought them." She stopped abruptly, a look of shock on her face. "My God, I've remembered! That was his name: Grannell. Christopher Grannell. From Oxford, like Stefan Kardos. I couldn't remember before, but that was definitely the name he gave me."

"Back up a minute, Mum," Em said. "How do you know the grapes were poisoned?"

She looked at him with a pleading expression on her face. "It makes sense, doesn't it? Your father was *getting better.* His temperature was back to normal; the doctor said he could get up for a little while just as long as he didn't overexert himself. He should have been back to teaching by the end of the week. Then he's visited by two complete strangers in a matter of days and dies after eating grapes one of them brought. Of course he was poisoned!"

"Did he eat all the grapes?"

"No, but he wouldn't need to, not if it was a strong poison. He might only need to eat one."

"What did you do with the grapes that were left?"

His mother stared at him for a long time before answering. "I threw them out," she said eventually. The stare turned fiery. "I didn't know they were poisoned, did I? How could I know? I was shattered by your father's death. I never even dreamed it was murder at the time; it was only later that I started to put two and two together: your father's nervousness, his secrecy, the two strangers, his sudden death. You don't believe any of this, do you?"

Em took a deep breath. "Actually, I do. There have been some very freaky things going on, Mum. Remember the break-in where they rifled Dad's study? Well, there's been another since you've been locked up here, and this time they rifled the whole apartment— Uncle Harold showed me. And why are you here anyway, in a psychiatric clinic? You're not mad and you haven't done anything, so why are you here? Then there were the strangers at Dad's funeral. You were a bit out of it and probably didn't notice them." What he meant was *drinking,* but thought it kinder not to say so. "But one of them was carrying a gun. A handgun in a shoulder holster."

His mother's jaw dropped. "A *shoulder holster?*" Em knew how she felt. Nobody in Britain carried handguns in shoulder holsters. That was something you only saw in Mafia movies. Somehow a shoulder holster was even more shocking than poison. Which was, of course, the reason why he'd chosen not to believe he'd really seen it.

"He followed me to France," Em said. "The man with the gun."

Somehow his mother seemed to shake off the effects of her drugs, stood up, and gripped his arms; but this time she wasn't holding on to him for support. "You were followed by a man with a gun?" she gasped. "Oh God, oh God!"

"It's all right, Mum. He might not even have had the gun when he followed me. I only really saw it at the funeral."

"It's *not* all right!" his mother told him savagely. "There's something dreadful happening here, something I don't understand at all. You need to get out of here, Em. You need to get out fast. This clinic is mixed up in the whole thing, I'm sure of it. You have to get out. And then you need to lie low. When I get out, I'll find you—you can leave word with somebody—Tom perhaps; we can trust him. There's money; I told you that. We can leave the country and hide."

They can keep you here for months, Em thought. "Mum," he said, "if they were planning to do anything to me in the clinic, they'd have done it by now." The only problem was, he didn't know who *they* were. He didn't know what they were after, or why they were posing a threat.

"No they wouldn't," his mother said. "That would attract too much attention. But they've put me out of harm's way, and now they're obviously after you. They know you're here, so they can track you when you go; and the longer you stay here the more time they'll have to put things in place. Get out now, get away and lie low. Tell Tom where you'll be so I can find you. Go *now.*" She stared earnestly up into his face. "And for God's sake, make sure you aren't followed!"

Em stole a bicycle. He'd never done anything like that in his whole life, never taken so much as a candy bar; but he was desperate and the bicycle was there, leaning against a gate by the edge of a path that wound away from the side of the clinic. He was fairly sure he hadn't been followed when he left the clinic, mainly because his mother had made him climb out through a window; but if she was right about the cameras, it would only be a matter of time before somebody discovered he had gone. He planned to be a long, long way away before that happened, longer than he was likely to manage on foot.

In less than a minute he was among the trees, and eventually found the perimeter fence. He abandoned the bicycle conspicuously, hoping it might be found quickly and returned to its rightful owner, then scrambled over the fencing and reached the main road. He didn't want to risk the bus stop; but a van driver pulled over on his first attempt at thumbing a lift, and luck was with Em big-time, for the man was headed almost exactly to the place he wanted to go.

Unlike many of the faculty, Tom Peterson did not live on campus. Just four years ago, shortly after his marriage break-up, he'd bought himself a nineteenth-century rectory on four acres of grounds just on the edge of town. Em, who'd been here before, slipped through a side gate, avoided the driveway, and stuck to the shrubbery until he came within sight of the house. He stopped and switched on his mobile phone.

Tom himself didn't seem to be there—no sign of his car, which he usually parked to one side of the front door—but Em had hopes someone else might be. He thumbed the number she'd given him in France.

"Do you know who this is?" he asked when Charlotte answered.

"Yes, of course, E—"

"Don't mention my name," Em cut in hurriedly. "I need to talk to you."

"So talk," Charlotte said. She sounded a little miffed, probably because he'd cut her off.

"Not over the phone."

"Are you all right?" Charlotte asked.

"I'm fine," Em said. "Can we meet?"

"When?"

"Now. Soon as possible."

"Where?"

"You remember Sam's Diner, the place we went with your dad on the way back from the airport?"

"I know the place you mean. I remember where it was. You had a revolting doughnut, right?"

"Yes. I mean, it wasn't revolting, but I did have a doughnut. Can you meet me there in an hour?" She'd have to leave now if she was to meet him there in an hour.

"Yes, I suppose so. Is this about the man—you know, the one we saw near the Louvre?"

"Might be," Em said. "Your father's not there, is he?"

"Not where?"

"Where you are now," Em said cautiously.

"I'm at home."

"He's not at home, is he?"

"No, he isn't. Do you want me to ring him?"

"No, don't do that," Em said quickly. "Just come to meet me. Without ringing anybody."

"Know what, Mr. I-Don't-Want-You-to-Mention-My-Name? You are getting seriously weird in your old age." She hung up.

Em stared at his phone for a moment, then dropped it into his pocket and waited. He watched from the cover of the shrubbery until Charlotte emerged from the front doorway and locked the door carefully behind her. She marched down the driveway, frowning.

"Pssst!" Em hissed as she drew closer.

Charlotte started visibly, and one hand went quickly

to the little bag she was carrying. Em stepped out from the cover of the shrubs.

She relaxed at once, but the frown actually deepened. "What do you think you're doing? I nearly Maced you!"

Em blinked. "You don't carry Mace, do you?"

"Standard issue for girls my age in California. Never mind the interrogation. What are you doing here? Why aren't we meeting at what's-its-name's like you said?"

"Sam's Diner. That was just to throw them off," Em told her. "In case my phone calls are being monitored." That was something else he'd have to do: get himself a different mobile phone. She was looking at him with an exaggerated expression of astonishment. Despite everything, he smiled at her. "How do you fancy Ropo's? I'll fill you in on everything over a cup of coffee." He remembered something and added, "Provided you buy the coffee."

"I'll buy the coffee," Charlotte said.

Ropo's was a trendy coffee bar much favored by teenagers, where young couples could go to cramped, two-person booths and hold hands. Em and Charlotte were in one of them now, drinking frothy mochas. Any hand-holding was conspicuous by its absence. Charlotte watched his face closely as he finished his story. "Wow," she said softly, "this is *way* crazier than what happened in Paris!"

"Yes," Em agreed. Except that what happened in Paris was *part* of what happened when he came home; he was sure of it.

"What are you going to do?" Charlotte asked. "You can't let them take you into care."

"No, I can't," Em said. "That's the main thing. If they get their hands on me, I'll never find out the truth about my father's death."

"Well," said Charlotte briskly, "you can't go home; that's for sure. They might even be waiting for you there now—the Social Services people. What about moving in with your uncle Harold?"

"First place they'd look."

"What about moving in with Dad and me?"

"Second place they'd look," Em said gloomily. "Your dad was my dad's best friend."

"All the more reason. When we tell him what's been going on, he'd never give you up to Social Services."

"He might not want to, but he'd have to," Em said. "He's not a blood relative, so he'd have no legal standing. I suppose he might apply to become my guardian; but that could take months, maybe years, and meantime I'm in a boys' home somewhere and Mum's in a psychiatric clinic pumped with drugs."

"He could hide you. Pretend you weren't with him."

Em shook his head. "That would never work. Besides, if he was found out, it could get him into big trouble— for obstructing Social Services or something. I wouldn't want that to happen."

Charlotte hesitated. After a moment she said carefully, "What about moving in with me then?"

Em stared at her. "Moving in with you?"

"I could hide you in my room. Dad need never know."

Em almost laughed aloud. "You *couldn't* hide me in your room! I mean, who's going to believe we weren't . . . ?" He let it trail off in embarrassment.

"Weren't what?"

He felt the flush crawling up from his neck, but fortunately the low blue lighting would have hidden it. He moved his hands about vaguely, wishing he'd never brought it up.

She let him stew for a moment, then said soberly, "All right, what *do* you plan to do?"

And Em, who didn't know what he planned to do, had no idea what he planned to do, heard his voice answer her: "Sleep on a park bench somewhere."

Em's luck. It began to rain. He felt the first drops as he left Ropo's, and it had turned into a steady downpour by the time he reached Nelson's Square. He was dressed in a T-shirt, jacket, and jeans; but the jacket was far from waterproof, and he had nothing to wear on his head. He was soaked through in minutes.

He passed the statue and turned right, headed for an unfamiliar, rougher part of town down by the canal. Where there was a canal there were bridges, and bridges gave you some shelter, somewhere to sleep when you were homeless; and thank God it was still summer, so he wouldn't die of exposure. At least that was his thinking before the rain started. Now he wasn't so sure how much shelter a bridge would give, especially if the wind picked up.

There was a Salvation Army shelter near the canal, on somewhere called Holt Street—he'd looked it up in Ropo's phone book before he left. But he wasn't exactly sure where Holt Street was, and he didn't know what happened at Salvation Army hostels. Did you just turn up and ask for a room? Did you have to pay; and, if so, how much? Did you have your own room, or did you share a dormitory with a bunch of smelly old men? Did they feed you? Were the lavatories clean?

He had money—quite a lot, actually. He had thirty euros in notes, left over from his holiday, which he supposed he could change into sterling when the banks opened tomorrow. He also had seventeen pounds sterling, the entire contents of Charlotte's purse, which she'd insisted on giving him after she paid for the coffee. In all, it probably added up to more than forty pounds, which was a lot of money for him. But the problem was, he didn't know how long it would have to last. Even if the Salvation Army fed him for nothing—which they might since they were a religious organization—he couldn't keep going back to the same place. That would be far too dangerous. Besides, they might be obliged to report underage boys to Social Services. He couldn't risk that either.

He found himself outside the Salvation Army shelter by sheer chance. The facade, illuminated by a towering streetlamp, looked as ordinary as it could get: a large house in a street of large houses, many of which had now been changed into offices. The only thing that marked this house as a shelter was the Salvation Army logo and the motto Blood and Fire on a discreet brass plaque. Above three shallow steps, the front door was open. There were lights on inside.

Although Em's coat collar was turned up, rain was trickling down the back of his neck. He felt cold and miserable. It occurred to him that maybe he should find out more about the Salvation Army just in case he decided to stay there some other time.

Em pushed through the door. He was in a large hallway with open doors leading off it. To his left was a desk, in charge of which was a gray-haired man wearing jeans and a sweatshirt. Apart from the Salvation Army logo on the man's sweatshirt, there was no religious symbolism on display anywhere.

The man swung his feet down from the desk as Em entered but kept the phone glued to his ear. He waved at Em with his free hand, a sort of cheery, semimilitary salute. "You got your troubles, I got mine; but they're nothing to these boys. Listen, Paul, I'll ring you back. Somebody just walked in." He cradled the phone without saying good-bye. "Hi," he said to Em.

It was warm inside the hallway, so warm that Em's clothes were already beginning to steam. He wasn't going to stay here, not if it cost money, not if the man had to report him to Social Services; but the thought of going back out into the rain was becoming less appealing by the minute. He should have thought through what he wanted to ask before he came in. He hesitated, staring dumbly at the man.

"Name's Jeff," the man said. "Fancy a cup of tea and a look around?"

He fancied something to eat a lot more, but anything warm inside him would be welcome. Em nodded.

"Common room through there," Jeff told him, gesturing toward the open door. "Say hello to the lads. They're a friendly lot on the whole, although some of them don't look it. Wouldn't recommend the coffee, but you might find yourself a sandwich, and there were a couple of bananas left when I last looked, if old Victor hasn't snaffled them. Want to check out the sleeping accommodation, it's through the common room and on your left. Come back to me when you're finished."

Em noticed Jeff hadn't asked his name or where he was from or what he wanted. He opened his mouth to say something, closed it, then opened it again like a fish. Jeff waved toward the open door again. "Through there," he repeated, then lifted his phone and pressed the redial button.

It was warmer still in the common room, and noisy. The place looked as much like a canteen as anything else, with men huddled around small plastic tables, drinking from mugs and talking loudly. They were a rough-looking lot on the whole. Em edged nervously toward a countertop with an enormous tea urn, a coffee machine, and a scattering of sandwiches on paper plates. There was an enamel bowl that might once have contained fruit, but it was empty now. Old Victor had apparently snaffled the last of the bananas.

Em found a mug and reached for the tea urn.

"Careful with that bloody thing," a voice said in his ear. "Scald you as soon as look at you."

Em turned to find an old man with bulbous eyes and an enormous, straggling gray beard standing behind him. He had a peculiar accent. "You hold the mug tight under the spout and press the red button. Go on—tight under the spout, and don't jump when it steams."

Em pushed his mug carefully under the spout.

"You get to appreciate strong tea," the old man remarked. "Milk's over there in the big blue jug. And there's sugar in the packet. Makes the tea almost drinkable if you put in enough sugar. Not like the coffee. Nothing makes the coffee drinkable. I'd keep away from the coffee, I were you. Have a sandwich. Cheese and Branston—very tasty."

"Thank you," Em said. He added milk and sugar to his tea, sipped it experimentally. The taste wasn't too bad. He reached for a sandwich. "You wouldn't be Victor, would you?"

The old man's face started a suspicious smile. "How did you happen to know that, young man?"

"Lucky guess," Em told him. He finished the sandwich, grabbed another, and took it with his mug of tea to inspect the sleeping accommodation. With food in his stomach he was beginning to feel a little more cheerful and a lot more confident. Maybe he could stay here for just one night. He could sleep under a bridge tomorrow when the rain had stopped. When *hopefully* the rain had stopped.

But the sleeping accommodation wasn't the series of rooms he had pictured. It was one large room, much the same size as the canteen, with cots squeezed in everywhere. There must have been forty of them at least, maybe even fifty. Although it was still relatively early, almost half of them were occupied by fully dressed men curled up, apparently asleep.

"It's not the Ritz," Victor's voice came from behind him, "but it's warm and dry, and they change the sheets before they allocate you a bed. Usually. You staying the night?"

"Thinking of it," Em admitted. He had to sleep in a dormitory at school, and this wasn't really so very much different.

"Better talk to Jeff then. Before it fills up. You'll find it fills up fast when it's raining."

Em hesitated. There was still the business about Social Services. One phone call and he could have bartered a warm dry bed for his freedom. At the moment, nobody knew who he was; and while anybody could guess he was underage, he still hadn't admitted it officially. He could walk away now and no one would be any wiser.

But walking away now meant walking into a wet night.

Em stared into the dormitory room. He'd never seen cots look more appealing. "Victor . . . ?" It would be okay to ask Victor. He'd never make the phone call. But would he know the answers?

"Yeah?"

"What happens if you're under eighteen? Do they have to tell anybody?"

"You mean like your parents?"

Victor thought he was a runaway. "Yes," Em said quickly. Then hesitated and added, "Or anybody?"

Victor shrugged. "They would if you were younger, like seven or something. But you could pass for older."

"Won't he ask my name and where I live?"

"Anybody asked your name yet?"

"No, but . . ."

"And where you live is the streets, Sunshine. You don't have a home; you don't have some *permanent address*"—he spat the words as if they were distasteful—"otherwise you wouldn't be in need of shelter, would you? Say anything you like. Don't you understand? Nobody checks up on you."

Em finished the last of his sandwich and brushed a crumb off his jacket lapel. "I think I'll go talk to Jeff."

Like Victor said, it wasn't the Ritz. Em's clothes had dried out in the heat of the shelter, and he was now curled under a blanket in one of the cots. Victor, by accident or design, was stretched out on another bed beside him, already asleep. It was far from dark. Light bled in through the windows from the street outside, through the open door, from the now-quiet common room. A surprising number of the men seemed to be reading by the dim glow of battery-operated night-lights.

The dormitory wasn't quiet either. All around Em, like the sounds of the sea, was a gentle dissonance of snoring, grunting, heavy breathing, punctuated by an occasional belch, fart, sigh, or moan. It should have been hugely irritating, but strangely, Em found it comforting. In the gloom, wrapped in heat and sounds, he began to drift. Fragments of dreams intruded on his waking consciousness. At one point he thought he saw the prophet Nostradamus, with his black beard and funny hat. At another he was back in the shelter dormitory watching a ratty little man drag a tattered canvas bag across the floor.

He awoke to a riot.

Victor was standing, minus his trousers, hurling abuse at a bullet-headed character with bulging muscles. The brute wore a T-shirt sporting one word: WINSTON. Several beds had been pushed aside, and the two antagonists were surrounded by a circle of excited men. "Fight!" shouted one of the men; and the word was taken up and transformed into a chant. "Fight! Fight! Fight! Fight!"

Em pushed himself hurriedly out of bed. "Bloody know you did!" Victor shouted. "You knew where I kept it!"

"Everybody knew where you kept it," Winston said. "Now leave me alone before I break your face."

"What's going on here?" Jeff was pushing through the crowd now.

"Bastard took my stash," Victor said without turning his head.

To Em, "stash" meant "drugs"—he'd heard users at his school talk about their stashes—but by the look of Jeff's expression, it had a different meaning here.

"Never touched it," Winston growled. "You probably gone and lost it."

"It'll be under his bed," Victor growled.

"All right!" Winston said. "You look and then apologize." He turned around and, without so much as a grunt, lifted his entire bed and held it clear of the floor. There was nothing underneath it.

"Was it green?" Em asked. Faces turned toward him, and his heart started to pound again. "Was it a small, green, canvas bag?"

Victor stared at him. "Yes, it was," he said uneasily. "You saying you saw it?"

Em looked at the ratty little man who was standing on the edge of the circle of onlookers a little to Winston's right. "Here," the man said at once, "what do you think you're accusing me of?" He began to back away nervously.

Em grabbed him. The man jerked free, ricocheted spectacularly off one of the onlookers, plunged over an empty bed, and scrambled gracelessly across the floor like an insect until another onlooker pressed down on him with a heavy boot.

"Just hold him there a minute," Jeff said. He dropped down to look under one of the beds, then drew out a green bag. "This it?" he asked Victor.

"That's it," Victor told him grimly. He glanced at Winston and added sheepishly, "Sorry, big fellow."

"So, what was in it?" Em asked curiously the next morning. "Has to be something special for you to face a bloke as big as Winston."

Victor shrugged slightly. "I could have taken him. I'm tougher than I look."

They were sitting together at a table in the corner of the common room, sipping mugs of strong, sweet, milky tea. Nobody had had breakfast yet. According to Victor, volunteer ladies would turn up with bacon and eggs, but not before eight. The squabble with Winston and the ratty man's subsequent eviction as the real culprit had woken everybody early. Now the common room was packed with anxiously hungry residents trying to fill up on liquids. Even the coffee machine was in use.

"Yes, I know," Em said diplomatically. "But what were you so worried about him stealing?" The bag was too small to hold much of anything; and given the circumstances, it was unlikely to contain wads of cash or pouches of diamonds. Em was betting on something of sentimental value, and he was curious. Whatever it was would tell him something about Victor, the old man who wouldn't back down from a fight with somebody half his age.

The bag in question was resting beside Victor's foot. He hooked the strap with one finger and lifted it onto the table. "Want to see what's in it? Are you sure? You may very well be disappointed." He turned the bag upside down and tipped the contents onto the table.

"That it?" Em asked after a moment.

"That's it," Victor said.

Em stared at the small, battered book, the tattered school jotter, the stub of a pencil, and the bundle of thin twigs held together by two rubber bands. "What is it?"

"That's the oldest book in the world, kid," Victor exclaimed portentously.

Em frowned. "It's a paperback."

"I don't mean this *actual* book, stupid. That's obviously a copy. I mean the book itself. Oldest book in the world. First written in ancient China around 3500 BC. It's called the *I Ching*." He pronounced it *yee jing*.

"What are the twigs for?" Em asked.

Victor's tone became even more scathing. "Those aren't twigs, my boy. Those are dried yarrow stalks. You need them for the oracle."

"So the book's an oracle? Some sort of fortune-telling? It can tell you the future?" Em was suppressing a grin. If a tattered paperback could tell the future, what was Victor doing in a homeless shelter? All he had to do was bet his boots on the three thirty at Newmarket and walk away with a million.

"It's not fortune-telling, and it's obviously not going to tell you who'll win the three thirty at Newmarket; otherwise I wouldn't be sitting here, would I?" Victor said as if reading Em's mind. "But it *can* guide you on what you should do in a situation to make sure of the best possible outcome."

"May I look?" Em asked, intrigued despite himself. The book and his funny bunch of sticks were obviously precious to Victor, judging by the fuss he'd made when they disappeared.

Victor shrugged and pushed the book across. "Knock yourself out, kid," he said in a spoof of an American accent.

Em flipped the first few pages and glanced at a

dense, academic introduction—Dad would have loved it!—before opening it at random somewhere toward the middle. Confusingly, the page heading read "61. Chung Fu/Inner Truth" beneath two Chinese characters Em couldn't understand and above a little diagram made up of broken and unbroken lines. Near the bottom of the page, under a subheading "The Judgment" was what looked like a four-line poem about pigs and fishes. It must have lost something in translation, because it didn't even come close to rhyming. Or making sense, come to that. "How's it work?" Em asked curiously as he pushed the book back across the table.

"You use the yarrow stalks," Victor told him. "You count them in a special way, and that gives you your hexagram. Then you look it up in the book and that gives you your oracle."

Em wished he hadn't asked. What was a hexagram anyway? "Why don't you show me?" he suggested.

"What? Cast you an oracle?" Victor stared at him soberly for a long time, then apparently made up his mind. "Very well." He started to peel the rubber bands off the yarrow stalks. "What's your question?"

Em looked at him blankly.

"Your question," Victor repeated. "The oracle answers your questions. No question, no answer." He absorbed Em's expression and sighed. "Imagine you're talking to the spirit of a very wise, very old Chinese sage. Somebody who's been around, somebody who knows the ropes. Somebody maybe a bit psychic. Now what question do you want him to answer for you?"

There were so many. Had his dad really been murdered? And if so, why? Who'd arranged to have his mother locked up? When would she get out again? Who broke into their home—twice? But he suspected the oracle wouldn't give him answers about stuff like that. Victor was watching him impatiently, so he said, "Could I ask something like 'Is my present situation going to work out okay?'"

"You can ask anything you like," Victor told him grumpily. "But you might be better off asking what sort of action you should take to ensure your present situation works out for the best."

"All right," Em said. "What action should I take to make sure my present situation works out for the best?"

Victor tapped his bunch of yarrow stalks sharply on the table, and Em wondered if that was the way the ancient Chinese called up spirits. He liked Victor, and they were surrounded by people and noise; but Victor's face had taken on a set, determined expression that somehow made the whole thing feel decidedly spooky.

It took Victor a long time to consult the oracle. When he had finished, he wrote something in his jotter with the stub of pencil. Em leaned across to see what it was and discovered a single, broken line. He grinned at Victor. "Well, what's it mean?"

"Nothing yet," Victor told him. "That's just the first line. Now shut up and let me concentrate."

Em sat back and shut up, watching Victor with

fascination. The process of counting—it was repeated five more times—took almost twenty minutes. When it was finished, Victor had drawn a peculiar diagram on the page of his jotter. "You've got moving lines," he muttered, half to himself. Then he reached for the book and flicked quickly through its pages.

There was a stir behind Em as the doorbell rang, and he glanced over his shoulder to see what was going on. Jeff was walking toward the front door. "That'll be breakfast," Victor said absently without looking up. "Might want to do this later."

"No, do it now," Em urged him. He was hungry, but just at that moment he was even more curious. "What are moving lines?"

"The first hexagram"—Victor pointed at the diagram he'd drawn—"that's this thing, represents the situation you find yourself in. Where you are now, so to speak. Sometimes that's all there is with the *I Ching*: just the situation you're in and some advice on how to handle it. But sometimes, like now, the situation you're in isn't stable. It can't hold for very long."

"What do you mean, 'can't hold'?"

"It's on the point of changing," Victor said. "When you're in *that* sort of situation, it shows up as moving lines."

"All right," Em said, "what's my current situation?"

"Conflict," Victor told him promptly.

From the corner of his eye, Em could see two men and a woman standing in the doorway deep in conversation with Jeff. All three were wearing conservative gray suits, and if they'd brought breakfast, there was no sign of it. "What sort of conflict?"

"Well, you'd best be the judge of that," Victor said. "According to the book, somebody is out to get you at the moment. Somebody powerful, I'd say. And if you push them too far, you're going to be in *real* trouble. A cautious halt halfway brings good fortune, according to this."

Em stared at him openmouthed. He was already in real trouble, but apart from that, everything Victor said was spot on. And he'd figured it out by fiddling with a pile of dried sticks!

As Victor turned to a later page in his book, Em heard his own name emerge from the buzz of conversation behind him. Not just his friendly nickname either, but his full name, spoken formally: Edward Michael Goverton. Em felt himself go cold. He'd given a false name to Jeff and told nobody else who he was. Even Victor didn't have a name for him other than "boy."

"Your development is hexagram thirty-three, which is called 'Retreat,'" Victor told him. "That says it all. The only way to deal with the dangerous situation is to get out of it. The good news is, you *can* get out of it. But only if you move quickly."

Em was already moving quickly. He was on his feet and headed for the back door of the shelter. Attracted by the sudden movement, the two men from Social Services—they had to be from Social Services—turned in his direction. "Hey," one of them called, "are you Edward

Goverton?" Except he wasn't from Social Services, he was the man from the train, the man who'd followed him to Paris.

Em burst into a run. The back door was through the dormitory and down a passageway past the lavatories. Behind him, Jeff started to protest as the two men sprinted across the common room without another word. The woman stepped in front of him, grabbed his arm, and said something sharply into his face.

As Em reached the open doorway of the dormitory, the men in suits were already halfway across the common room. He glanced behind in time to see Victor casually trip one up as he raced past the table where Em had been sitting just seconds before. The man careered against another table, fought briefly for his balance, then crashed heavily to the floor. His companion leaped over the body and redoubled his speed.

The dormitory was a jumble of temporary beds that slowed Em down as he zigzagged between them. But it slowed his pursuer even more, so he was only a third of the way through as Em reached the far side of the room. Em jerked open a door and raced down the dingy passageway, praying that the back door at the end was not locked. He reached it as the man following entered the passage, then experienced everything dissolve into slow motion as he turned the handle, tugged experimentally, felt the first hint of a catch before the door pulled open.

Em was outside now, in a narrow back street, and time was running frantically again. He could hear the heavy footfalls behind him, fancied he could hear the man's labored breathing as he slammed the door. His whole instinct screamed at him to keep running, to run like the wind; but for some reason Victor's voice was echoing inside his head with a sentence he'd quoted from *I Ching*: "A cautious halt halfway brings good fortune."

Despite his every impulse, Em stopped to look around. Beside the back door was an empty trash can. He threw the lid away with a clatter, then forced the rim of the can under the knob of the door. He kicked it savagely into place so that it jammed tight. Seconds later his pursuer was rattling the door furiously, shrieking with frustration.

But by then Em was disappearing down the side street on his way to freedom.

Em blew the whole day in a mixture of worry and fear. How had they found him? No one knew he was staying in the shelter. He'd only decided to go there when he found himself standing outside it . . . and even that had been an accident. He'd lied to Jeff about who he was and told no one else. He should have been absolutely safe, absolutely anonymous, yet the man who'd followed him to France had found him in a single night and turned up with his friends to get him first thing in the morning. Who the hell were they? Until he figured that out and how they'd found him, there was every chance they would find him again. Not to mention the fact that the *real* Social Services must still be after him. His life was turning into a chase movie.

He slid into a coffee shop and bought coffee and a

ham roll to go, then caught a bus to carry him out of the district. He disembarked at random and headed into a nearby park, trying desperately to shake off the sensation of invisible pursuers.

Eventually, late in the afternoon, he walked out of town altogether and climbed a grassy hillside to a spot where he could see anyone approaching half a mile away. He knew it was an overreaction, but he felt safer here, more able to think.

He tried a trick his father had taught him: laying out his problems in his mind one by one in the hope he might get some idea what to do next. The overall sequence was simple enough. Someone had killed his father. There had been strangers at the funeral, one in a car with diplomatic plates, one who carried a handgun. Someone had rifled his father's study. The man with the handgun had followed Em to France. While Em was away, someone had persuaded two doctors to commit his mother to a mental clinic, and someone had rifled their entire home. This was obviously tied up with the fact that he was being followed, but where was the pattern that made sense of it all?

It had started to rain again by the time he got back into town. Not the downpour of the night before, but a steady drizzle that somehow managed to be just as wetting. It focused his mind on where he was going to spend the night.

There was no question of returning to the Salvation Army shelter. Or any other local shelter, come to that. If he wanted to sleep in a warm bed tonight, he needed to leave town and find a shelter somewhere he wasn't known, somewhere that had too many shelters for his pursuers to check them all. London was the obvious choice.

Em hesitated. He thought he probably had enough money to cover his fare to London; but once he paid it, he'd have very little cash left over. In fact, now that he came to think of it, what with wandering and worrying, he'd forgotten to change his euros in a bank that day, so he might not have enough for the fare after all. More to the point, just staying free was hardly enough. He had to find out what was going on, and he wasn't going to do that in London. In fact, traveling to London just to get shelter had to be really stupid since he'd just have to travel back again, and he wasn't sure he had the funds for that. He pulled out his phone and dialed Charlotte's number.

By the time he reached the central depot, the last bus was gone (at 11 p.m., according to the timetable posted outside). But by now he'd more or less decided against London anyway. There was no sign of Charlotte yet; and after ten minutes waiting in the shadow of an archway, he was beginning to wonder if she was coming at all. Then a taxi drew up and she stepped out of it.

"Over here!" Em whispered urgently as she stood frowning at the closed gates of the station.

"Are you all right?" Charlotte asked anxiously as she joined him in the archway. "You sounded weird on the phone."

"I'm fine. Did you bring the money?"

Charlotte nodded. "Yes."

"How much could you get?"

"A hundred pounds."

Em almost choked. He needed money badly, but this was way more than he'd expected from her. "A hundred pounds?!"

"It's all I had," she snapped angrily, obviously mistaking his tone. Her own tone softened into an anxious "You will give it back when all this is over? I'm saving for an iPad."

"Every penny. I promise." He impulsively kissed her on the cheek, and she blushed.

After she'd gone, he walked around the corner to the train station, which was still ablaze with light although not exactly packed with people, and discovered his luck had changed. There were several late-night shops still open, plus an all-night fast-food bar. To his delight, one of the shops was Camping World; and a huge sign in the window was advertising a sale.

He spent £9.99 on the cheapest sleeping bag in the store: SALE, screamed the sign, LESS THAN HALF PRICE FOR THIS ITEM. He had money now, thanks to Charlotte, but he still had to watch his spending or the extra hundred wouldn't last very long. He went around to the fast-food bar and spent fifty pence to buy a bag of chips, which he ate on a bench on one of the platforms. He dropped the greasy bag into a litter bin, then headed down a broad flight of steps to the underground passageways.

There were seven passages in all, each one leading to

a different platform. Four of them were fully lit to show their platforms were still operational. In the remaining three, the lights were dimmed: the platforms they led to were closed for the night. Em picked one of the dimmed passageways at random.

He walked until he was out of sight of the entrance, then unfolded his new sleeping bag and began to climb inside it. He wasn't the only one sleeping here. He'd already passed a large cardboard carton with a huddled shape inside, and a little farther on from him there was a sleeping figure under a tattered blanket. Em settled himself against a wall, cradled his head in his arm, and closed his eyes.

The passageway was a good choice. It was dry and reasonably warm despite a constant draft. There would be no one wandering past to disturb him before the platform reopened in the morning. It was possible, he supposed, that some railway official might turn up to move him on, but he doubted it.

But sleep didn't come easily, even though he was tired out from his day of walking. He kept thinking he'd wasted a day, a day he could ill afford to waste, when he should be making plans. He'd started out with the bold idea of discovering the truth about his father's death, finding out who caused it and all the other hassles. But since then all he'd really done was run. Worse, he still couldn't think what else to do.

Everywhere he might think of going would certainly be thought of by the people after him, so it was really only a matter of luck whether he'd be undisturbed wherever he picked. The yawn stretched his jaw without warning, all his niggling thoughts turned fuzzy, and he sank into a comfortable darkness.

A woman screamed.

Em sat bolt upright. There was no sense of time passing, and for an instant he had absolutely no idea where he was. Then he remembered and looked around frantically. Something was terribly wrong. The scream came again, followed by a stream of swearing that echoed from wall to wall. He started to scramble from his sleeping bag, fumbling with the zipper in his haste to get it open. A man's voice tried to cut across the woman's shrieks, but Em could not make out the words. He shook free of the bag eventually, moved quickly to the corner of the passage, and peered cautiously around it.

The men who'd chased him from the Salvation Army shelter were engaged in a ferocious altercation with a tiny, white-haired woman—the sleeping shape in the cardboard carton Em had seen earlier. The carton itself was tipped over on its side now, and the woman's belongings—they looked like old rags and shoes—were scattered. One of the men had hold of her arm, but only in an attempt to stave off her furious attack. Even so, she managed to pummel him with her free hand while trying desperately to kick his legs and keep up a stream of abuse. Em could have kicked himself for not listening to his fear and moving on. It was only dumb luck that they'd disturbed this feisty little woman before they found him.

Em turned and ran. The shouts of the woman would cover any sound of his footfalls, so he had a real chance of getting away. He reached the steps with no sign of pursuit and took them two at a time. He emerged onto a darkened platform, slick with rain—this part of the station had no roof. A single, self-illuminated sign promised the next train at 6 a.m. Em ran to the end of the platform, breathing in waterlogged air, then dropped down onto the track and followed it all the way out of the station before climbing a fence into somebody's backyard and then opening a gate that took him into an alley. Minutes later, he was back on the main streets.

He felt elated. He knew where his pursuers were tonight. If they were checking the station, it meant he would be safe somewhere else—*anywhere* else. Except possibly the shelters where his description might be circulated. His mind went back to the first thoughts he'd had when he went on the run. He could head for the canal and shelter under one of the bridges. His sleeping bag was waterproof and zipped up all around his head so that only his face would be exposed. That made a big difference. Although the weather was wet, it was still mild, so he'd be just as cozy as he'd been . . .

The thought remained unfinished as Em realized he'd left his sleeping bag in the passage at the railway station.

The canal proved a mistake. He found a bridge quickly enough, but the wind blew rain right under it, so he might as well have lain down in the open. Worse still, somebody had been using this tiny stretch of canal bank as a toilet, and the smell was awful.

All the same he trudged along the bank in search of another bridge until the streetlamps ran out and darkness forced him to retrace his steps. It was well into the early hours of the morning now, and since he'd slept a little in the station passageway, he was beginning to wonder if he shouldn't forget about shelter altogether and start a new day early. But it was just a passing thought. He knew he needed more sleep.

He found what he was looking for by accident. A stretch of canal bank ran parallel to a railway line . . . just where the railway entered a tunnel. Em climbed up the embankment, made a slippery descent down the other side, and headed straight for the tunnel.

He discovered there was a concrete apron on one side of the track broad enough for him to sleep on. He placed the palm of his hand against one wall of the tunnel and used it as a guide until all light faded and he was standing in pitch darkness. Then he slid down, curled up in a fetal position, and tried to settle himself for sleep.

He awoke with a light shining in his face.

Em scrambled to his feet, his mind racing. He was blinded and confused, but his instinct was to make a run for it. He could worry later about how they'd found him. He hit out blindly, somehow managed to slap the flashlight aside, and headed off like a rabbit. He caught his foot on the railway line and fell heavily. His pursuer—there only seemed to be one of them—was on him at once. Em tried desperately to struggle, but a knee in the small of his back pressed him down effectively. "Stop wriggling!" a voice hissed in his ear. "Look at me!"

Em turned his head as the man turned the flashlight to shine on his own face. "Victor?" Em gasped.

The pressure on his back eased abruptly as Victor climbed off him. "You never stop to think, do you? Same thing in the shelter: first hint of trouble and you're off."

Em brushed himself down. He'd grazed the palm of one hand but was otherwise unhurt. "What are you doing here, Victor?"

"Looking for you," Victor said.

"How did you find me?"

Victor shrugged in the gloom. "Followed the boys chasing you. I don't have time to explain. Where's your mobile phone?"

There was a faint vibration underfoot.

"Why do you want my mobile phone?" Em asked suspiciously.

"Oh, for God's sake, Em!" Victor snapped. "They're using it to track you."

Em's eyes widened. "How do you know my name?" He'd been very, very careful not to mention it to Victor while they were in the shelter.

"I'll explain later." Victor held out a hand. "Phone?"

The vibration transformed itself into the distant sound of an approaching train.

"They can't use it to track me," Em said stubbornly. "It's switched off." His last call had been to Charlotte, and he'd switched it off afterward to save the battery.

"You really don't know what you're up against, do you, Em? Just give me the bloody phone. I managed to divert them, otherwise they'd have had you by now; but they're not far away, and it's only a matter of time before they pick up your signal again."

"I told you," Em protested. "I switched it off." All the same, he pulled his phone from his pocket.

The train was closer now. Em could see the approaching lights and hear the rattle of the carriages echoing through the tunnel. He stepped back to flatten himself against the wall and instinctively reached out to pull Victor with him. Victor gripped his hand and took the phone. "Off or on, it's still transmitting a signal," Victor said. "Not many people know that, but they can use it to track you anywhere you go. The only thing that's saved you so far is your habit of going underground. That confuses the signal and slows them down."

The train was almost upon them now. The phone had cost Em's father a hundred and forty pounds. Em watched in horror as Victor tossed it casually onto the track. Seconds later, in a rush of air and noise, the train crushed it to smithereens.

"There," Victor said, "that'll buy us time. But we still need to get out of here. Come on." He grabbed Em's arm, and together they began to walk down the track after the receding train.

"Where are we going?" Em asked. They were standing in a deserted street outside a grocer's and a heavily shuttered pawnshop. Victor was in the process of inserting a key into the lock of a doorway between them. Em could imagine a stairway behind the door leading to rooms, or even flats, above the shops. But Victor shouldn't have a key to anywhere. Victor lived in Salvation Army shelters. His only possessions were his *I Ching* paperback and the yarrow stalks.

But the key wasn't the only odd thing about Victor. Now that they were out of the railway tunnel and into a part of town where the streetlights let Em see properly, Victor was a different man. He no longer had the look of a tramp. His clothes—jeans, sneakers, and Windbreaker—were casual but clean, and the sneakers looked positively new. The beard was no longer the matted, straggling bush of gray and white Em saw in the shelter. It had been neatly trimmed and, though Em couldn't quite believe it, seemed to have been dyed, for it was now predominantly brown, with only the slightest hint of gray. The result was that Victor looked younger—quite a lot younger. And not just because of the beard. His walk was more confident, not an old man's walk at all; and casting his mind back to the tunnel where Victor had easily held him down, it was clear to Em that Victor was far stronger than an old man ought to be.

"Safe house," Victor said.

That didn't make much sense either. Like most boys at his school, Em read thrillers despite his teachers' disapproval. A safe house was where spies hid when they were on the run. But Victor couldn't be a spy, unless he was spying on the Salvation Army.

The door opened, exactly as Em expected, on a cramped hallway and a flight of narrow wooden stairs. He hesitated.

"Come on," Victor said. "The sooner we get you off the streets and hidden away, the happier I'll be." Even his voice had changed. It was firmer, more confident, although his accent stayed the same.

The staircase smelled of dust, and the flats it led to looked shabby. But only from the outside. When Victor used another key on the nearest door—there was a battered aluminum figure 1 screwed into the peeling paint work—it opened into a bright, well-furnished apartment. Em looked around in bewilderment. This wasn't a rich man's flat, but there was carpet on the floor and a dishwasher, washing machine, electric cooker, and breakfast bar in the kitchen area. There was even a small piano in the living room. Did Victor *own* this place? So what was he doing sleeping in shelters?

There were dead bolts on the inside of the door, and Victor slammed all four of them across before turning back to Em. "It's steel lined," he remarked. "Need a battering ram to get through it, so you'll have plenty of time to escape if they do find you. Which they won't." He moved over to the window and twitched the curtain aside. Behind it was a small, brushed-steel lever set into a metal plate. "Releases an escape chute," Victor said. "You can be out of here and on the street in seconds. It's mechanical, so it will work even in a power cut."

"Who are you?" Em asked soberly. By now only a muppet would have failed to work out that Victor wasn't what he seemed to be—or at least not what he *had* seemed to be. This was no down-and-out, wherever he'd been sleeping lately.

"Would you like coffee? There's some quite decent Costa Rican in the cupboard."

"Is this one of those 'if you tell me who you are, you'll have to kill me' deals?"

Victor smiled for the first time. "Something like that."

"You're MI5, aren't you?" Em blurted. It was like something out of a movie, and even as he said it, he didn't believe it; but it was no more unlikely than everything else that had been happening to him since his father died.

Victor shook his head. "No. No, I'm not. Let's just say I work for something called Section 7. It's a bit more secretive than MI5."

Em blinked. "More secret than MI5? More secret than the Secret Service?"

Victor shrugged. "You can find MI5 headquarters in the phone book; they even have a website. Nothing very secret about that, is there? But you won't find Section 7 listed anywhere; and if you could persuade anybody in authority to talk about it at all, they'd deny our existence."

"So that's all you're going to tell me?"

"Actually, no, it isn't. If you give me time to make the coffee, I'm going to tell you a great deal. Including some stuff even MI5 doesn't know about."

The smell of percolating coffee reminded Em that the last thing he'd eaten was a small bag of chips in the railway station the night before, and suddenly he was ravenous. He began to open cupboards in the kitchen area.

"There's the remains of a cooked chicken in the fridge," Victor told him. "I need to stock up properly now that there are two of us, but it'll keep you going." He began to pour the coffee into two large mugs and handed one to Em. It bore an inscription in multicolored script: YOU'RE JUST JEALOUS BECAUSE THE VOICES ONLY TALK TO ME.

Em skipped the knife and fork to savage a chicken leg held in his fingers. Victor watched him over the rim of his coffee cup with an expression of amusement. After a moment, he opened a drawer in the table and threw across a paper napkin. Em used it to wipe his mouth, then his fingers as he asked, "Did you dye your beard?"

If Victor was surprised by the question, he didn't show it. He shook his head. "This is my real color. I washed out the white and the gray. Didn't need it anymore."

"Why didn't you shave it completely?" Em took his first sip of coffee. It was excellent.

"I have rather a distinctive scar. The beard hides it." He reached across to pick a sliver of meat from the chicken. "Facial scars are rare—they mark you out. But lots of men wear beards."

"Is Victor your real name?"

"No, but you can keep using it."

"Do you live here?"

"At the moment, yes."

"Why were you in the Salvation Army shelter pretending to be homeless?"

"I was looking for you."

Em stared at him. The old familiar feeling of sinking out of his depth came back full force. There was so much going on he didn't understand. "How did you know I'd be there?"

"I didn't," Victor said. "When I found out that you were on the run, it seemed a homeless shelter would be a good place to start looking. I got lucky." He shrugged. "There aren't very many shelters in the town."

"I was going to sleep under a bridge," Em said inconsequentially.

Victor gave him a cynical glance. "I don't think so," he said. "Sleeping outdoors sounds easy until you actually try it. Then you head for the nearest shelter. It's only when you can't get in anywhere that you end up under a bridge or on a park bench. But you were a quick learner with the railway station and very brave trying the tunnel."

Em didn't want to think about finding a place to sleep tonight (except that he was going to sleep here, wasn't he, in this safe house, with Victor?), didn't want to think about the people chasing him. What he wanted was answers. "Victor," he said, "what's all this about?"

"Have you ever heard of the Knights of Themis?" Victor asked.

21

"The year was 594 BC; the country was Greece; the city was Athens. . . ."

"What was the weather like?" Em asked.

Victor glared at him. "Do you want to know what's going on or don't you?"

"Sorry," Em said contritely.

"There were actually riots in the streets," Victor continued. "The poor in Athens were tired of being pushed around by the nobles and having no say in what happened to them. So the Athenians called in a man named Solon to act as mediator, and he set up a whole series of reforms—new laws, what amounted to a new constitution, really. These laws were the first steps toward political democracy, the first time such a thing happened anywhere in the world."

"Good for him," Em murmured.

"Solon was a very wise man," Victor remarked. "But unfortunately, his reforms pleased nobody. The nobles thought they went too far; the poor thought they didn't go far enough. Solon went off on a world tour—that's when he discovered the Egyptian records of Atlantis that Plato wrote about—and left them to sort themselves out. While he was away, a group of the most conservative nobles banded together to form the Knights of Themis."

Em frowned. "Knights of . . . ?"

"Themis. She was one of the ancient Greek Titans, the embodiment of divine order. She represented the old laws and customs. The Athenian nobles liked her because they wanted to go back to the way things were before Solon stuck his nose in. Specifically, they wanted to get rid of this newfangled democracy business. The Knights of Themis was a political movement in the form of a secret society dedicated to the overthrow of democracy. The society itself was organized something like today's Masonic Lodge, with initiations into various degrees. There were oaths pledging obedience to the superiors of the order and binding members to absolute secrecy about their plans, aims, and methods."

Em frowned. "And I should be interested in this because . . . ?"

"Because the Knights never went away," Victor told him bluntly.

"Wait a minute," Em cut in. "A political movement founded in Greece more than two and a half thousand years ago is still in existence today?"

Victor shrugged. "Why not? Democracy was a political movement founded in Greece more than two and a half thousand years ago, and that's in existence today. Believe me, the Knights of Themis are still very much active. Antidemocratic movements have always been able to attract influential people. Their main goal now is a unified world under a single government."

"No more wars," Em murmured.

"No more democracy." Victor scowled. "Their ideal world government is one completely controlled by themselves."

After a moment Em said cautiously, "Yes, but we don't have a world government, democratic or not; and not much sign of one."

"We have a united Europe," Victor said.

"Yes, but that's just trade. The European Union is just trade."

"That's certainly the way it was sold to the voters, but it's not just trade anymore. There's a European parliament and a European legislature, and the laws they bring in are binding on all the member states. They don't call it a United States of Europe yet, but that's where it's heading; and it's getting stronger and more powerful every year."

Em began to smile. "You're not trying to tell me that the Knights of Themis—"

"Were behind the European Union?" Victor interrupted him. "That's exactly what I'm trying to tell you. Just like they were behind the two world wars. The next step for Europe will be to abolish national governments and create a single, central, all-powerful government for the whole continent. And guess who'll be running that?"

Victor obviously wanted him to say the Knights. Em actually said nothing.

Victor knuckled his eyes tiredly. "In fact, their plans for Europe are so far advanced, they've now moved on to the second stage: the establishment of a new world order."

"What's that?"

"The abolishment of *all* sovereign states everywhere and the creation of a single world government."

Em finished his coffee in a single gulp. "Hard to swallow."

"The coffee or the concept?"

"The concept. The coffee's fine."

"They're not doing it all at once. The idea is to integrate various countries into greater unions, then unify the unions. You already have the European Union. There's also an emerging Asian Union: China, Japan, Korea, Taiwan, Hong Kong, and Singapore. It's all economics at the moment, but that's the way the European Union started. There are also proposals on the table for a Central Asian Union to unify Kazakhstan, Kyrgyzstan, Tajikistan, Turkmenistan, and Uzbekistan; and for a South Asian Union that would be bigger than the rest of them put together. That one's going to bring together *forty-three* different countries all the way from Saudi Arabia to the Philippines . . . and the creepy thing is, the South Asian Union includes major players from the Asian Union and the Central Asian Union, so you're *already* seeing a potential union of the unions."

Em opened his mouth to say something, but Victor was in full flight.

"Once you take an interest in the world as a whole, you can see the hand of the Knights everywhere. But the really interesting part is what they're doing to America."

"The Land of the Free," Em murmured.

"Not anymore," Victor told him.

"After 1945," Victor said, "the Knights decided to take over America."

"They *what?*" Em gasped.

"You heard me," Victor said. "America is unusual among modern democracies in that so much power is concentrated in the hands of one man: the president. Much more than our own prime minister, you can be certain. Put a Knight of Themis in the White House, and you effectively take control of America for at least four years—eight if you play your cards right."

"But they haven't done it, have they? They haven't put a man in the White House?"

"Oh, yes, they have."

Em stared at him in disbelief. "The current president?"

Victor shook his head. "Not him. They couldn't control the backlash against their plans to expand America's involvement in the Middle East. But the Knights have their own men in the Senate and the House of Representatives, and there are a whole host of lobby groups that secretly support their aims. They've also infiltrated the commercial and financial sectors big-time. Apart from that, they've had their men in the White House off and on since Washington. They even went public about it in 1957."

"What happened in 1957?"

"They issued the current dollar bill." He obviously caught Em's blank look, for he asked, "You don't have a dollar bill about your person, do you?"

"I've never even seen one."

"Your education has been sadly lacking," Victor said. He extracted a bill from his wallet. "Souvenir of my last trip to New York. Now look . . ." He placed it facedown on the table and smoothed it flat. "What's that say?"

Em glanced at the banknote. "'In God we trust.'" Em looked up at him. "All others must pay cash." As he said it, he realized it was only the second joke he'd cracked since his father died. He was still desperately sad, still missed the old boy terribly; but the coiled spring inside his gut seemed to have eased when he wasn't paying attention. He was returning, very slowly, to something like his old, cheerful self.

"Very funny," Victor said sourly. "To the left of that—the Latin."

Em looked to the left of the ONE on the dollar bill. Within a circle there was a drawing of an eye inside a pyramid with some wording around it. The drawing looked vaguely familiar, but for the life of him he couldn't think why. He forced himself to concentrate on the wording. *"Annuit cœptis,"* he read slowly. *"'Novus ordo seclorum.'"*

"Which means?"

"Bit rusty on the old Latin, I'm afraid," Em told him.

"Annuit cœptis means 'favors the beginning.' *Novus ordo seclorum* near enough translates as 'new world order.' Put the whole thing together and you have the message: The Knights of Themis want to start a new world order. And since it was printed right there on a dollar bill, the implication is that the USA *also* wants that."

"Does it?" Em asked. He was beginning to feel at sea. Politics at home had never been an interest of his, and American politics was a complete mystery. He believed what Victor was telling him, but he couldn't seem to get any overall picture into his head.

"There are signs," Victor said. "It certainly wasn't long before that message came out into the open: the first President Bush publicly announced that he favored a new world order in 1990 during an address to the United Nations. By that time, Themis even had the Russians on board. Premier Gorbachev was calling for a new world order as early as 1988."

"Yes, but talking about it and doing anything about it are two different things."

"Ever hear of the North American Union?"

Em shook his head. "No."

"Neither have most of the American people. It's a Themis plan to set up a union of the United States, Canada, and Mexico. There's going to be a common currency called the amero. It's just like the European Union, and it's the first step toward a single state that will take in the whole of the Americas, north and south. Nobody's ever voted for it, but plans are moving ahead just the same. That's what I mean about taking over America. Anybody who criticizes the idea is accused of political scare tactics—I quote President George W. Bush on that."

"You're saying," Em said carefully, "this North American Union is part of a new world order?"

"I've told you how these people work. First you unify countries, then you unify the unions. We've already got a European Union; we're well on the way toward one or more Asiatic unions. Add in a union of the Americas, centralize power, and you've got a world government."

Em went back to a much earlier thought. "Would that be such a bad thing?"

"What, with the Knights of Themis running the show?"

Em shrugged. "They can't do much worse than the politicians we have now: wars . . . famines . . . crime . . . drug running . . . people smuggling . . . bank crises . . . global warming. . . . Some of those are bound to get better under a world government."

"You're right," Victor said. "Most of those problems *will* disappear—all of them, in fact. But I doubt you'll like the way the Knights plan to make them go away."

"I don't understand."

"Primarily through population control," Victor said firmly. "Last time I checked, there were nearly seven billion of us on the planet—far too many for effective totalitarian government. The Knights plan to cut that figure down to approximately fifty million worldwide and keep it there."

Em decided he'd misheard the figure. "You mean five hundred million?" Even that sounded ludicrously small.

"I mean fifty million," Victor said. "About what it was at the time of ancient Egypt. Instant cure for famine as a start: enough food to go around, but not enough humans to pollute our environment—great idea, don't you think? And if you structure the world government to be run by a few thousand Themis elite, with the rest of the population effectively functioning as their slaves, you abolish war. The really scary thing is that they've started the process of taking away people's liberties already, to pave the way for their eventual slave state."

Em blinked. "Have they?" He vaguely remembered his father complaining about the government and civil liberties, but what Victor was saying seemed a lot more serious.

Victor shrugged. "The Patriot Act in America allows the state to search through your emails, bug your phone conversations, examine your bank records and your medical records. You can also be arrested and held without trial, just like the good old Soviet police states. But it's even worse here in Britain. You can now be arrested and held without trial, denied access to your own money, have your activities restricted for no reason whatsoever, and have samples of your DNA taken against your will. And the Knights of Themis are only really getting started."

Em hesitated, then decided he didn't believe it. Victor was talking about antiterrorist legislation that would probably only be temporary anyway. And it was one thing talking about a small, manageable population, but getting to it was a different matter. "How do you reduce the world population from nearly seven billion to fifty million?" Even as he asked it, a chilling idea occurred to him, and he added softly, "Start a nuclear war?"

But Victor was shaking his head. "A nuclear war would destroy the planet, leave it a miserable place for the survivors to live on. The Knights don't want that. Their aim is a new Garden of Eden, with themselves enjoying the benefits and a slave population to look after them. One plan for the population reduction is a combination of sterilization for the young and euthanasia for the old. It won't happen until they have a world government, and even then it will be introduced gradually. But there's a faction of the Knights who thinks that's too slow. They say we need to cut the population now before global warming gets out of control. Their favored method is a bioengineered virus designed to kill off most of the population and then die out itself, leaving a bright new world for the survivors. The problem, of course, is how you stop the virus from attacking the Knights themselves. They have scientists working on that already."

Em stared at him in something close to horror, then shook his head violently. "How do you know stuff like this? I mean, most people have never even *heard* of the Knights of Themis."

"I'm betting your father did," Victor said.

Em blinked. "What's my father got to do with it?"

"Your father was a world authority on Nostradamus, I gather?"

"Yes," Em said cautiously.

"Not just the prophecies, but the man's whole life?"

"Yes . . ."

"Nostradamus was a Themis initiate," Victor said bluntly. "It's the sort of obscure fact some scholars would know but nobody else cares about. There's a theory that he used his prophecies to predict a future world where democracy no longer existed; and if you read them, it's hard to argue with that."

"But that was back in the sixteenth century," Em protested. "You seem to know exactly what they're up to *now*."

"Wish I did," Victor told him. "But I do know more than most. Section 7 was set up specifically to combat the Themis threat. I've spent most of my working life investigating the Knights."

Em glanced at the clock on the kitchen wall. Victor

had been talking about his Knights of Themis for more than an hour now, and it was fascinating to listen to. But Em wasn't sure he had the time to listen much longer. The Knights might be plotting to take over the world, but right now Em had more personal things on his mind. Like how to keep clear of the man with the gun and his friends. Or how to get his mother out of the psychiatric clinic.

"Look, Victor," he said heavily, "what do the Knights of Themis have to do with me?"

"They're the ones who are after you," Victor said.

His room was a cramped monk's cell with a single bed, a tiny wardrobe, and a kitchen chair; but it was better than a dormitory and a *lot* better than sleeping in a railway tunnel. It was now well past midnight, and Victor was anxious for him to get some rest. But Em was too excited—too worried—to think of sleep. "Any chance of more coffee?" he asked Victor.

Victor sighed and headed back to the kettle. "Okay," he said, "maybe it was a bit unfair to spring it on you, but the *I Ching* advised directness."

Em had been about to push him on the important stuff but sidetracked himself. "You asked the *I Ching* how to deal with me?"

"I asked for help in locating you, then how to deal with you." He shrugged. "Hey, it works for me!" He turned on the tap to refill the kettle. "One more cup, then we get some sleep. I must get my head down even if you don't—we need to be fresh tomorrow. There's a lot we have to do."

"Right," Em said, not knowing what he was talking about and not much caring. "But for the moment, let me get this straight. There's this big, really scary secret organization that's trying to take over the entire world, but they're taking time out to chase me? Because . . . ?"

"I don't know why because," Victor told him. "I wish to God I did—it would make life a lot easier. I just know they had a serious interest in your father—a *very* serious interest—and now they have an interest in you."

"My mother thinks my father was murdered."

Victor glanced at him uncomfortably. "She may be right. They've had her sectioned, which would suggest she knows something they don't want made public. Did she talk about it a lot—that she thought your father was murdered?"

"I suppose she might have," Em said.

"It's standard Themis procedure when people get troublesome. If need be they're murdered, assuming that can be done without raising suspicions. If they can't be murdered—and they wouldn't want to kill a second member of your family so quickly: might arouse police interest—having them sectioned is the next best thing. Once you're in a mental institution, nobody believes anything you say."

"Yes, but how do they get the doctors to—" Em

stopped abruptly. He'd suddenly remembered where he'd seen the eye-in-the-triangle design that Victor had shown him on the dollar bill. It was the logo on the map the nurse had given him. "My God," he said, "the Knights of Themis own the clinic!"

"Where they're holding your mother?" Victor nodded. "Yes, they do." He poured boiling water into the percolator. "I'm making this weak. You really need some sleep. So do I."

Em had never felt less like sleep in his life. "Why did they kill my father, Victor? He had no interest in politics. He wouldn't give a toss about some new world order so long as they left him alone to study his books. The only thing he really cared about was Nostradamus, for heaven's sake!"

"He must have been a threat to the Knights of Themis, otherwise they wouldn't have taken such drastic action," Victor said bluntly. "They're absolutely ruthless, but that doesn't mean they go around swatting people like flies. Above everything else, they want to preserve their secrecy. So they're careful. Murder is very much a last resort, and they only do it when they're certain nobody will suspect their involvement."

"You still haven't told me why they murdered my father!" Em's voice rose. "Last resort or not, it doesn't make any *sense*. He couldn't have been a threat to them. He couldn't have been a threat to *anybody*."

"I don't *know* why they murdered your father," Victor said quietly.

"All right." He made a massive effort to pull himself together. "All right, why are they after me, then? I can see they would want to put my mother away if she was blabbing about Dad's death, but I haven't been talking to anybody. I didn't even think he was murdered after I heard Mum talking about it. I thought she was just being, you know, paranoid, or miserable or something. So why come after me?"

Victor handed him the fresh cup of coffee. "I don't know that either." He sighed. "Drink it down. Go to bed. I need you fresh in the morning."

But Em wouldn't leave it alone—*couldn't* leave it alone. "You're going to help me—right?"

"We're going to help each other, kid," Victor told him tiredly. "You could have information I need to know—I still haven't debriefed you. But believe me, we're both on the same side. I hate the Knights of Themis, hate everything they stand for."

"Debrief me now," Em offered.

"In the morning," Victor said. "I'm too tired now. *Early* in the morning, if you like."

"What else are we going to do tomorrow?"

"What do you mean?"

"Are we going to rescue my mum?"

"Who do you think I am—James Bond?" Victor demanded. "We don't just burst into a psychiatric clinic guns blazing and drag your mother out by the ears. You'll find that her commitment papers are perfectly legal. If we did try to take her out by force, we'd have every police station in the country on our case, as if we haven't enough problems already."

"Can't just leave her there," Em muttered. He was annoyed by Victor's attitude.

"That's exactly what we do," Victor told him firmly. "What we *will* do. What we're going to do tomorrow is debrief you properly, then make our plans."

"Can't you *start* to debrief me now?"

"No. Have you finished your coffee?"

"Do you have a gun, Victor?"

"Yes, I have. What do you want to know that for?"

"Can I see it?" Em asked.

"No, you can't."

"What sort of gun is it?"

"Czech CZ-TT 15-shot semiautomatic. Polymer frame so it won't trigger airport metal detectors."

"Can't we just *start* the debriefing tonight?" Em asked again. "That way you can sleep on it, and we have a head start in the morning. We can make plans, and you can clarify any stuff that comes up that you need to clarify. Don't you think that makes sense, Victor?"

Victor released a long, defeated sigh. "All right," he said. "We try to get a handle on the situation. But I need to get some stuff from my room. If we're going to do this, we may as well start off right."

Em sat staring into his coffee, heart thumping, until Victor returned with a small, solid-state recording device, hardly larger than a credit card, and an old-fashioned notebook and pen. He set them all down on the table and sat facing Em like a policeman about to start an interrogation. "The last few months before he died," Victor began without preliminary, "did you notice anything unusual in your father's behavior?"

Em took a deep breath and began to tell him everything he knew.

They reviewed their situation over a breakfast of bacon, eggs, sausages, tomatoes, sliced fried mushrooms, baked beans, and a piece of toast each. Between the good night's sleep, the place to stay, the first-class food, and a professional agent (with a gun!) to help him, Em felt almost optimistic.

"The problem," Victor said thoughtfully, "is we don't know who we're up against. I mean, we're up against the Knights of Themis, we know *that*; but that's like saying we're up against the Russian army. We might know all about the generals in Moscow, but it's the sniper in the next tree we actually have to worry about. You don't know the name of the man who followed you, nor the men who broke into your father's study. I don't suppose you remember the license plate number of the black

Mercedes at the funeral."

Em shook his head. "Sorry."

"Didn't think so. As I see it, we have two choices at the moment. We can sit tight, wait for them to make another move, then play it by ear, take things as they come. Or we can try to find out *specifically* who we're dealing with in the Knights of Themis and take the fight to them."

Neither option appealed very much to Em, but he couldn't think of a better one. "How do we find out who we're dealing with?" Something struck him, and he added, "Hey, we could start with the clinic! The one where they're holding Mum."

Victor poured himself his third mug of coffee. "I already know the names of everybody involved in running that clinic—Section 7 has had it under investigation for nearly three years. It won't do us any good. The clinic is a genuine medical practice mainly looking after rich neurotics. These special patients' backgrounds are on a need-to-know basis, and the clinic's shrinks have only telephone contact with the Themis cell that sent them. They don't even know the name of the Knight involved: he gives them a code word when he calls."

"You're telling me none of the doctors in the clinic knows why Mum's being held there or the names of the people who had her sectioned?"

"That's what I'm telling you," Victor said.

"What about the other doctor?" Em asked at once.

Victor looked nonplussed. "What other doctor?"

"Alexander Hollis," Em exclaimed excitedly. "Our family doctor. He was one of the two doctors who signed the papers. We've known him for years. He can't be a member of the Knights—"

"*Anybody* could be a member of the Knights, believe me," Victor interrupted. "That's their strength."

"All right, either he's a member of the Knights of Themis, or he was forced to do what he did by them. Either way, he's worth talking to." He hesitated. "I think Uncle Harold said something about him being out of the country, but only for a few days. He might be back by now."

"You know what?" said Victor thoughtfully. "You may have something there." He stood up. "What did you say his name was?"

"Hollis. Dr. Alexander R. Hollis. His office is on Oakland Avenue, near the university."

"Okay, I'll go call, find out if he's back at work. You do the dishes."

Em blinked. "How come I get to do the dishes?"

"I cooked breakfast."

"Yes, but I could call them."

Victor gave him a long, slow look. "You really don't know what you're up against, do you? These people want to rule the world, and they've *already* gone a long way toward doing just that. They've infiltrated every power structure on the planet. They have money to spend— more money than some entire countries. They're looking for you. Do you really imagine it's beyond them to run a voice recognition bot throughout the British phone system? They could trace your call from *any* phone, including phone booths and the one in this apartment. Until this thing is over, until we know exactly what's going on, it's no more phone calls for you, my boy."

Em stared back for a moment and then said, "You make the calls. I'll do the dishes."

Victor took his time getting through to Dr. Hollis's surgery. Em rinsed and stacked the dishes, turned on the portable radio beside the sink, discovered he was listening to some boring news channel—there was a holdup in the distribution of Death Flu vaccine—and switched it off again when he couldn't find any music he liked. Victor returned, frowning slightly. "He's still not back at work, but he's back in the country. I got that much out of his dragon of a secretary. What she wouldn't tell me was where he lives. I don't suppose you know?"

"I do, actually," Em said. "Been there for supper twice with Mum and Dad."

Victor instructed the cab to drop them off on a corner several blocks away from Dr. Hollis's home. "How come we're getting out here?" Em asked him at once.

"Just a precaution," Victor told him as he paid the cabbie.

"Precaution against what?"

"Listen," Victor said impatiently, "I spend most of my life undercover, hiding from Themis. You pick up certain habits—it's the only way you can survive. For example, I don't own a car: too easy to trace. That's why we travel by cab. But I never give the final destination in case somebody questions the driver and he happens to remember us. I don't use credit cards because they leave an electronic trail. The Section keeps me supplied with cash, and I wouldn't buy so much as a cinema ticket under my own name. That way nobody can track you."

"Okay," Em said, chastened.

They walked together through the quiet morning streets to the head of the avenue where Dr. Hollis lived; and suddenly it wasn't quiet anymore.

"What's going on?" Em asked.

Victor gripped him by the arm and pulled him back a pace or two. There was an ambulance and two police cars parked, lights flashing, about two hundred yards ahead. Paramedics were carrying a stretcher up the steps of one of the Georgian houses that made up the avenue. "That's not the Hollis house, is it?" Victor whispered urgently.

"Could be," Em said. "Hard to be sure from here."

"Get around the corner," Victor said firmly. "I want you out of sight."

"Where are you going?"

"To try to find out what's happening. I don't like the look of this."

"Can't I come with you?"

"Haven't you heard a thing I've said? You're the one they're after, not me. Just stay out of sight, and I'll fill you in when I get back. If I find out anything."

It was nearly fifteen minutes before he did reappear,

looking grim. "He's dead," he said without preliminary.

It came as such a surprise that Em said foolishly, "Who's dead?"

"Your Dr. Hollis. His wife's still out of the country, but their housekeeper found him hanging from a beam in his study when she arrived to tidy up this morning."

"Like . . . suicide?" He couldn't think why Dr. Hollis would commit suicide—he'd always seemed a cheerful soul. Unless, Em thought suddenly, it had something to do with sectioning his mother. Maybe the doctor felt guilty.

"That's the police theory. There's apparently a note, but they wouldn't let me see it."

Something in Victor's tone made Em say, "But you don't believe it?"

Victor shook his head. "Damn right I don't. I've seen this happen before. I think he was murdered."

Victor wanted more coffee. They found a tiny café along a narrow alleyway and picked a table as far away from the counter as possible so they could talk. At this hour of the day they were the only customers.

"Listen, kid," Victor said. "I'm sorry for springing that on you. I should have eased you into it."

"Don't call me 'kid,'" Em muttered.

"So what should I call you: Edward?"

"Em. Everybody calls me Em. It's, like, my initials: E. M. for Edward Michael."

"Okay."

Em declined coffee and tea, and felt like throwing up when Victor suggested a doughnut. He was frightened, jangled, and nervous, and was finding it difficult to sit still. What he wanted was to keep on the move. What he *really* wanted was to run. Except he didn't know where, and he didn't actually know what from. He licked dry lips. "Why do you think he was murdered?"

"It's a familiar pattern. My guess is your Dr. Hollis wasn't a Knight himself, probably not even a Themis sympathizer. I think they had something on him and used it to force him to sign the papers for your mother."

"What would they have had on him?" Em found himself watching the doorway as if he expected the Knights to pile through it at any minute.

Victor frowned. "How should I know?" he asked crossly. "The Knights are experts at ferreting out dirty little secrets. But if I'm right, they blackmailed him with *something* until he agreed to sign the papers."

"Why didn't they kill him right away then?"

"My guess is they couldn't find him. He left the country, remember? His big mistake was coming back. He obviously had no idea what he was up against."

Em sat looking at Victor for a long moment. Eventually he said, "What do we do now?" He licked his lips. "Dr. Hollis was our best lead." And whether he'd been murdered or killed himself, he was still dead.

Victor leaned forward in his seat to stare at him earnestly. "Listen, k— Listen, Em, I want you to think really hard. This whole mess comes right back to your father. I know it hurts you to talk about him, even think about him, and I'm sorry, but we have to face this if we're to get any further. Section 7 is certain the Knights of Themis killed him. What we don't know is why. Now they're after his son—you. What does that suggest?"

Em thought about it for a moment. "That he had something or knew something or found something, and they're worried he might have passed it on to me?"

"Exactly!" Victor exclaimed. He leaned back and took a long drink of his coffee.

"But he didn't!" Em protested. "At least, if there was something he'd discovered, he didn't pass it on to me. He didn't talk to me about stuff that much. He was a university professor, for cripe's sake. He lived in his head most of the time. Or with his nose stuck in a book. I don't think he talked to Mum much either—maybe that was one of the reasons she drank too much. I promise you, he didn't tell me *anything*."

But Victor wasn't ready to leave it alone. "I want you to *think*," he said again with emphasis. "Before he died, maybe even weeks or months before he died, did he talk to you about anything unusual, anything at all?"

"No," Em said firmly.

"Did he give you anything for safekeeping? A paper or a folder or an envelope; anything like that?"

"No," Em said again.

"How about a gift of some sort?"

Em frowned. "You mean something valuable?"

"Not necessarily. But something you could conceal something in—a box or a case or even a book; you can slip a sheet of paper between the pages of a book. Anything like that? The Knights obviously think your father communicated something to you. I'm trying to figure out how he could have done that—tried to send you a message—without your realizing what he was up to."

"Dad never gave me *anything* before he died," Em said. "I mean, not immediately before he died. Like, I got presents from time to time the way everybody does. I mean, he gave me stuff the Christmas before, but that was months—"

"What did he give you for Christmas?"

"Oh, come on!"

"I'm serious," Victor said.

Em thought about it, trying to remember. Finally it came to him. "Pair of gloves and a scarf. And a box of chocolates. Wasn't very imaginative when it came to Christmas. He gave Mum a frying pan. I thought she was going to hit him with it."

"Did you eat the chocolates?"

"Well, I shared them. With Mum and Dad. But, yes, we ate all of them."

"There was nothing else in the box? Note? Slip of paper?"

"Just chocolates."

"Did you ever wear the gloves?" Victor asked.

"Yes, of course. And the scarf. It was cold last Christmas."

"There was nothing stuffed into the fingers of the gloves?"

Em shook his head. "No, nothing. Of course not. Look, I told you; he didn't give me anything before he died. Why would he? It's not like it was my birth—"

He stopped suddenly, then finished slowly, "—day . . . or anything. Listen, Victor, there *was* something. He gave it to Mum to give to me for my birthday. This was when he had the high fever and I suppose he thought he might not make it, so he gave it to her to . . . you know . . . Thing was, my birthday isn't until October, and Dad was always a last-minute merchant, so why would he get me something that far in advance?"

Victor was sitting forward again. "What was it?"

"It was an iPod. He even had it engraved. But that wasn't exactly sending me a message, was it?"

"What did the engraving say?" Victor asked quickly.

"Just 'Happy birthday from your loving father.'"

"Nothing else?"

Em shook his head. Then, "Something about 'good listening.'"

"What did he mean by that?"

"Nothing," Em said. "Just *good listening*, I suppose. You use an iPod to listen to music."

"And did you? Listen to your iPod?"

Em shook his head again. "No. I never even switched it on. I was sort of . . . sad, you know. Mum gave it to me after my dad died. I just couldn't cope with . . . I mean, it reminded me too much . . ." He could feel the tears beginning to well again.

"Where is it now? Do you have it here?"

"No, I left it at home. I put it away after Mum gave it to me. Didn't look at it since."

"Put it away where?"

"At home. I told you. In my room." He'd shoved it in among his CD collection, some sort of mad thought that an iPod should be with his music. He supposed he'd thought he would take it out and use it one day when he got over the pain of his father's death.

"We need to get it," Victor said.

"You really think Dad may have sent me a message in the iPod?" It was possible, he supposed: he hadn't even looked in the box properly. There could be a card in there—a whole letter for all he knew. He felt a curious sensation in the pit of his stomach. A message from his dad, maybe even a message about the Knights of Themis.

"I really think it's worth finding out." Victor looked at him thoughtfully. "The question is, how do we get hold of it?"

Em frowned. "I'll go and get it."

"They'll be watching the house," Victor said. Em didn't have to ask him who he meant. Victor drained the last of his coffee. "What we need is somebody who can get the iPod for us, somebody who can enter the house without causing suspicion."

"Uncle Harold," Em said. "He has his own key, and he's been sort of caretaking the place since they took Mum away."

"Do you trust him?"

The question stopped Em short. He wasn't sure he *did* trust Uncle Harold. From where Harold was standing, Em had gone off to visit his mother a couple of days ago and then simply vanished off the radar. Harold might even have reported him as a missing person. So how would Harold react to a message from Em asking for his iPod? He *might* just bring it, but he might just as soon tell the police the good news that his nephew had turned up again.

"Is there anybody else? Some other relative? A friend? It would have to be somebody who could go into the house without raising suspicion."

Em thought about it. "Charlotte," he told Victor.

"Who's Charlotte?"

"A friend. She knows about my mother, and she knows I'm on the run. She was the girl who was with me in France when we were followed by the man with the gun."

"The one who spilled the coffee?"

Em nodded. Victor grinned slightly. "A resourceful young lady. You think she'll help out again?"

"Definitely—she's already loaned me money. The thing is, her father works at the university, so she has an excuse to be on campus."

"Do you have a key to your apartment?"

"Yes."

Victor chewed his bottom lip thoughtfully. "Wonder what would be the best way to get it to her . . ."

"We don't have to," Em said. "I know where Uncle Harold leaves his spare—under a flowerpot on the windowsill to the right of the door."

Victor shook his head in disbelief. "No wonder you were burgled twice." He pushed back his chair. "Do you have her number?"

Em nodded.

"Call her now," Victor said. "Have her pick up the iPod and deliver it to you. Tell her to make sure she's not followed, but we can't really trust her about that since she's not a professional, so we'd better make the drop someplace open where we can watch her before we make contact, make sure nobody has tagged along."

"How about the Leslie Memorial?" Em suggested. Leslie Memorial Park was a two-hundred-and-fifty-acre parkland in the center of town, fifty acres of which were taken up by a picturesque man-made lake. Vast swaths of the site were open grassland with meandering pathways and little in the way of cover.

"Sounds good to me. If you meet by the memorial itself, we should be able to spot anybody following her half a mile away."

"Okay." A thought struck Em. "Hey, wait a minute—I thought I can't make phone calls?"

Victor gave him a wicked grin as he pulled something from an inside pocket and handed it across. It was a black, almost featureless touch screen cell phone with no manufacturer's logo. "Nobody will trace you when you use this little monster," Victor said. "Special Section 7 issue."

Em took the phone without a word, stared at it for a moment, then began to dial Charlotte's number.

The Leslie Monument dated back to the Second World War and featured a tall aviator in the cockpit of a Spitfire. Although only half life-size, it was set on a high granite plinth that dwarfed Charlotte as she stood at their appointed meeting place, impatiently consulting her wristwatch.

"I think we should go and see her now," Em said. "She's not going to hang around much longer. You know what girls are like."

"Not for a good many years," Victor told him. "But just hold fire—I want to be certain."

They were standing together inside the overhang of a clump of bushes, one of the very few in this area of the park. Apart from Charlotte and an old woman seated on a park bench feeding bread to pigeons, there was no one else in sight. "Certain of what?" Em demanded. "There's just Charlotte."

"Certain she hasn't been followed. Can't be too careful. I just want to be sure of the woman on the bench."

"She's an old lady," Em protested. "Hardly Themis material."

"First time we met, you thought I was an old man."

"Okay, point taken. But she was here before Charlotte arrived. That doesn't suggest following."

"Mmm," Victor said noncommittally. Then, "You're probably right. Off you go."

"Aren't you coming?"

"Fewer people see me the better," Victor said. "Just get the iPod and get back here. Don't hang about chatting." He caught Em by the arm. "One more thing: you mention nothing about me—understood? I told you about Section 7 on a need-to-know basis. She doesn't need to know."

"What do I say if she asks me what's going on? She's bound to. She knows about Mum. She'll want to know where I've been hiding. She already knows about the man with the gun—should I tell her about the Knights?"

"Tell her you've been sleeping on park benches. It's almost true." His tone softened. "Em, we can't afford to tell her the whole truth, for her own sake. This is a dangerous game. You're involved through no fault of your own. I'm involved because I'm a professional. But there's no need for her to be involved. We've put her at enough risk already just asking her to get the iPod."

Em shrugged. "Okay."

Charlotte looked none too pleased as he approached. "What kept you?" she asked. "I thought you weren't coming."

"Sorry," Em muttered. He'd decided to say as little as possible rather than get into a convoluted explanation that would only lead to further questions.

Charlotte sniffed. "I very nearly went home."

"Sorry," Em said again. He glanced around him to ensure that no one else was about and realized that hanging around with Victor was making him paranoid. Even the old lady had wandered off, although her pigeons still clustered around the bench, mopping up the last of the bread crumbs. "Did you get the iPod?"

"Yes, of course I got the iPod. Did you realize the police are watching your apartment? There was an ugly, great police car parked right outside with a uniformed sergeant and a uniformed constable."

"They didn't cause you any problems, did they?" It was a stupid question. Of course they must have caused her problems. The police were *paid* to cause people problems, especially people who were letting themselves into houses that weren't their own. He wondered how Charlotte had managed to get past them.

Charlotte smiled for the first time. "With my honest face? Of course not. When I saw them parked there, I went straight across and asked the sergeant if he had a key to your house."

Em's jaw fell. "You did *what?*"

"I told him your uncle Harold asked me to collect something for him. It was nearly true, except it wasn't your uncle Harold who asked; it was you."

"What did he say—the sergeant?" Em gasped.

"He said they didn't have a key—they were just keeping an eye on the house. I said that was all right, because Uncle Harold had said something about a spare key under the plant pot and would they like to come in with me, help me look."

"Oh my God!" Em exclaimed. "You didn't tell them about the iPod?"

"They didn't ask. They didn't want to come in with me either. I suppose I looked respectable, and I think I may have mentioned that my dad was with the university. Anyway, they just sat in their comfortable police car while I found the key and let myself in." She gave Em a disgusted look. "Your room is a dreadful mess."

"Yes, I know," Em said. "But you found the iPod?"

"I told you I found the iPod." She produced a red-striped box from the pocket of her jeans but snatched it away when Em reached for it. "No you don't. I want to know what's been happening. I was really worried about you, Em. I thought you would have phoned me before now and not just because you wanted me to do something."

"It's not all that easy," Em said vaguely. "I've been sleeping on the street."

"Could have fooled me," Charlotte said. She looked

him up and down. "You're clean, and you've had a change of clothes."

Girls missed nothing. The change of clothes had come out of Victor's wardrobe in the safe house, and he'd showered that morning. Em thought on his feet. "I washed in the public restrooms," he said. Charlotte would have no idea what sort of facilities there were in men's restrooms: she'd probably never been in one in her life. If she asked, he'd tell her that truck drivers showered there all the time. When Charlotte didn't ask but continued staring at him, he licked his lips and went on with the first thing that came into his head: "I stole the clothes."

"You what?" She contrived to sound shocked, the girl who'd just told him how she lied to the police.

"Off a clothesline," Em added.

"Oh, you poor, poor thing!" Charlotte exclaimed.

He had to wait until she was out of sight before returning to Victor.

"Did she get it?" Victor asked quickly.

Em nodded.

"Not too much hassle?" Victor asked.

Em shook his head. "Just the right amount."

Victor looked at him blankly, then said, "Okay, let's get back to the safe house and take a look."

When they reached the door of the apartment, Victor did not unlock it at once. Instead he knelt down and peered closely at the doorjamb.

"What are you doing?" Em asked curiously.

"Just making sure we've had no visitors in our absence."

"You haven't fixed a thread down there?" Em asked incredulously. "Boy, you really take this seriously."

"Have to," Victor told him. "This is survival we're talking about. I'd have thought you'd have realized that by now." He stood up. "All clear. The thread is intact."

They went inside; Victor closed the door and went directly to the window to draw the curtains. As he did so, there was a knock at the door.

Em froze, his heart pounding. Suddenly Victor was holding a gun, clasping it with both hands, pointed upward the way they did in cop movies. He stepped to one side, behind the table. "I want you to open it, Em," he said quietly, his eyes never leaving the door. "But the second you do, I want you to step back and to one side, leaving me a clear shot." He brought the gun down so it was pointing at the door. "Unlock it, then pull it quickly wide-open so you're shielded behind the door. It's metal lined, remember, so you'll be safe. Got that?"

"Got that," Em said. He wasn't sure about the *safe* bit, but it never occurred to him to question Victor's instructions.

"Go," Victor whispered.

The knock came again, loud and insistent, as Em moved to the door. He uttered a silent prayer and then, before he could lose his nerve, unlocked the door and pulled it wide-open, stepping behind it as he did so. He couldn't see who was outside; but he had a clear view of Victor, his hands rock-steady as he aimed the gun, and Victor's expression went from grim determination to openmouthed shock. "What the *hell* are *you* doing here?" he gasped. But slowly, cautiously, he was lowering the gun.

Em risked a glance around the door, and he too froze with shock.

"Won't you introduce me to your friend?" Charlotte asked him as she walked inside.

"How did you know we were here?" Victor demanded. Em noted that the gun was still in evidence, although no longer pointed in Charlotte's direction. Victor had set it within easy reach on the tabletop.

"Followed you," Charlotte told him calmly. She pulled up a chair and sat down. "In a taxi." She gave Victor a sidelong look. "I wish you'd put that thing away. You must know I'm a friend of Em's."

Victor slid the gun off the table and into his pocket, but continued to stare at Charlotte.

"You haven't told me who you are," Charlotte said.

"His name's Victor," Em said. He ignored Victor's warning glance. "Come on, Victor. Charlotte's a friend. She knows about the man with the gun. She knows I'm being followed. She's already helped me twice. And now she knows where we live. We may as well tell her the rest. She could be of help. I think we need all the help we can get."

Victor continued to glare at Charlotte for another moment, then his shoulders slumped and he turned to Em. "You're right. Fill her in while I make some coffee." He glanced back at Charlotte. "Just remember, this isn't a game. You've blundered into something very dangerous—potentially lethal, in fact."

"I'll take my chances," Charlotte said, tight-lipped.

Since there wasn't really very much to tell, Em brought her up-to-date quickly while Victor made the coffee. She proved one of those rare people who didn't ask silly questions—didn't ask questions at all—until he had finished. Not even the news that Victor was an agent of Section 7 seemed to faze her. "And that's about it," he said in conclusion.

"You think the iPod I collected might have some clue to what this is all about?"

"Victor does," Em said.

"Then maybe we should have a look at it," Charlotte said.

Em opened the iPod box as Victor took fresh coffee mugs from the cupboard. He dropped the iPod into the palm of his hand, then checked inside the empty box for a card or note, but there was nothing. Next he examined the iPod itself. On the front, the gray-black touch screen was blank. Reluctantly he turned it over. Etched into the silvered back, above the Apple logo and the name iPod, was the inscription: *Good listening. Happy birthday, Edward, from your loving father.* Loving father. Em felt his eyes begin to brim again.

Victor walked over. "Did you say you wanted coffee?" he asked Charlotte. "I made you a cup anyway." He set her mug beside her on the table, then turned to Em. "Anything?"

"Nothing in the box. I haven't switched it on yet." He pressed the button on the top edge and watched while the Apple logo appeared center screen. It seemed to hang there for a long time before it was suddenly replaced by a color photo of planet Earth taken from space above the message SLIDE TO UNLOCK. Em ran his thumb across the bottom of the screen, dragging the slider icon with it. The iPod screen flared into a grid of icons. Across the bottom, four were labeled MUSIC, MAIL, SAFARI, and VIDEOS.

"There's Wi-Fi in this apartment," Victor murmured. "Switched off at the moment, but I can turn it on again if we need it."

"I don't think we will," Em said. "If Dad did leave me any sort of message, it wouldn't be on the Net. It'll be in the device itself."

"How about that thing labeled NOTES?" Charlotte suggested. "He may have left you a note."

Em thumbed the icon, and a lined yellow page expanded to fill the screen. But the page was blank. "Nope," Em said.

"What else might he have used?"

"I don't know," Em said. "I'll do a bit of a search."

The search took more than fifteen minutes as he checked icon after icon. Things like SAFARI and MAIL didn't work without the Wi-Fi connection, but he decided to come back to them a little later. It was Charlotte who pushed the issue when she said suddenly, "Maybe he sent you an email."

"I'd have picked it up on my PC ages ago," Em said.

"Not if he set you up with a special email account on the iPod."

Em looked at her in sudden admiration. A special email account was certainly a possibility. It would be easy enough to set one up under Em's name, or an assumed name for that matter, then change the iPod's settings to download any mail that went there. Even a Luddite like his father might have managed it if he was desperate enough. "We'll need the Wi-Fi if we're to check."

"The router's in my bedroom," Victor said. "I'll plug it in." He came back only moments later. "Should be up and running now."

Em thumbed the MAIL icon and stared at the screen in disappointment when he discovered the factory settings were intact. "Great idea," he told Charlotte, "but he didn't do it. I'd have to plug the iPod into my PC at home to transfer my email settings, but that would just give me my normal account—Dad didn't set up a special one."

"I'll leave the network on for a bit; you may need it later," Victor said. "Keep trying."

Em kept trying with no luck whatsoever. After another five minutes, he decided Victor must be just plain wrong: Dad had left no message at all, at least not on the iPod. Out of curiosity, he thumbed the MUSIC icon and opened a screen headed PLAYLISTS. Only one showed, an item labeled ON-THE-GO, but he knew from past experience that this one would be empty. Until he synched with his home computer, none of his music would be on the iPod.

There were five icons along the bottom of the Playlists screen. The first, highlighted, repeated PLAYLISTS. Next to it were ARTISTS, SONGS, ALBUMS, and MORE. The first three had to be blank as well, but he thumbed the last one curiously. It opened a new screen listing: AUDIO BOOKS, COMPILATIONS, COMPOSERS, GENRES, iTUNES, and PODCASTS. Podcasts was the only one that sported a small gray arrow. Em felt his stomach tighten. "There's a podcast on here," he said quietly.

"Shouldn't there be?" Victor asked.

"Not unless somebody downloaded one. Which would have had to be my father."

"It's not a demo that comes with the player?"

"Not a podcast," Charlotte broke in. "You have to download them."

"So your father downloaded one for you?" Victor said to Em. "Something he thought would interest you?"

"Either that or . . ." Em didn't want to finish the sentence in case the thought he'd had proved to be wrong.

Victor waited for a moment, then said, "Can we listen to it?"

"Hold on," Em said. He found the ear buds that came with the iPod and plugged them into the socket on the bottom edge of the device. He pushed one bud into his own ear and held the other out to Victor. "You won't be able to hear anything without this." To Charlotte he said, "If you squish your ear up against mine, we should both be able to listen from the same earpiece."

Charlotte pulled her chair close beside his and leaned across without a word until her cheek was pressed against his, her ear against his ear. She smelled of lightly perfumed soap. Em reluctantly dragged his attention back to the task at hand and tapped the Podcast heading. He watched the screen slide sideways to reveal a title, the single word DISCOVERY.

"Something from the Discovery Channel?" Victor asked.

Em doubted it. As Victor sat down and began to fiddle with his ear bud, Em tapped the screen again.

There was no video, but his father's voice emerged from the tiny speaker in his right ear.

28

Professor Edward Goverton sounded exactly as if he were in the university lecture hall facing an audience of students. His tone was dry and precise; his voice was strong. But as his first few words confirmed, he was lecturing to an audience of one.

"*Since you are listening to this, Em, I fear I must be dead. Doubtless this will upset you—I am none too pleased myself— but neither of us can afford the luxury of self-pity. I have made a dangerous discovery. In sharing it, I am aware that I place you in danger as well; but for the sake of our future, for the sake of the world, someone must stop what is planned. Although you are far too young for such responsibility, I know of no one else I can trust. I have already discovered that the enemy we face is ubiquitous and faceless. I suspect it has infiltrated many positions of power. I fear it has infiltrated my university. Thus, even academic colleagues and friends fall under suspicion.*

"As you know, I have long been fascinated by the life and works of the sixteenth-century French prophet Nostradamus. What you do not know, because I did not choose to tell you before now, is that during my research for that book, I came across some textural references to a hitherto undiscovered prophecy by Nostradamus."

Em stared beyond the iPod at the tabletop. *No, but you told your best friend, and he chose to tell me after you went and died. So now I'm going to hear it for the second time.* For some reason the thought made Em feel sad. It wasn't right, somehow, that he should have heard about his father's great discovery from anybody else.

"And what you certainly don't know, because I have shared this with no one, is that I managed to discover the full text of the prophecy itself."

So Charlotte was right! Dad *had* discovered the secret prophecy. But she couldn't have been right about him stealing it. Em really did know his father better than that.

Or thought he did.

"'Pendant les jours de la peste menacée . . .'" said his father's voice on the podcast. "'Quand des enfants seront percés avec la lance mince . . . un nouveau monde se lève de la douleur du monde vieux . . . et toute l'humanité soutiendra le joug de esclavage pour toujours.' *That is the prophecy, exactly as Nostradamus wrote it. I committed it to memory. I had to. The original text, the actual document, is in the possession of a Masonic Lodge in Toulon. One of their most closely guarded secrets. But the Grand Master happens to be a good friend of mine. I mentioned to him that I had reason to believe a secret prophecy existed. He made no comment at the time; but one evening, after he had too much Cognac, he confirmed the existence of such a prophecy and claimed to have seen it for himself. He even agreed to show me the document in question on condition I did not photograph or copy it. I held it only for a moment—just long enough to confirm the handwriting as that of Nostradamus, which was what he wanted. It never occurred to him that I could memorize it in so short a time. But it was only four lines of Early Modern French, not all that difficult, really. How's your French these days, Em? Can you translate it for me?"*

Not a chance, Dad, Em thought.

"No matter. I have never believed you were cut out for a life as a scholar, nor would I wish you to become one. I have made my own translation of the quatrain, which I am reasonably certain captures the sense of what Nostradamus was trying to say. What he wrote was . . . 'In the days of the threatened plague . . . when children shall be pierced with slender lance . . . a new world rises from the suffering of the old . . . and all mankind shall forever bear the yoke of slavery.'"

Whatever that means, Em thought. The prophecy said as little to him in English as it did in the original French. Although he'd never shared his father's fascination for Nostradamus, he knew enough to realize that a whole raft of his prophecies were like pictures in the fire: they were so vague, they could mean almost anything you wanted them to mean. Then, suddenly, he remembered what Victor had said about Nostradamus's connection to the Knights of Themis. Was this one of the prophecies that was meant to hasten the demise of democracy? But if it was, he couldn't quite see how . . .

"Now, you must have suspected I might believe Nostradamus to be a genuine prophet. That's to say you must have suspected that I believed—in certain instances at least—that Nostradamus could see the future. Let me confirm that you were right."

For the first time, Professor Goverton's voice lost its lecture hall edge. It became at once more intimate, confessional, and, if Em read it right, maybe just a little bit guilty. "This is a difficult area, Em. When I first began my study of Nostradamus, it seemed that some of his prophecies were genuinely predictive. So I decided to investigate the whole question of prediction and joined the Society for Psychical Research in London. Their records showed me it really was possible to foresee the future. But the very best precogs who were scientifically tested did not manage it every time or even most of the time.

"This was a more exciting discovery than it sounds, because the prophecies of Nostradamus follow exactly that pattern. But it occurred to me that even if only one in a hundred of his predictions was correct, would that not be worth investigating?"

On the iPod, Professor Goverton released an involuntary sigh. "Which is why, having discovered what was in effect a brand-new Nostradamus prophecy, my immediate instinct was to try to find out whether this was one of those rare instances in which he predicted accurately. I began my own historical research in the hope of finding a set of circumstances that would provide a perfect fit for his words.

"At first I thought the appearance of the word plague in the quatrain narrowed my field of investigation. I assumed it would refer to the period of the Black Death. But try as I might, I could find no *circumstances matching the words of the prophecy. So I turned my attention to later centuries. Eventually my research brought me right up to the present day, but still with nothing to match the prophecy. I decided I was on a wild-goose chase.*

"Then something happened to change my mind."

"Listen," Victor said, "this ear bud is giving me a crick in my neck. If that gizmo has a standard audio jack, I can rig it up to a set of speakers. That way we can all listen to it properly, and I can start taking notes without having to lean at an angle of forty-five degrees and you two can stop looking like Siamese twins."

Em tapped the button that paused his father's voice in midsentence. "Okay," he said. He was finding sharing the ear bud a bit of a trial himself.

"What do you think about the message so far?" Charlotte asked quietly as Victor left the room.

"Don't know," Em said. "I don't think he's come to the point yet." He stared at the iPod a little gloomily. Nothing his father said so far had thrown the slightest light on what was going on.

Victor returned from the other room after a moment carrying an old-fashioned set of powered speakers. He plugged them into a wall socket and then separated them out, wires trailing, on the table. He picked up the iPod. The connector fit. Victor made a couple of final adjustments to the speakers. "Okay, start it going, and we'll see if this works." Em thumbed the little START triangle on the screen.

Professor Goverton's voice emerged as if he were

standing with them in the room. "—*secret prophecy at this stage,*" he was saying, "*but this seemed like a promising—*"

"Hold on," Em said. "I'll rewind. I must have scrubbed the slider." There was no way of telling where his dad was at any point in the podcast, but he fiddled around using trial and error until he found the place he wanted. As he sat back, Charlotte reached out to give his nearest hand a sympathetic squeeze.

"*Then something happened to change my mind,*" said Professor Goverton soberly. "*One morning while I was shaving, it occurred to me that there were many forms of plague. Indeed, the word was often used loosely to describe any form of epidemic disease. This seemed like a promising new approach. I began to research historical references to any epidemic disease—the influenza pandemic after the First World War and so forth—but there was still nothing that matched the words of the prophecy.*"

"Goes on a bit, doesn't he?" Victor remarked. "He's doing a pretty thorough job of telling us what he *didn't* find."

Em smiled despite himself. "He'll get to the point eventually." He'd begun to feel a fizz of excitement, because it was clear that in the next few minutes they would have the answer to all their questions: why his father had been murdered, why he was being followed, why his mother had been sectioned, why an obscure but powerful secret society had taken such a terrifying interest in the Goverton family.

"*It was then,*" said Professor Goverton, "*that I made my big breakthrough. Remember our last family holiday together, Em?*"

The voice stopped. Em waited for a moment, then said, frowning, "Have you unplugged the speakers?"

Victor shook his head. "No." He waited a beat, also frowning, before adding, "Is that all?"

Em scrubbed the slider, on purpose this time. His father's voice came through loud and clear. *"—pandemic after the First World War and so forth—but there was still nothing that matched the words of the prophecy. It was then that I made my big breakthrough. Remember our last family holiday together, Em?"*

"Is that it?" Victor asked. "Is that all there is?"

Em was staring at the slider. The tiny icon that represented the playhead had not quite reached the end. He tapped the triangular PLAY button and watched the playhead crawl the last few centimeters before stopping again. There was not so much as a breath from the speakers. "Did you check the volume?"

"Volume's fine," Victor said.

"You didn't accidentally mute it, did you?" Charlotte put in.

Em checked. "No." He replayed a second or two of his father's voice. "See? It's working okay. Not mute." He readjusted, hit the PLAY button again.

"It was then that I made my big breakthrough. Remember our last family holiday together, Em?"

"What's he mean by that?" Charlotte asked. "What has your last family holiday got to do with anything?"

Em looked at her helplessly. "Haven't the faintest idea," he said.

Since he hadn't been planning for the extra guest, Victor insisted they go out for lunch instead of rustle up something in the safe house. The café he picked stood in stark contrast to the coffee bar of that morning. It was jam-packed with student types, and the noise level was through the roof. Victor had to lean across the little table to make himself heard.

"Where did you go on your holidays?"

"Ireland," Em told him through a forkful of lasagna. He and his parents had driven to Wales and taken the ferry to Rosslare, then endured a further drive west across Ireland to the Beara Peninsula in Kerry, where his mother had organized a holiday cottage rental. His father had been behind the wheel the whole time, with the result that he'd arrived tired and grumpy. He wasn't the only one, Em recalled. Dad's driving was pretty lethal on a motorway. On the narrow, potholed country roads of Kerry, it was positively terrifying.

"How was it?" Charlotte asked. "I mean, did anything unusual happen?"

"It was okay," Em replied without enthusiasm.

"What did you do?" Victor put in.

Em shrugged. "This and that."

Victor glared at him. "Come on, Em! This isn't a social inquiry. Your father was trying to tell you something on that iPod, and the clue is in your holiday. I'm going to quiz you until we find out what. Better get used to it."

It was fair enough. But the problem was, Em couldn't think of anything out of the ordinary that had happened on the holiday. It wasn't a patch on France where he'd been followed and got to see Paris and visited the very room in which Nostradamus made his prophecies. But he knew Victor wasn't going to let him alone; and under the circumstances, he also knew he should be cooperating instead of pouting like a spoiled kid. Which wasn't likely to impress Charlotte either. He took a deep breath. "Okay. Mum rented a thatched cottage in Kerry. We drove across. It wasn't fun. Getting to Wales takes four hours, then the ferry takes four hours, then getting to Kerry takes four hours. Too much time in a car and the ferry crossing was rough. Dad couldn't find the cottage even though they'd sent a map, so we were late and then there was some mix-up about the fridge that was supposed to be stocked but wasn't so we had to go off looking for a restaurant that was still open. Mum and Dad bickered the whole time; and when we did find a place to eat, Mum drank too much wine."

"Did it get any better after that?"

It had, actually. They had slept the sleep of the terminally exhausted and woke feeling wonderfully refreshed. They'd gone out to explore and found a funny little supermarket near a crossroads where they loaded up on gossip and supplies. They came back to the cottage and had a fried breakfast together outside on the tiny veranda to celebrate the fact that the sun had come out. Even Mum had looked cheerful. Em actually smiled at the memory. "Yes, it did."

"So what did you do? What was the highlight of the trip?"

What they'd done was not a lot, really. There was a sculpture garden open to the public that was really cool. And Mum had insisted on buying Em a sports jacket that wasn't exactly *cool* but was okay for something your mother would pick. Was that the highlight of the trip? It was difficult to say. The real highlight, he supposed, was that Dad was there to talk to him for a change and that Dad and Mum didn't argue very much. "Dad took a lot of photographs," Em said inconsequentially.

"What?" Charlotte sat up, suddenly interested. She glanced at Victor.

"Pictures," Em repeated, frowning. He glanced from one to the other. "He had a new digital camera. I don't know if he bought it for himself or somebody gave it to him. But it was the first time he took it out, and he was very newfangled with it. He took pictures of everything we did. *Everything.* The trouble was, he didn't have a printer—Dad was funny about a lot of new technology—so we never saw the pictures. Except on the camera, of course. While we were there, he was always showing us stuff on the camera screen: 'Look at this, look at that, see the shadow of that seagull.'"

Now Victor was looking interested. "Where is the camera now? Do you know?"

"At home," Em said, thought about it, then corrected himself. "No, last I heard, he'd taken it to the university."

"We need to get that camera," Victor said.

Em frowned. "Why?"

"Communications device," Victor said shortly.

Charlotte, who seemed to be following what was going on a lot better than Em, said, "Your father asks if you remember the holiday. His camera contains a record of that holiday. If there's a clue to the mystery in the holiday, we're going to find it on the camera. Or at least you are. Don't you see what he was doing, Em?"

Em shook his head and mouthed a bewildered No, since that was as good a way as any of talking over the background din.

Victor leaned closer to take up her point. "He had something to tell you, something he couldn't even trust with your mother. He must have known he was being watched, being followed, under threat or whatever, so he couldn't just write you a note—might be intercepted and read, which would give the game away. So he had to find a way of telling you that nobody else would know about. He starts by sending you an early birthday gift—nice little iPod touch MP3 player. Music machine—all the kids have them. Not something you'd immediately think of as a way of passing a message. Clever man, your father."

Em said, "What do we do now?"

"Get our hands on that camera," Charlotte and Victor said in unison.

"How do we do that?"

"You say it's at the university?" Victor asked.

"I said *likely* at the university. I don't know where else it could be."

Victor spotted a passing waitress and snapped, "Bill, please." Somehow she heard him above the noise and acknowledged his request with a smile. He turned back to Em. "Your father has an office there or something? A filing cabinet where he keeps things?"

"Office and rooms," Em said. "Where he can see students one-on-one." He realized with a dull jolt that they were talking about his father in the present tense, as if he were still alive. His father *had* had an office. His father didn't have an office at the university anymore, because his father was *dead*. "Wait a minute," he said to Victor, "I can't just walk in and claim it. They're still after me."

"I wasn't thinking of you claiming it; I was thinking of breaking in."

"What?" Em exclaimed. Despite the noise, he lowered his voice. "What?" he repeated.

"Shouldn't be too difficult," Victor said. The waitress was en route to their table, carrying a slip of paper on a saucer. He opened his wallet and extracted notes for the bill.

"But you don't even know where the office is," Em protested.

"That's why you're coming with me," Victor told him.

"Me too," Charlotte said.

Em was still arguing as they climbed the stairs to the safe house apartment. "It's finished if we get caught; you know that!"

"We won't get caught. I've burgled lots of places—required skill for a Section 7 operative."

"But I haven't," Em protested. "I'm not burglar material. I'm clumsy. I'm noisy." He glanced briefly at Charlotte and added, "I'm scared."

"University campuses are easy," Victor said as if he broke into them all the time. "Always people about, day or night. You blend in if you're dressed right. Nobody suspects for a minute you might be a thief."

"What's dressed right?"

"Well, you avoid the mask, the striped jersey, and the sack marked SWAG."

"Come on, Victor—I'm serious."

"You're making a big thing about this and you shouldn't, Em. You dress in whatever you usually dress in, whatever kids wear these days. Nothing trendy or flashy or making you stand out. Sort of gear Charlotte's wearing. Except she's not coming."

"Thanks a bunch!" Charlotte muttered, although Em wasn't sure whether she felt insulted about her dress sense or was carrying on her long argument with Victor about why she should go with them to get the camera.

"And what do *you* wear?" Em asked Victor to divert them into calmer waters. "A jacket with leather patches on the elbows?"

Victor turned to look at him. "Very *good,* Em. Academic uniform. Now you're thinking like an agent. But I'll stick to a tailored three-piece pinstripe. Nobody ever questions you if you're dressed like a wealthy city gent. Don't suppose we'll have to climb a drainpipe to get to your father's office?"

"No," Em said. "But, listen, the camera might not be there. I was thinking, they could have given his office to somebody else by now. I mean—"

They were at the door of the apartment, and Victor was kneeling to inspect his security thread. "Shut up, Em," he said in an urgent whisper.

"What's wrong?" Charlotte asked.

Victor stood up slowly, his finger to his lips. Although he hadn't answered, it was clear that something was very wrong indeed, and Em had no trouble guessing what.

He watched while Victor placed the palm of his hand on the face of the door and applied gradual pressure. The door remained closed. There were two obvious locks: a Yale and a large mortice that triggered all four dead bolts from the outside. Victor already had the keys in his hand. He inserted one into the mortice—a complex thing with spikes—and turned it gently. He withdrew it again and pushed a second key into the Yale lock. He turned it softly, leaving the door closed but needing only a push to open it.

"Stand well back, you two," he said quietly. He pointed. "Over there. First sign of trouble, you run. Got that?"

Em wanted to ask what sort of trouble Victor was expecting, but there was something in Victor's tone that stopped him cold. Besides, Victor had drawn his handgun from his pocket. Em stepped back swiftly to the spot appointed, dragging Charlotte with him.

Victor moved like a pro. He slammed the door open with a flat-footed kick and was inside the room in a single fluid movement. Em steeled himself for gunfire, but none came; nor was there any sound of a scuffle. He waited for a moment, felt his muscles begin to relax. Then all hell broke loose.

A burst of gunfire was followed by a scream, then a single shot. There was the sound of a heavy object falling, like a body, then a long moment of silence. Victor did not reemerge.

Em looked at Charlotte. Should he call out? Run for

help? Instead he gestured her to remain where she was, then moved slowly, cautiously, toward the open door. In his mind, masked raiders with Kalashnikovs would burst out spraying bullets everywhere, but in reality none appeared. He reached the edge of the door and peered around it into the room just in time to see Victor emerge from the kitchen, pushing his pistol back into his pocket. There was blood on his shirt.

"You're hurt!" Charlotte was pushing past Em despite his clear warning to stay put. She walked directly toward Victor, completely uncaring of whoever had shot him.

Victor must have read his expression. "They've gone, I think." Then to Charlotte, "Just a graze."

"You *think*?" Em gasped. He moved a few steps into the room in case Charlotte thought him a wimp and looked around cautiously in case Victor was wrong.

Charlotte said, "You're covered in blood." To Em's astonishment, she began to unbutton his shirt.

To Em's even greater astonishment, Victor let her. "It's nothing really," he said. "I just bleed easily. The bullet scarcely broke the skin."

"We need to get that cleaned up," Charlotte told him. "Somebody tried to kill you!"

"Yes," Victor agreed. He winced as she used his shirt to dab away blood from around the wound.

"You're sure they've gone?" Em asked.

"Two of them. Through a back window. They've definitely gone."

Unless there was a third one, Em thought. He moved

inside reluctantly and began to search systematically. There were remarkably few signs of the intruders. A back window had been opened, as Victor had said; but unlike his father's trashed study, nothing seemed out of place. He wondered what might have happened if Victor hadn't examined his security thread.

"Check your belongings," Victor called briskly. "They came in looking for something, and I want to know what." He was seated in the kitchen now. Charlotte had found some dressings in a drawer and was cleaning his wound.

When Em checked his stuff, the iPod was missing.

Victor spent more than an hour in his bedroom talking quietly into his secure cell phone while Em, nervously, brought him cups of coffee. He noticed that each time he entered, Victor would stop talking, then begin again as the bedroom door closed. Em was filling the kettle for the umpteenth time when he emerged, still looking pale and shaken. The shooting had obviously upset him badly. "Okay," he said without preliminary, "put your stuff together. We're moving out."

"Where to?" Em asked.

"Another secure location." The look on Victor's face matched the anger in his voice. He glared at Em as if it were all somehow Em's fault. "This place must have been compromised before we moved in. They let themselves in through the front door, which they had a duplicate key. The Section locksmith tells me the lock's impossible to pick, and now that he's described how it's put together I believe him. Worst of all, they knew exactly what they were looking for: your nifty little iPod touch. You know what that means, don't you?"

Em looked at him blankly. "No."

"It means this place is bugged!" Victor turned his face toward the ceiling and yelled, "Are you still listening, you creeps? Well, you won't be listening for long!" He turned back to Em and went on in a more modulated tone. "There's an electronics team from the Section on their way. They'll strip the place after we leave, change the locks, put in a few extra securities: classic stable door maneuver. But we need to find another place. So grab your socks, as they used to tell us in the army, and let's get moving."

"Where are we going?" Charlotte asked.

Victor turned his eyes upward in exasperation. "Aren't you listening? I just said the place is bugged! But in any case, you're not going anywhere except home, young woman. Now that the guns are out, this whole situation has become far too dangerous for a kid."

"Firstly, I'm not a 'kid,' as you say," Charlotte snapped in her coldest tone. "Secondly, Em's going with—"

"Em's *involved*," Victor cut her off. "He's already in the middle of all this. You're not."

The argument went on for some time, but Charlotte proved more stubborn than Em would ever have believed possible. To his astonishment, she continued to argue with Victor until his stamina wore out and he proposed a compromise. "You can stay with us for now—at least that way I can keep an eye on you. But any more signs of trouble and you're going home. And you're not, positively not, playing any part whatsoever when we go to get the little item we discussed earlier. Is that clearly understood?"

"Yes, of course, Victor." Charlotte nodded sweetly.

"Where are we going now?" Em asked as they emerged into the street.

"I know a place where we can hide out until we've done what we have to do. I have to cut all communications with Section now that there's been a breach—standard security procedure. They'll make contact again when they've investigated; but that could be weeks, maybe as much as a month. Meanwhile, there's absolutely no way the Knights will be able to find us. That's the good news."

"What's the bad news?" Em asked.

"Until Section makes contact again," Victor said, "we no longer have any help or backup. We're entirely on our own."

Victor let them in through the back door of a terraced house in the poorer quarter of town. The
place looked nondescript, with minimal—cheap—
furnishings and worn linoleum on the floor. It had that
slightly damp smell places get when they haven't been
lived in for a while. "A poor place, but mine own," Victor
murmured. He pulled down a blind on the window set
in the back door, then turned the key to lock it.

"Where are we?" Em asked.

"Hopefully in a safer safe house," Victor told him.
"Doesn't even have anything to do with Section 7. I
bought it four years ago under an assumed name, told
nobody, just in case. Now . . . I suggest you look the place
over, find out where things are, settle in, gather your
strength after all the excitement. We have a busy night."

He gave Charlotte a piercing look. "That's to say, Em and I have a busy night. You're staying here and keeping your head down."

"Yes, of course, Victor," said Charlotte meekly.

Em felt weird walking onto the university grounds. He knew every inch of the place, of course, probably better than its students, most of whom attended for four or five years at most. Thing was, it felt as if he'd been on the run for months, so coming back was scary, like listening to the creaks as you walked across thin ice. But what Victor had said proved right. Even at this late hour there were people about—students, staff, faculty—and nobody paid them the slightest attention.

Victor himself, true to his word, looked like a stockbroker up from London for the evening. His beard was tightly, neatly trimmed, his shoes were highly polished, and he really was wearing a three-piece pin-striped suit in a very sober shade of blue. Not one person in ten thousand would have guessed that the personal tailoring concealed a handgun (that couldn't be detected by airport security) and, although Em hadn't actually seen them, lock-picking tools.

They entered the main building side by side. "Is the office far?" Victor asked casually. He might as well have been inquiring about the weather. His whole demeanor oozed a confidence Em was working hard to match.

"Not far," Em grunted. The number of people about had begun to worry him now. It might mean no one questioned them while they kept moving, but once they reached the office itself—the darkened, closed-up, door-locked office—it would surely be a different matter. They could hardly just hang about outside, not without looking suspicious however well Victor was dressed. And what happened when he started work with his lock picks? Em had no idea how long it took to pick a lock, but he imagined it must be at least ten minutes. How did you disguise what you were doing for all that time? The first person to wander past would spot what was going on at once.

But even before they turned into the corridor that housed the offices he noticed there were fewer others in their vicinity, and in the corridor itself there were none. It was something he should have anticipated. There might be activity on campus twenty-four hours a day, but not concentrated around the empty offices.

"Which door?" Victor asked. Just the barest hint of tightness had crept into his voice.

"Second right," Em said tersely.

Without breaking stride, Victor extracted a small leather pouch from an inside pocket. On a quick glance, it could have passed for his wallet. "When we reach the door, I want you to stop, kneel down, and pretend to tie your shoelace. But keep an eye to the corridor and tell me at once if there's anybody approaching. When I pick the lock, we both go inside. You show me the places where the camera is most likely to be—this cupboard you mentioned, desk drawer, wherever: all you need do is point. Then you come back out and hang around in the corridor. Cough if anybody appears, and I'll stand quiet until they've passed. Got that?"

"What am I supposed to be doing in the corridor? If somebody comes?"

"Nothing. You're supposed to be looking like innocence personified. Whistle. Stare up at the ceiling. Tie your rotten shoelace again if you have to. Or walk off if need be—you can always come back. God's sake, Em, you're an intelligent boy. Improvise. Once I have the camera I'll join you, and we're out of here. Okay?"

Em took a deep breath. "Okay," he repeated.

They reached the door. "Whoops," Em said, sliding into character. He dropped to one knee and began to fiddle with his shoelace.

Victor stopped and turned toward the door. "Come on," he said quietly.

Em glanced up to see him politely holding the door open. "How did you do that?" he gasped. What he meant was, how did you do that *so quickly*?

"Standard lock," Victor said, as if that explained something. "Don't hang about. I want us inside."

They entered the office together, and Victor switched on the overhead light. "What are you doing?" Em demanded in sudden panic.

"What do you want me to do: use a flashlight?"

That was exactly what Em had expected him to do. "Yes. People can see we're in here." There were two windows between the office and the corridor. Both were of frosted glass, but with the overhead light on you could still see shapes inside.

"People could see that light as well. Which looks more suspicious: a darkened office with somebody fumbling about by flashlight or a well-lit office with somebody inside obviously going about their legitimate business— otherwise they wouldn't have the light on?"

"Oh," Em said.

"Show me where to look, then get out," Victor said.

Em pointed wordlessly to the cupboard, the filing cabinet, and then, after a moment's thought, to his father's desk. Both the cupboard and filing cabinet locked. As far as Em remembered, the drawers in the desk did not.

"Okay, lookout duty. Off you go," Victor told him. "Remember—cough and I go into my masterful disguise as a university executive working late."

Em slipped through the door and closed it quietly behind him. There was no one in the corridor. He stood, feeling nervous and stupid, not knowing what to do with himself. He was worried about what he would say if anyone asked him what he was doing here. The corridor was *still* empty, but in his head he was standing under the full glare of an enormous spotlight, carrying a notice: SHOULD NOT BE HERE!

Em dropped on one knee, undid his shoelace, and began—slowly—to do it up again, taking care to allow the knot to slip out so he could pretend to tie it again. After a moment he realized a drawback of his position. To make the action look natural, he was facing along the corridor, with the result that he could only see people coming from one direction. But it was only a small drawback, because he was confident he would hear anyone who approached from behind. He fiddled with his lace, allowed it to flop open, fiddled with his lace again. Maybe the camera wasn't there at all. Maybe his father had left it somewhere other than his office. Maybe he'd had the use of a locker, or loaned it to a friend. Maybe—

"Playing cat's cradle with your shoelace?"

Em started so violently he almost toppled over. He swung around in panic to find Charlotte looking down on him, grinning broadly.

"What the hell are you doing here!?" he gasped. "Victor said you weren't to come!"

"Like I was going to pay attention to that."

"How did you find us?"

"I've been to your father's old office before. With Daddy. Is Victor inside?"

"No!" Em glanced through the frosted window at the figure plainly moving inside. "Yes. Listen, you can't stay here . . ."

"I thought I might help."

"Well, you can't. Victor will *kill* you if he finds you here."

"You think so?"

"Know so!" Em exclaimed fiercely.

"Soon find out," Charlotte said, still grinning. "It looks like he's finished inside."

The office door opened, and Victor slid through it. If he was surprised to see Charlotte, he didn't show it. "Thought you'd never stay behind," he muttered. "Right, let's get out of here before we're spotted."

Em asked, "Did you find the camera?"

Victor's face broke into a smile as he pulled the camera from his pocket and waved it under Em's nose.

The living room in Victor's personal safe house was little larger than a postage stamp, poorly lit, badly decorated, and uncomfortably furnished. Em sat in a lumpy two-seater sofa at one side of a miserable coffee table while Victor occupied an armchair of sorts at the other.

"How do you work this bloody thing?" Victor demanded, pressing buttons on the camera apparently at random. "It's not at all like mine."

"Let me try," Em offered.

Victor ignored him and continued to work on his buttons until frustration got the better of him and he pushed the camera across the table. "Here, you try. See if you can find the holiday pics."

Em gave him a look, then turned his attention to

the camera. He hit what he thought had to be the right icon and was rewarded by the little screen flaring into life with a photograph. He found himself looking at the happy little family grouping gathered in the Irish sunshine for their outdoor breakfast that first morning of their holiday. For a moment, all he could do was stare, feeling the catch in his breath, the knot in his stomach. Then he swallowed and said quietly, "Got it. Want to come around and look?"

"You've found the holiday pictures?" Victor was already out of his chair and heading around the coffee table. Charlotte slid beside Em on the other side.

"Yip." He waited until Victor was settled beside him. "That's us at the cottage." He pressed the FORWARD button, and the photograph slid stylishly to one side to reveal an out-of-focus picture of a mountain split by a bar on the left-hand side. "Mum must have tried to take that from the car. I don't know where it is." He thumbed the button again, and the screen transformed to a shot of a Labrador flopped sleepily in the doorway of a country pub. "We had lunch there a couple of times." Then the main street of Kenmare . . . then a view of a lake in a valley that might have been taken from a helicopter but was actually shot from high up on a mountain road . . . then forests on the Ring of Kerry . . . then boats in a harbor . . . The final one was a picture of the ferry in Rosslare, its decks rain-swept by a sudden squall.

Em looked up at Victor and frowned. "That's it. That's all the holiday pictures I remember us taking."

He glanced back at the camera screen again. The icon on the bottom right was a filled triangle. If there were no pictures left, the triangle would be empty. "Wait a minute." Em pressed the button again.

The photograph was in sharp focus, with no sign of shaking, as if the camera had been attached to a tripod when it was taken. It showed a wooden table, but not one Em remembered from the holiday. On the tabletop was a vase of wilting flowers. Beside them was an assortment of objects: a cup and saucer, a scrap of paper, an open fountain pen with its cap set neatly beside its nib, a small china ornament of a sleeping cat, an open notebook, and a box of matches. It looked for all the world like the cartoon for a still life painting arranged by an artist with neither taste nor talent.

It was the scrap of paper that drew Em's eyes like a magnet. Charlotte spotted it at much the same time, for she reached across to point and murmur "Look at that!" Even on the tiny screen what was drawn on the paper was evident. It was the same symbol Em had seen in the clinic where his mother was a prisoner, the same symbol Victor had shown him on the back of the one-dollar bill: the eye within the triangle used as a sign by the Knights of Themis.

Victor bent over to take a closer look. "This is what he wanted you to see," he said with certainty. "This is the message your father sent you."

Em stared at the scrappily planned still life in bewilderment. "I don't get it."

"Neither do I," Victor admitted. "Not yet." He stood up. "Does this camera have a standard computer connection?"

"I think so."

Victor made for the door. "We need to take a closer look at that picture."

Victor's laptop was one of the new MacBooks. A bar crawled swiftly across the screen as Victor downloaded the entire camera content. In a moment, the whole of his laptop screen was filled with Kenmare's main street. Victor tapped a key, and they were looking at the mystery still life. The eye in the triangle stared back at them balefully.

"He's written in the notebook," Charlotte said at once.

Em followed her gaze. On the tiny camera screen, the open notebook had displayed what looked like an empty page with faint ruled lines. Now, on the laptop, it was evident that each line supported a message in the tiniest example of Professor Goverton's cramped, neat handwriting Em had ever seen. Even with the larger screen, it was impossible to read what it said. "Can you zoom in?"

Victor was already tapping keys. "Think so."

The screen zoomed, blurred, then cleared to pin-sharp focus. At the top were the words CURRENT READING, followed by the professor's translation of the lost Nostradamus prophecy. The remainder of the notebook page was filled with what looked like a random series of numbers, which meant nothing to Em at all. He scanned the first line:

12 6 9 8 3 6 57 1 2 10 4 7 13 34 6 (53 15 3-4) 197 2 9

"I don't understand," Em said. "Do you?"

"Secret message?" Charlotte suggested.

Frowning, Victor said, "Obviously a secret message— Em's eyes only. Looks like a cipher of some sort." He hesitated. "Or possibly a code."

"Aren't they the same thing?" Em asked.

Victor shook his head. "A cipher substitutes something for each letter of the alphabet. A code substitutes something for every *word* of the secret message. This is almost bound to be a cipher."

Em felt as if he was trapped by Victor's gaze. The iPod had been engraved with a message. The one about good listening. Maybe there was more engraving on it somewhere else; they hadn't really searched. Or maybe if he listened to every song, one of them would be interrupted by his father saying, *The key to your cipher is A equals* three. Em swallowed. "Maybe there was something else on the iPod."

"Yes," Victor said slowly. "I was wondering about that myself. But the iPod's gone missing, almost certainly into the hands of the Knights. So our friends on the other side could easily have the key." He shrugged suddenly. "But so far we're the only ones who have the message, which puts us ahead."

Em didn't see how. "If they can't decipher the message without the message and we can't decipher the message without the key, that puts us about even, I'd say."

"Not quite," Victor said. "If we just had the key, there's no way on God's sweet earth we could guess the message. But since we have the message, there's a chance I might be able to crack it *without* the key."

"You could do that?" Em asked. He was beginning to think his luck had taken a real upturn the day he met Victor.

"Probably. Ciphers were part of my basic training. But the real question isn't whether I can do it; it's whether I can do it in a reasonable time. My guess is, we don't have a month or two to work on this one."

"It could take a month?" Charlotte put in.

Victor sniffed. "It could take a *year*. Depends on how complicated Em's father made the cipher. I'm hoping he didn't use a computer to create it. That could really slow us down."

Em felt just the smallest swelling of relief. "Dad was a Luddite," he said. "There's no way he would have used a computer."

"That could be a help," Victor said. He turned back to the laptop and pulled a notebook and ballpoint from his pocket. "Okay, the first thing to find out is whether or not this actually *is* a cipher. After that we can worry about what it means."

"How do you do that?" Em asked curiously. "Find out whether it really is a cipher?

"Frequency analysis," Victor said without raising his head from the screen. "On average, every letter of the alphabet appears with a given frequency in any piece of text. *E* is the most frequent—turns up nearly thirteen percent of the time. *T* is the next most frequent, then *A*, then *O*, then *I*. Your father seems to be substituting numbers for letters in this cipher, so if I find a number that appears more often than any other, it's likely to stand for *E*. After that I look for *T*, then maybe *A* and work out their actual frequency in relation to the whole message. If the percentages stack up, that means we're definitely dealing with a cipher."

"Won't that let you decipher the message?" Charlotte asked at once.

"Possibly. Depends on how sophisticated Em's father was in setting it up. For the moment I want to confirm that we're dealing with a cipher. Now, do you think you could manage to shut up for five minutes and let me get to work?"

In fact it took him nearly ten, and Em knew they were in trouble from the depth of his frown. Eventually he threw down his ballpoint. "It's not a cipher," he announced.

"Are you sure?"

"Of course I'm bloody sure!" Victor responded angrily. "He must have created a code. Which means he must have sent you the key in advance."

"In the iPod?" Em asked.

Victor nodded. "Probably."

"In which case—" Em began.

"We're dead," Victor finished for him. "I'm not saying

codes can't be broken, but without the key it's going to take far longer than I think we have available. Especially since I can't send it to our experts in the Section. But there's no way I'm going to risk that." He knuckled his eyes tiredly.

"Maybe he didn't send the key in the iPod," Charlotte suggested.

Victor looked at her. "Go on."

"Maybe the clue's in the camera."

"We went through all the pictures in the camera."

"No you didn't," Charlotte told him. "You went through the holiday file, because that's what he told Em to do. 'Remember our last family holiday . . .' But you didn't go through pictures in any other file."

"You're right," Victor muttered. He pushed the camera toward Em. "Have a look. You work it better than I can."

Em shook his head. "You've downloaded everything onto your laptop. If there's anything else, it'll be on there already."

Victor nodded, then pushed his finger across the trackpad and began to tap keys.

Em leaned across to watch. There were two more files of photographs apart from the holiday pictures they'd already examined. One seemed to be more holiday shots, although not one featuring people. On the third one Em suddenly realized what he was looking at. "That's the Nostradamus Museum," he said excitedly. "Dad must have taken these on one of his French trips to research his book."

"Okay," Victor said, "let's examine each one of these carefully. If there's a Nostradamus connection, it might well be where he hid the key."

That made sense to Em, but even though they examined every picture in the file minutely, there was nothing that would help them with the message. Victor brought up the second file, only to discover that it was a series of old woodcuts. He paged through them slowly, but none showed any sign of additions or tampering. "I think those may have been for a presentation to his history students," Em said.

Victor turned away from the computer. "We're missing something," he said. "We need to put ourselves into your father's head. He has a vital message he needs to communicate to you; but he can't afford to have it read by the wrong people, so he hides it carefully away and writes it in code. But at the same time he has to make sure *you* read it, so the code has to be easy for you to crack. Which means either you already have the key and don't know it. Or . . ." He frowned thoughtfully. ". . . or the key is contained in the message itself! That could be it." He brought up the notebook page again and pushed the laptop toward Em. "Have another look at those numbers and see if any of them rings a bell. A birthday or some significant date—that sort of thing.

Em stared at the figures, then shook his head. "No."

"Come on!" Victor exclaimed impatiently. "Really try. There has to be something in there."

Em looked again. The figures remained figures, just

a series of numbers without logic or pattern. "I wonder what 'current reading' means?" he said.

Victor blinked. "What?"

"He wrote 'current reading' at the top," Em said. "I just wondered what that meant."

"It's a book code," Charlotte said suddenly.

"Presumably it's a reference to some book he was—" Victor stopped, his mouth open. "What did you just say?"

"It's a book code," Charlotte repeated. "I saw something about them in a movie once."

Victor stared at her for a long moment, then abruptly thumped himself on the forehead. "My God, how could I have been so stupid? Of course! I must be going senile."

"You know how he made up the code?" Em frowned as he looked from one to the other.

"Of course I do!" Victor said. "Well, I do now, thanks to Charlotte. So obvious. A book code takes time to set up, but once you've done it, it's absolutely unbreakable without the key. But you can pass on the key very easily. If it's somebody you know, you can even pass it in such a way that it would mean nothing to anybody who intercepted it."

"So are you going to keep me in suspense?" Em asked him. "Or is one of you going to tell me what a book code is?"

Victor grinned. "Simple. I want to send you a secret message that nobody else could possibly decode. So the first thing we do is agree between us on the book that will be the key. It's quite a good idea to pick something fairly big, like the Bible or the complete works of Shakespeare; but the actual book doesn't matter so long as we both have a copy. I then compose my message *using words taken from the book we agreed on.* But instead of sending you the message itself, I send you the exact location of where each word appears in the book. Page number, followed by line number, followed by position in the line—word number three or four or whatever. All you do to reconstruct the message is follow my instructions using your own copy of the book."

"What happens if somebody else has a copy of the book? Couldn't they just look up the words as well?"

Victor gave him a withering look. "They don't know which book we agreed on, do they?"

Em hesitated. "But Dad and I didn't agree on any book," he protested. "We never talked about sending messages in code."

"Maybe not, but he sent you the clue right along with the message. 'Current reading.' We know he must have composed the message sometime after he got ill. All you have to do is remember what you were reading around that time. Maybe something you were set to study at school: Dickens or Chaucer or something. Something he would have noticed you reading at the time." He leaned forward eagerly. "Can you remember?"

Em remembered all right; and it wasn't Dickens or Chaucer. He felt his face begin to flush. "It was Harry Potter."

"Which one?" Victor asked. "Haven't read them myself, but I understand there's more than one."

"Harry Potter and the Goblet of Fire." Em's flush receded. Victor clearly didn't think there was anything much wrong with reading Harry Potter. "I missed it first time around."

"Big book?"

Em nodded. *"More than six hundred pages."*

"Perfect for a book code. Six hundred pages is a lot of words. Couple of hundred thousand by my reckoning. Well, well, well . . ." He grinned broadly at Em. "Don't suppose you have a copy with you?"

Em shook his head. "No way."

"Doesn't matter. There's a bookshop around

the corner; I can slip out and buy one. Hardback or paperback?"

"They're both the same, aren't they?"

"Same text, but you sometimes get a variation in layout or type size. Can lead to different page numbers. Even a page or two difference is a nightmare when you're decoding. I'd rather we were all singing from the same hymn-sheet."

"It was the hardback," Em told him. "Mum bought me a copy."

Okay," Victor said, "I'll see if I can find us the hardback."

Em and Charlotte were paging through the holiday photographs on the laptop again when they heard Victor's key in the lock. Moments later Victor appeared in the living room waving a fat hardback with a skinny dragon on the jacket. "Got it!" he exclaimed triumphantly.

Em felt a tingle of excitement intermixed with a distinct undertone of fear. If Victor was right about the code—and Em didn't doubt for an instant that he *was* right—they would soon know what Em's father had been trying to tell him so secretly. That was dangerous knowledge. It would almost certainly call for dangerous action. "What do we do now?"

"We get to work on the code. Should be quick and easy if we go at it together."

"What do you want me to do?" Em asked. The fear racked up another notch, but he hid it successfully.

"You can do the book bit since you're the Potter fan. I'll call out the page numbers and so on from the picture on the computer. You find the word and call it out to me. Charlotte will write it down. We'll soon know what your father was trying to tell us."

It was an innocent enough phrase, but it got to Em a little. Dad wasn't trying to tell *us* anything—he was trying to tell *me.* He pushed the reaction down. It was stupid. Victor only meant that they were in this whole mess together; and, frankly, Em was glad of it. He knew with absolute certainty that he would never have gotten this far without Victor's help. Or Charlotte's. Actually, without their help, he would probably be a prisoner of the Knights by now. "Okay," he said, and held out his hand to take the book.

"Right," Victor said briskly as he leaned over the laptop, "turn to page twelve."

Em opened the book.

"Got it? Now count down to line six. You there?"

"Yes."

"Now the ninth word on that line . . . ?"

Em counted, using his forefinger to keep his place. *"My,"* he said. "'There is a little more in the bottle, my Lord.' Ninth word is *my.*"

Charlotte wrote it down as Victor consulted his laptop again. "Turn back to page eight," he instructed. "Sixth word in line three."

Em found the page and scanned the line. "Oh," he said.

Victor looked up quickly. "What's the problem?"

"There's a hyphenated thing here. 'Grown-up.' Does that count as one word or two?"

"Count it as one," Victor told him decisively.

"Then the sixth word is 'son.'"

Charlotte wrote that down as well. "'My son'—good start. He wants to send a message to his son, so he begins it 'My son.' I think we're on the right track, Em. Couple more words should tell us whether the message really makes sense. Okay, find page fifty-seven."

Em flipped quickly through the book. "Got it."

"First line, second word?"

"'The.'"

"Back to page ten, line four, seventh word."

"'Riddle.'"

"Page thirteen, line thirty-four, sixth word?"

Em missed his line count and had to start again, but eventually he said, "'Disguise.' The word is 'disguise.'"

Charlotte scrawled *disguise* in his notebook. "Something tricky now. He's put four sets of numbers in parentheses, and there's a hyphen in front of the last one. Haven't seen that in a book code before."

"What's it mean?" Em asked.

"Not sure," Victor admitted, "but I'm going to assume the first three number sets refer to page, line, and word position like the others. Look up page fifty-three, line fifteen, word three. We'll worry about the *hyphen four* later."

Em did as he was told. "The word is 'sneer.'" He

looked up when Victor failed to respond and repeated, "The word is 'sneer.'" To Charlotte he added, "Are you writing this down?"

Charlotte nodded. "Yes."

"I'm thinking," Victor told him. "The message isn't making a lot of sense after 'My son.'" He frowned. "'The riddle disguise sneer.' Just random words. Yet 'my son' seems spot-on."

Charlotte leaned over to look at the screen. "Why did he put it in brackets?"

"I was wondering that myself. And why *hyphen four* at the end?"

"Maybe it's not a hyphen," Em suggested.

"What else would it be?"

Em shrugged helplessly.

"Maybe it's a minus sign?" Charlotte said brightly.

Victor stared at the screen. "By God, you're right, Charlotte. That's exactly what it is. 'Sneer' minus four. Take away four letters from 'sneer' and what do you get?"

"Depends which you take away. If you take away the first four, you're left with *r*. If you take the last, you have *s*," Em told him

"Last would be my guess, because *s* makes sense. Listen to this: 'My son, the riddle disguise' . . . then *s* in parentheses, which means it's not really a part of the message, just something he added in to make the rest of it read properly. Trust an academic to come up with something like that. So what we've got is a prophecy and a secret message about the prophecy. 'My son, the riddle disguises' . . . the riddle being the prophecy."

"The riddle disguises what?" Em asked.

"That's what we're about to find out," Victor said with another wide grin.

It took them longer than Em expected to decode the remainder of the message. His father had clearly lost patience leafing through Harry Potter and created several words using his minus-four principle to spell out every letter. It was a habit that slowed the decoding process down considerably. But they got there eventually.

"That's it," Victor said, pushing away the laptop.

"What's it say?" Em asked. He'd been so focused on the individual words that the overall sense of the message hadn't reached him.

Charlotte read aloud from her notebook: "'My son, the riddle disguises a planned vaccination program for Death Flu. Supplies contaminated. New lethal pandemic within six months provides solution to the population problem. Documented proof from Bederbeck Foundation three one point two eight seven oh six minus one one ten point nine oh two five one nine. Obtain proof at toe of blind man. Release to press.'" She hesitated for a moment, then added, "'Your father.'"

"He put that into the code? 'Your father'?"

Charlotte nodded. "Yes."

Em wiped one eye quickly with the back of his hand. It was a bizarre farewell. He swallowed the lump in his throat and forced himself to say briskly, "I'm not sure I understand what he means, Victor." Some of the message made no sense at all. Who was the blind man? What was the Bederbeck Foundation? And why was there a whole string of numbers spelled out in words?

"I think I do," Victor told him confidently. "You have to put this in context. Actually, you have to start with the secret prophecy."

"What do you mean?"

Victor must have memorized the prophecy, for he quoted it without having to check anywhere. "'In the days of the threatened plague . . .' Your father seems to have interpreted that as this so-called Death Flu the media has been making such a fuss about. Don't know if you've heard about it. Started with vultures in Africa, and they're worried that it might turn into a pandemic. Not that it would matter since it doesn't seem to be a particularly dangerous strain, but people are panicking because it's called *Death* Flu."

"So Death Flu is the threatened plague?" Charlotte asked.

"I believe Em's father thought so. But there's a lot more. You have 'When children shall be pierced with slender lance.' You could see a 'slender lance' as the needle the doctor uses to give you your shot. So when you get vaccinated, you're 'pierced with a slender lance.' The World Health Organization has pinpointed children as the highest risk group and recommended mass vaccination of all youngsters under the age of sixteen to prevent the disease from spreading. That's why they're concentrating on the under sixteens—not yet at the age of consent—but the vaccine will be made available to all age groups, of course; and the fear factor will ensure widespread uptake."

Em remembered Tom's remark about having Charlotte vaccinated and the comment that Em himself should have a vaccination too. If he hadn't got caught up in one crisis after another and the shots had been available, he was certain he would have been vaccinated by now . . . and with contaminated vaccine, according to his father. He gave a low whistle. "And Nostradamus managed to predict all this five hundred years ago?"

Victor shrugged. "Maybe he did and maybe he didn't. The point is, your father *thought* he did. Or maybe he was investigating several possible meanings for the prophecy when he stumbled on something very nasty. The really creepy thing is that there are hints of this in the prophecy as well: 'A new world rises from the suffering of the old . . . and all mankind shall forever bear the yoke of slavery.'"

"I'm not sure I follow that. . . ."

"Remember what I told you about the Knights of Themis?"

Em nodded.

"They talk about a 'new world order' to describe the slave states they want to set up." Victor shrugged and shook his head. "I don't know whether Nostradamus predicted this or not; it might all be pure coincidence. But it started your father on an investigation. He was a very, very clever man, and I think he turned up something certain people didn't want him to know."

"You're telling me he found out about the Knights?"

"I'm telling you he found out about a Knights of Themis plot. Whether he knew who was behind it, I don't know, although I suspect he might have from one part of the message." Victor turned to face him directly. "Here's how I read it. One of the Knights' most cherished aims is a drastic reduction in world population. By *any* means. I know for a fact they've encouraged wars in the past just so hundreds of thousands—millions—of people could be wiped out. But the problem from their viewpoint is that wars won't hack it anymore. World population is now so high that even a few million dead hardly dents the statistics. So they're always looking for new ways to reduce it."

"And you think my dad found out about one of them?"

Victor had a hot, excited look in his eyes and hardly seemed to hear the question. "If you were one of the Knights, Em, how would this sound to you? You pick a new strain of flu—the virus mutates a lot so there's a new strain nearly every winter. You pick one of these and give it a really scary name: bird flu or swine flu or, better yet, Death Flu. Then you get your tame experts to say it might turn into a pandemic, and you make sure the media plays this up. Remember, the Knights have huge influence on the media. They actually *own* some of our most important newspapers; and they have control of several other news outlets, including some TV networks.

Next thing is Themis politicians or politicians in their pay are encouraged to call for something to be done. A lot of them might even believe something *needs* to be done because they don't know the whole story, and they may well believe the medical experts and the newspapers. With everybody making such a fuss, the government agrees to underwrite a large-scale vaccination program—maybe even make it compulsory."

Charlotte said a little stiffly, "I thought you said it was the World Health Organization that recommended vaccination?"

"You think the Knights have no influence on the World Health Organization?"

"Okay," Em murmured thoughtfully. He looked up to catch Victor's gaze. "So, what then?"

"What then, if you're a Themis bad guy, is that you get one of your pharmaceutical companies to manufacture a very special batch of vaccine, which they then offer to world governments at a fraction of the cost any other producer could manage. This vaccine claims to protect children, who are supposed to be most seriously at risk from Death Flu. Except that what it actually does is kill them."

"Kill them?" Charlotte echoed. "Like . . . poisons them?"

But Victor shook his head. "Hardly. If kids dropped dead after they had their shot, the vaccination program wouldn't go very far. The Knights are nothing if not subtle. My guess would be bioengineering."

Em looked at him blankly. "What has bioengineering got to do with it?"

"Do you know how a vaccine is made?" Victor asked him.

"Some sort of antibiotic injection, isn't it?"

Victor shook his head again. "Not even close. To make a vaccine, you take the disease virus or bacterium or whatever—and you weaken it. Then you introduce it into your patient."

"You give people the disease?" Em asked, appalled. He'd *been* vaccinated when he was little—against measles, mumps, and German measles. He'd been vaccinated again—against cholera—when he was a lot older prior to a trip abroad. He was only in his teens now, and he'd already been exposed to all those diseases! Cholera was supposed to be deadly.

"You give people a *weakened version* of the disease. Their immune system recognizes it for what it is and attacks it vigorously. And because the disease is weak to begin with, your immune system kills it off easily. But by then your immune system is stronger precisely *because* of the fight, and it has in place all the strategies it needs to defeat the same disease if it appears again. So when the normal version of the disease comes along, even though the disease *hasn't* been weakened, your body beats it off before it gets a grip. You've developed an immunity because of the vaccine."

"What's that got to do with bioengineering?"

"Well, weakening the disease is *sort* of bioengineering,"

Victor said. "But that's not what I was getting at. Suppose instead of a weakened version of Death Flu, you make the vaccine from a bioengineered strain of some other completely different disease . . . and you *don't* weaken it. Now, remember two things, Em. The first is that no vaccine is a hundred percent effective. You expect a few failures, so some patients who've had the vaccine will still get the original disease. The second is that your vaccination program is designed to stop the spread of Death Flu. If it does that, or seems to do that, it's successful."

It was horrible, but some really nasty ideas were beginning to creep into Em's head. Suddenly he thought he knew exactly where Victor was going with all this. But before he could comment or ask another question, Victor went on: "So you pump the world's children full of something you claim to be a vaccine against Death Flu. A few of them still go down with the disease, but everybody expects that anyway. But not very many people actually get it, because it's not a vigorous strain to begin with—you've only convinced people that it would be. And almost nobody dies from *Death* Flu, which allows you to announce that the vaccination program has been a complete success: it reduced fatalities, reduced infections, and prevented the spread of a deadly disease. Except that it was never deadly to begin with—the whole thing was just one big con game."

Em was getting confused. "But if Death Flu doesn't kill anybody, or hardly anybody, how does it reduce the population?"

"You haven't been listening," Victor told him. "Death Flu was never meant to reduce the population. Death Flu was just an excuse to introduce your vaccine. And your vaccine is bioengineered to work like a time bomb. It incubates very slowly in the body for months—your father says six months—long enough for people to have forgotten all about Death Flu and the vaccination program. Then suddenly, young people start dropping dead from a whole new disease. This one really is a pandemic; this one really is a killer. And worst of all, there's no way you can vaccinate against it because the Knights have *already* introduced the disease to a whole generation of children, and it's now erupting fully formed. No time to develop a vaccine, no time to find a useful treatment."

"Oh God," Charlotte murmured.

"Think of it. Can you imagine a more effective way of population reduction? You don't just kill off millions and millions of people, although that's a nice start; you specifically target the millions and millions of people who are most likely to have families in the not-too-distant future. You not only wipe them out, you wipe out their descendants as well. Take the long view, and you suddenly have a huge gap in population growth." He paused. "Plus the possibility of introducing another bioengineered disease targeting a different generation, which is why I think your father may have known about the Knights. His message talks about a so-called solution to the population problem."

Em said soberly, "We have to do something about this."

"We most certainly do," Victor agreed.

Em held his gaze. "What?"

Victor tapped Charlotte's notebook. "I think your father's told us that, don't you? 'Documented proof from Bederbeck Foundation.' God knows how he got hold of that." He looked at Em admiringly. "Your old man must have been some sort of Indiana Jones."

It was difficult to think of his father as any sort of Indiana Jones, but that wasn't what concerned Em at the moment. "What's the Bederbeck Foundation?" he asked. "Do you know?"

"Yes," Victor told him soberly. "It's one of the largest and most secretive bioresearch companies in the world. Section 7 has been keeping tabs on it for years. The actual ownership is hidden behind a maze of shell companies, but we've been able to establish that it's funded exclusively by the Knights. It all ties together. That's what makes me think your father's message is genuine."

It had never occurred to Em to think his father's message was anything other than genuine; but for all Victor's explanation, there was about half of it that he still didn't understand. "Who's the blind man?" he asked.

Victor shook his head. "No idea. I've no idea what a lot of his message means." He caught Em's expression and added, "Yet."

They were still wrestling with the message over a snack when a sudden burst of pop music stopped Victor in his tracks. "What the hell's that?" he gasped, looking around in panic.

"Sorry," Charlotte murmured, fishing out her cell phone. She thumbed a button and the music stopped. "It's Dad," she whispered, looking at Victor.

Victor nodded, "Take it. He's probably wondering where you are. Say you're with friends. Keep it vague."

Charlotte spoke softly into her phone for a moment, then covered the mouthpiece and looked up. "He wants me to come home."

Victor, who seemed to have changed his mind about the value of having Charlotte with them, said quickly, "Get back now—he'll just be worried about you staying out overnight. We can get together again here tomorrow morning and do some more work on the message."

"Okay," Charlotte said.

"Tell him nothing," Victor snapped fiercely.

"No, of course not," Charlotte said, a little impatiently. She uncovered the mouthpiece. "On my way, Daddy."

The following morning, before Charlotte reappeared, Victor's secure phone rang. He stared at it for a moment, frowning. "It's the office," he said.

By "office" he obviously meant Section 7. Em waited a moment, then asked, "Aren't you going to answer it?"

"This is too soon," Victor muttered. "We're not supposed to communicate until they've investigated how our last safe house was compromised. Like I told you, that usually takes weeks. Something's happened." He thumbed the ANSWER icon on the touchpad. "Yes?"

Em had a bad feeling too, although he didn't know why. He watched Victor's face carefully, but it showed nothing.

"Yes," Victor said again, in agreement this time rather than as a question. "And the apartment? . . . Mmmm . . . Okay . . . Okay . . . Okay, understood." He thumbed the DISCONNECT, slammed the phone down on the table, and spat, "Damn!"

"What's the matter?"

"They've taken Charlotte."

For a moment the words made no sense to Em. Taken? Taken where? Who'd taken Charlotte somewhere? Then the implications crashed in on him, and panic swept across him like a wave. "The Knights? They've *kidnapped* her?"

"That'd be my guess. Section thinks so too."

"They can't have," Em protested. "She was with us yesterday." Victor gave him a hard look and said nothing. "Okay, okay, that was stupid. Tell me what Section said."

"Charlotte's father reported her missing to his local police station early this morning when she didn't come home last night."

"But she left to go home. After her father called."

"Try to wake up, Em. Section 7's linked into the central police computer system. Everything's monitored. She didn't get home."

"What are the police doing about it?"

"Nothing. They have calls from anxious parents all the time. Teenager staying out all night isn't exactly headline news. Drunken party . . . new boyfriend . . . you name it. They filed a report, told her father to contact them again if she was still missing in forty-eight hours, and probably forgot about it. I should have followed my instinct, not let her get involved in this mess."

"You think the Knights have taken her?"

"Who else?"

"I didn't think they'd be especially interested in her," Em said defensively. "I'm still not sure why they would take her . . . if that's really what's happened."

"Look at it from their point of view. She was with you in France. Her father was a friend of your father.

She brought you the iPod. She followed us to the safe house. She was part of our discussion about the code and the camera. If you were a Knight of Themis and you even knew half of that, wouldn't you think she might be worth talking to?"

"Okay, but where did they snatch her? I mean, they can't have known she was here with us."

"I don't know," Victor said. "But logically it had to be somewhere between here and her home. My guess would be the taxi stand I sent her to last night. Maybe there were no cabs. Maybe she had to wait. Maybe the Knights were looking for her and just got lucky. How should I know? But that's where we start to investigate."

Em watched Victor in action with unspoken admiration. Victor had changed into a neatly tailored suit and adopted an easy, confident style that positively commanded respect. The drivers at the taxi stand were practically tripping over themselves to help him, but unfortunately none seemed to have seen anything of a young girl the night before. Until, that was, the fifth one Victor talked to.

"Nice-looking kid in a red sweater?"

"That's her," Victor said, suddenly alert.

"Saw her all right, Governor. She was walking from the direction of Railway Street. I was next in line for a fare, so I was watching out. You get a feel for people who are looking for a taxi, even before they come up to you."

"Where did you take her?" Victor asked.

"Didn't take her anywhere, Gov; that's the point. She was picked up before she got to the stand."

"By another cab?"

The driver shook his head. "Naw, the boys here are decent skins, wouldn't try to steal your fare. What happened was, this car pulled up—black Merc—and the driver calls out something to her and she bends down to talk to him and I thought, 'There goes my fare; somebody she knows is giving her a lift.' Next thing, this big bloke was helping her into the back—"

"The driver?" Victor interrupted him.

"No, somebody else in the car. Only it was more like he was, you know, sort of pushing her, like maybe she didn't want to go. But she didn't shout or fight or anything, and he got in beside her, so I figured she must have known him. Anyway, the Merc took off and that was that."

"None of your colleagues mentioned anything like this," Victor said, nodding back toward the other cabs.

"Wasn't on last night's shift, was they? Plenty of people seen it, if that's what you mean."

"I don't suppose you got the car's license plate number?" Victor asked him.

The cabbie shook his head. "Naaw, why should I? Didn't do anything wrong, did he? Not like they carried her off kicking and screaming." He hesitated, with a sudden look of concern. "Isn't something wrong, is there?"

Listening to him, Em had a picture in his mind of

the black Mercedes that had turned up at his father's funeral. And in his mind too was the absolute certainty that the big man who had bundled Charlotte into the back was the same man who'd carried the gun.

"Nothing wrong," Victor reassured him. He extracted a ten-pound note from his wallet and slid it in the man's direction. "Thank you. You've been a great help."

"Thank *you*, Gov!" The cabbie smiled as he pocketed the note.

"That had to be the Knights of Themis," Em told Victor as they walked away.

"No doubt," Victor grunted sourly. He had an absent look on his face.

"So what do we do?"

Victor shook his head. "I don't know. Maybe we just wait."

Em stopped dead to stare at him. *"Wait?"*

"What else can we do?" Victor said patiently, "We know she's been taken off in a black car, but we don't know where. We don't know the plate number. We can question cabbies from the night shift and any other witnesses we might find, but frankly, that's the longest of long shots. Would you note down a number in those circumstances? Waiting for developments may be our only option."

"But they might kill her!" Em protested wildly.

"They won't kill her," Victor said. "Worst they'll do is interrogate her."

"About us?"

"Yes, indeed. Not that they'll get anything very useful. We still haven't figured out all of your father's message."

"But they might . . ." Em hesitated. "Suppose they . . ." He trailed off, unwilling to say it.

"Torture her?" Victor finished for him. "That what you're worrying about? We're not dealing with a bunch of half-witted muggers here, Em. The Knights have access to the most sophisticated interrogation techniques on the planet, and torture certainly isn't one of them. The intelligence you get from torture is rubbish. People tell you what they think you want to hear just to stop the pain. They might drug her, but that's the most harm she'll come to."

It made sense, but Em still couldn't believe where it led to. "She'll be frightened. We can't let her go through all that and just hope they'll turn her loose afterward."

"I'm not sure it isn't the best course," Victor said.

But he changed his mind later that afternoon when Section 7 called with the news that Charlotte had been taken out of the country.

"One of our agents spotted her at Heathrow," Victor told him. "Lunchtime flight; but he was slow reporting in, and they've only just got around to telling me."

"How did he know it was her?" Em asked, a little desperately.

"He didn't. I suppose *we* don't for sure. But the girl matched Charlotte's description, and she was with two Themis personnel. Not actual members, but known employees of the organization. I'm fairly sure one of them is your famous man with the gun. His name is Stefan Kardos. Trained killer, good at his job, and likes it. I had my suspicions that it might be him following you, but I couldn't be sure until now. I don't think there's any doubt it was Charlotte."

"My God," Em gasped. "That's the man who visited my father just before he died! Where did they take her?"

"They boarded British Airways Flight 177. Eight-hour transatlantic, landing JFK in New York."

"They've taken her to *America*?"

"Looks like it," Victor said.

"What are we going to do?"

"Go after her, of course," Victor told him. "This is the first time the Knights have come out in the open with a direct move against you. I know they locked up your mother, but that was covert—and completely legal. This is kidnapping. It means they're beginning to panic, and *that* means we're getting close to something. If we can get Charlotte back, we can find clues to what's worrying them in the questions they've asked her. I don't suppose you have your passport?"

"Yes, I do," Em said, surprising himself. For some reason he felt the need to explain. "Mum insisted I take it to France even though you're not supposed to need it for EU borders; and then when we came back, I never took it out of my wallet." He hesitated. "It needs to be renewed soon."

"How soon?"

"Can't remember exactly." Victor looked worried for some reason.

"Less than ninety days?"

"Oh yes," Em said. "More like a month or six weeks." He began to scrabble for his passport in order to check the exact expiration date.

"Could be a problem." Victor frowned.

"Why?"

"The Americans waive entry visa requirements for British citizens, but only if your passport is valid for ninety days from the time you arrive in the United States. Which means you have to renew your passport or get a visa, and we don't have time for either," Victor murmured. "I'll have to organize fakes."

"Fake what?"

"Papers," Victor told him calmly.

Em stared at him appalled. "You want me to travel to America on fake papers?" Since 9/11, the Americans had gone security mad at airports. They probably shot you if they found you with fake papers.

"Don't worry," Victor said. "Our forger is really excellent. Have you been to America before?"

Em shook his head. "Never." He'd always wanted to visit New York, but he didn't suppose there'd be much time for sightseeing.

"Don't worry," Victor told him in that reassuring tone he used just before he dropped one of his bombshells. "I'll make all the bookings and have someone meet you."

For a beat Em said nothing. What Victor just said hadn't really made sense to him. Then it did. "Aren't you going too?" he asked.

"Yes, of course, but we have to travel separately."

"Why?" Em demanded.

"Security," Victor said. "I'll meet up with you in New York."

"You can't wear those socks," Victor told him sternly. They were in a menswear shop, where Victor was allowing him to choose new traveling clothes.

Em stared down at the socks in his hand. So far as he could see, they looked the soul of sobriety. "Why not?"

"Nobody in America will take you seriously if you wear black socks," Victor said.

Eventually Em found himself in a check-in queue at Heathrow Airport, a single suitcase by his side, and his ticket, passport, and forged visa clutched in one sweaty hand. His heart was thumping like a jackhammer. He wished he had Victor with him. He wished Charlotte were free. He wished the Knights would leave him alone. He wished he had a proper visa. At the rate the line was moving, he calculated that he had perhaps seven minutes before he reached the check-in clerk. That was when his phony visa would be discovered. That was when it would all go wrong.

Except it didn't. The clerk barely glanced at his passport, processed his ticket on the computer, then handed him back his documents with a brief smile.

The customs officer in New York proved a lot scarier.

The customs officer in New York was a burly black woman who didn't know how to smile. She was wearing a blue uniform and, to Em's discomfort, a sidearm. She glared at him as he approached, scowled as he reached her desk, and growled "Papers" when he attempted a grin.

Em watched her nervously as she examined his documentation.

"Purpose of visit?" she snapped.

To rescue my friend from the clutches of the world's most powerful secret society. "Holiday," Em said, following the instructions Victor had given him in London. "To see your beautiful country."

"Vacation?" asked the woman, frowning. She somehow managed to convey disbelief and disapproval of the word *holiday* both at the same time.

"Yes," Em nodded. Then repeated "Vacation" just to be on the safe side. He hoped this wasn't going to take too long. His nerves were stretched to the breaking point, and he was beginning to need a restroom.

"Where's your visa?" the woman demanded.

Em's mouth suddenly went dry. He fought down an urge to bite his lips. "Brit—" He coughed to clear his throat and began again. "I'm a British citizen."

"So?"

"We don't need visas."

"That so?" The woman stared at him for a moment, then flicked open his passport. "Edward Michael Goverton. That your name?"

For the first time he noticed the name tag balanced on her ample bosom. *Her* name was Hilda Bolden. He nodded. "Yes, ma'am."

"And this is your own passport?"

Em felt a moment of total panic. Why was she asking about his passport? He swallowed. "Yes."

She glanced from him to his picture and back again, then said, "One moment." There was a weird-looking box attached to her computer on the desktop, and she pushed the open passport into a slot in the front. A green light came on, and the box hummed briefly. Hilda Bolden leaned forward to check something on the monitor. "One moment," she said again. She picked up the telephone and murmured something he couldn't catch. Then she cradled the instrument, favored him with one of her most ferocious glares, and said, "This passport is forged. Come with me, please, Mr. Goverton."

Em thought of making a break for it, taking to his heels and running for his life past the customs desks and through the airport concourse into the busy streets of New York. But he knew he would never manage more than fifty yards before Security had him pinned to the floor. With his insides churning, he followed her through a door marked PRIVATE and down a corridor into a windowless room furnished only with a desk, two chairs, and a filing cabinet. To his horror, Hilda Bolden locked the door behind them.

"Well, Em," she said, "time to give up this little charade, don't you think?"

Em hadn't thought he could feel any more frightened, yet somehow he managed it. But despite his fear, a question burst through. "How did you know my name?" She *couldn't* know he was called Em. The only name on his passport was Edward Michael.

She smiled for the first time. "Victor told me."

"You're . . . ? You're with . . . ?" Em spluttered.

"Section 7? Right in one. Give that boy a fat cigar. Why the surprise?"

Em blinked. "I suppose I— I mean, I thought Section was— I mean, this is America, so I thought—"

There was a knock on the door. "That'll be Victor, I expect," Hilda said. As she unlocked the door, she said to Em over her shoulder, "The Knights of Themis are an international organization. Section 7 has to be international as well in order to fight them. Originally we were set up as a joint project between America and Britain, but now we're in every country in the world. Every one that matters anyway." She swung the door open, and Victor stepped in. He was wearing a very sharp suit.

"You made it then?" he said to Em.

"What's going on, Victor?" Em asked. He was furious that Victor hadn't warned him about what would happen when he reached the States. His experience with Hilda had rattled him. Even now that he knew she was on his side, she still seemed scary.

Victor said, "This place has been swept for bugs, so we can speak freely; but don't take that for granted once we leave here. Clear on that, Em?"

"Clear on that, Victor," Em confirmed tiredly.

"Hilda's introduced herself, I presume? She's one of Section 7's best international field operatives and our initial liaison in America. She's the one who arranged to have our friends followed when they landed in New York. I'll let her tell you."

Hilda picked up the story without a moment's hesitation. "Victor called as soon as he got the news about your friend. Just in time, as it turned out—the flight was circling, waiting clearance to land. I had Air Traffic Control delay them a bit until we could put surveillance in place; and sure enough, when the plane came down, we were able to identify two Themis operatives—"

"One was your old friend Stefan Kardos," Victor interrupted softly.

"—traveling under assumed names. They had a young girl with them I assumed was Charlotte."

"Was she all right?" Em asked at once. "Do you think she was hurt?"

"Frankly, I think she was drugged. She wasn't making

any fuss about going with them."

"What did you do? Did you arrest them?"

Hilda parked her ample behind on the corner of the desk. "Section 7 doesn't have powers of arrest—it would have to have been a snatch operation, and we didn't want to risk a run-in with the airport authorities . . . or show our hand. Besides which, we wanted to be sure they had time to interrogate her—"

"You wanted to *what?*" Em exploded.

Hilda frowned in surprise. "Victor's orders," she said, as if that explained something. "We wanted to know what questions they would ask her, and they wouldn't have a chance to interrogate her on the plane. Girl didn't seem to have been harmed, so we decided just to put a tail on them until further instructions from Victor."

Em looked at her for a moment as the information sank in, then asked cautiously, "Does that mean you know where they went?"

Hilda nodded. "Yes. Midtown apartment the Knights use as a safe house."

Em turned from Hilda to Victor. "Can't we do something to rescue her?"

"Ahead of you," Victor told him. He opened the door behind him, and Charlotte walked in.

The Michelangelo had leanings toward red leather and thick carpets. "Posh place," Em remarked. He was experiencing emotions that had nothing to do with the hotel. They'd started with a flooding of relief when he had seen Charlotte at the airport, the intensity of which almost frightened him. Now, looking at her across the table in the suite Victor had arranged for, he was becoming aware of an undercurrent of disappointment. It took him time to work out where it was coming from. Somewhere in his most secret heart he had wanted to be part of her rescue—heck, he'd wanted to be the hero who rescued her himself. To fly all the way to America only to discover the deed had already been done was . . . well, stupidly disappointing.

"Good coffee." Victor shrugged in response to Em's

remark about the hotel.

Em was looking at Charlotte. "What happened?"

"They grabbed me while I was waiting for a taxi," Charlotte said. "I didn't know one of them, but the other was the man we saw in France, the one with the gun—"

"Stefan Kardos," Victor put in.

"They injected me with something, and the next thing I knew, I was on a plane. It was all sort of confused until I was in a room being questioned—"

"We've debriefed her on that," Victor put in again. "Absolute confirmation we're dealing with the Knights, absolute confirmation they're worried sick about what your father discovered."

"Talking of which," Charlotte said, "Victor says you're still not sure where to find the proof of what he did discover?"

"We still haven't cracked the whole message," Em said gloomily.

"Maybe I can help with that," Charlotte said. "Can I take another look?"

Minutes later they were poring over the notebook. "We got stuck on this three one point two eight seven business," Em reminded her. "That didn't seem to make any sense in any code."

"My guess would be map coordinates: latitude and longitude," Charlotte said without a moment's hesitation.

Em and Victor looked at each other. Then they both looked at Charlotte. Could it have been that obvious? Could they both have been that stupid?

"What made you think of map coordinates?" Victor frowned.

Charlotte shrugged. "I don't know. There were maps lying about in the house where they took me, and I was thinking about map reading for some reason when the drugs wore off. I suppose they were in my head."

"Why didn't he write them as numbers if they're map coordinates?" Em asked cautiously.

Charlotte shrugged. "Not all that many numbers in a Harry Potter story I'd imagine. He had to spell them out."

Dumb question, Em thought. But it didn't stop him from asking another one: "What are they the coordinates *of*?"

Charlotte gave him that long-suffering look of hers. The one that asked why she had to do all the brain work. "You'll have to check that out on a map."

"I'll get the hotel to send one up." Victor moved toward the phone. "But if he stole the documents from the Bederbeck Foundation, my guess is he would have tried to get them safely hidden as quickly as possible, especially if there was any possibility that he would fall under suspicion. He must have known what he was up against by that stage. So, now that we're thinking map coordinates, my guess would be the location has to be somewhere quite close to the foundation itself."

"Where's the foundation located?" Em asked. For some reason, he thought it might be back in London. He hoped it wouldn't be somewhere in the North or, heaven forbid, even Scotland. He didn't have much stomach for another lengthy trip after the flight back.

"Arizona," Victor told him tersely.

The hotel supplied one of the largest maps of North America Em had ever seen. Victor pored over it while Charlotte watched him and Em watched Charlotte, although he tried very hard not to make it obvious.

"They're in the Sonoran," Victor announced eventually. "Striking distance of the Bederbeck Foundation. Just as I thought."

"What's the Sonoran?" Em asked.

"The Sonoran Desert," Victor told him. "Bit of a wilderness. If he hid the documents out there, nobody would find them without instructions. Sort of place where you could die trying."

Lucky we have directions then, Em thought. Maybe his dad really had been like Indiana Jones. Just a little.

"Is that where we're going next?" Charlotte asked Victor brightly. "To the Sonoran to find the proof Em's father hid?"

"*We* aren't going anywhere, young lady." Victor frowned. "I'll go ahead to set things up, but you've been through a traumatic experience—"

Charlotte, who'd clearly guessed what was coming and didn't like it, said quickly, "I wasn't at all upset, not really. I mean—"

"—and the only place *you're* going is home. We've told your father you're safe, and he is flying over to collect you."

"Yes, but Dad—"

"I may have given him the impression that you were rescued by the FBI, and I'd be obliged if you continue to let him think that. But even if you tell him differently, you won't make it stick. The FBI is prepared to back up Section's story."

Charlotte actually pouted, rather prettily, Em thought. "But I want to go with you to find the proof. This isn't fair—you didn't even know it was map coordinates until I suggested it." The pout changed to a winning smile. "Come on, Victor, you know how helpful I've been. You know how helpful I *can* be."

But Victor was buying none of it. "Too late for that. Your father will be landing soon." He gave a very small smile of his own. "Besides, I'm going to have enough problems keeping one kid out of trouble."

That would be me, Em thought. But he didn't really mind being called a kid. At least it meant Victor was taking him along.

E m had only the most fleeting impression of Phoenix before catching a connecting flight to Tucson. He had only a fleeting impression of Tucson as well, which was a pity, since he'd been into Country and Western in the days when he had time to listen to music and it was featured in many of his favorite songs. But he doubted he'd have appreciated it much anyway. He was unused to flying and by now had entered an unreal state of gray exhaustion that was almost worse than jet lag.

Somebody met him at the Tucson airport with the mention of Victor's name. From that point, his trip took on an increasingly surreal aspect. He was bundled onto an aircraft that surprised him by taking off straight up until he realized it was a helicopter. Although he'd never been in a helicopter before, he actually fell asleep until a hand shaking his shoulder dragged him reluctantly back to consciousness.

"Time to get out, Em," a voice said in his ear. So he got out and walked across the tarmac, vaguely aware that somebody had an arm around his shoulders, holding him crouched so he wouldn't be decapitated by whirling blades.

There was a large car waiting with deep, comfortable backseats. All this, the chopper and the car, was laid on by Section 7. Must have been. Victor seemed to be able to arrange anything over here. Who was he anyway? This sort of stuff was way beyond a simple field agent surely. Or was it? Em was still wondering when he fell asleep again. He dreamed that somebody helped him check into a hotel where the room was air conditioned, the sheets were cool and clean, and the mattress was welcoming. Then the dream turned to a velvet darkness.

Em woke to sunlight, wondering where he was. It had the feel of a hotel room. There was an oversize television at the bottom of the bed, and he could see a bathroom through an open door. He found his watch on the bedside table and discovered it was almost noon. As he completed the long swim into consciousness, he saw an envelope beside the watch. His name was written in a flamboyant, open hand he recognized at once. He tore open the envelope. The single sheet of paper inside lacked any letterhead. The message read:

Welcome to Arizona! I've arranged a place for us, but you looked so shattered when you arrived I thought it best to let you sleep over in town before bringing you out.

I'll collect you at the motel at 3 pm tomorrow. (Or today, I suppose, since you'll be reading this in the morning.) Any problems, call the local number listed at the bottom of this sheet. Anything you need, call reception at the motel and charge it to the account of Harlan Benson (name I'm using here).

Yours sincerely,

V.

Em pulled himself out of bed and headed for the bathroom. His body still felt like lead, but his head was mercifully clear. There was no bath, of course—*Welcome to America!*—but the shower controls looked like they belonged at Cape Canaveral.

By the time he emerged from the shower he was feeling not just human, but lively and hungry. He lifted the phone and dialed reception. "This is going to sound silly, but where exactly am I?"

"Easy Rider Motel, sir," a male voice told him as if guests got confused every hour of the day.

Em said, "I was also wondering about the name of the town."

"Nogales, sir. The town's called Nogales. Only around here folks think it's a city."

Em finally got to the point. "Is there somewhere I can eat? Like breakfast?"

"Motel has a fine restaurant, sir. Just follow the signs when you come out of your cabin. I can recommend the flapjacks."

The motel restaurant was functional and clean. The waitress looked Spanish but didn't have the accent. "Hi, honey, you on your own?"

Em nodded. "Think so."

"You must be Harlan Benson's boy. He told me to take good care of you."

Em remembered in time what Victor had decided to call himself and suppressed the blank look. "Thank you."

"My name's Donna. Harlan's a doctor—right?"

So Victor had passed himself off as a doctor for reasons best known to himself. Em nodded. "That's right." He was surprised how easily the lie came. He was getting used to thinking like a secret agent.

"I'd like to be a doctor, but I never had the brains. Don't know what it's like back where you come from, honey, but over here doctors make a fortune. You'll never meet a poor one. You hungry?"

"Starving," Em told her.

By the time Donna brought eggs, then the recommended flapjacks, Em decided he knew her well enough to ask, "Do you know anything about the Bederbeck Foundation?"

"Know it's over thataway," Donna said, jerking her head in an indeterminate direction. "You figuring on paying them a call?"

Em smiled. "Not today."

"Glad to hear it. Those boys are so secretive they got machine-gun posts."

Em's eyes widened as he stared up at her. "Seriously?"

"Heck, no! But they like to keep themselves to themselves, and they do have a load of security. Wander too close to the facility and their musclemen turn up out of nowhere to escort you back the way you came. What's your interest in Bederbeck?"

Em shrugged casually. "I was only wondering if you knew what they did there."

"Sure do, honey. Is this a test or what?"

He hesitated, then said, "I think I passed a sign on the way in. I was just curious." What the hell, he'd probably be telling a lot more lies before he finished what he had to do.

Donna laughed. "You and a lot of other people. Whole place is supposed to be a big secret, but you can't keep nothing to yourself in a place the size of Nogales. They're doing research into plants out at the facility; that's what it's all about: food crops you can grow in dry conditions, like the real bad parts of the Sonoran. Won't talk about it because that sort of thing could be big money now that the world's getting hotter and all."

It was as good a cover story as any, Em thought.

He was waiting outside the motel reception at three o'clock when a battered red off-roader truck pulled up beside him and the driver leaned across to open the passenger door. It took Em a moment to realize he was looking at Victor, who'd shaved off his beard. The scar wasn't as pronounced as Em had imagined it would be, but it was pronounced enough. It gave Victor a vaguely sinister look but made him look younger and, in an odd way, more sophisticated. Would never have mistaken him for James Bond though. He was wearing jeans, brown riding boots, and a Stetson—none of them new. "Throw your case in the back and climb in," Victor said.

Em did as he was told. "Where are we going?" he asked as he slid into the passenger seat.

"Good afternoon, Victor," Victor said. "Nice to see you again, Victor. Thank you for making all the arrangements to get me here, Victor."

"I thought your name was Harlan."

"Touché!" Victor said.

They drove south, then east, away from Nogales, then went off-road into the desert. "Couple of Border Patrol officers were shot out here the other week," Victor remarked casually.

Em blinked and scanned the shrub and rocks around them. "Shot dead?" He knew nothing about this part of the United States, but already it was sounding like the Wild West.

Victor shook his head. "One in the leg, one in the hand. So I'm told."

"Then why are we coming out here?" Em demanded. He would have thought they had enough problems hiding from the Knights of Themis without heading into bandit territory.

"Because two Border Patrol officers were shot here the other week," Victor told him, face blank. "I wanted to find a base for us somewhere we aren't likely to be disturbed."

The old truck creaked, rattled, and bucked in protest

at the rough terrain but held together until Victor somehow found a narrow dirt road heading deeper still into the desert.

"What are we going to do," Em asked, "camp out?"

"All mod cons, actually," Victor said. "I rented a log cabin. As Harlan Benson." He jerked the wheel to avoid a pothole. "That's *Doctor* Harlan Benson, by the way, in case anybody asks."

"So I gathered," Em murmured.

Victor threw him a quick look. "Gathered where?"

"Waitress at the motel."

Victor gave a small smile. "Donna?"

"That's right. You talked to her, told her to look out for me."

"One of our best agents," Victor said. He swung the truck sharply right onto a side road that was little better than a track.

The heat in the van had been lulling Em into a torpor despite the conversation and the bumpy road. Now he sat up with a jerk. "She's with Section 7?"

"She'll deny it, and you'll never prove it," Victor told him. He slowed the truck and let it roll to a halt on the top of a ridge. "Take a look to your right."

Em turned. His surroundings fell away into a wasteland of shrub and cactus. "What am I looking for?"

"The fence," Victor said. He waited a beat. "Got it?"

The fence—now Em saw it—ran along the far edge of a dip, then vanished over a rise. It looked about six feet high, composed of thick metal mesh staked by concrete posts, with a capping of razor wire to discourage climbers. He nodded. "Got it."

"That marks the edge of Bederbeck property. The foundation bought up a huge swath of badlands to surround its facility."

Em let his eyes drift along the visible length of the fence. No machine-gun posts, no guards; not even a sign saying BEWARE OF THE DOG. He reckoned that with thick gloves and a bit of care, he could have climbed over.

"It's electrified," Victor told him as if reading his thoughts. "Won't kill you, just enough of a jolt to discourage intruders." He turned the key in the ignition and the truck's engine roared to life again. "But I'll tell you something: if we tried to get over it, or even if we stay parked here for too long, we'll have a couple of armed security goons from the foundation strolling over to ask what we're doing."

"How'd they know we were here?"

"Security cameras. They're hidden along the fence every hundred yards, and the fence runs for *miles*." Victor leaned toward him. "Not to mention . . ." He pointed through the window. ". . . See there, top of the next ridge?" Em followed the finger and was rewarded by a flare of sunlight on glass, although nothing else was visible. "We've been under surveillance since we pulled up," Victor said. He withdrew to push the lever into drive, and the truck bumped into motion again.

As they drove off, Em discovered he was feeling uneasy. But the odd thing was, it had nothing to do with the watchers on the ridge.

The log cabin proved as fake as Em's travel documents. It looked like the real McCoy as they approached on a track that might have been made by goats, but failed close inspection by the time they drew up at the pocket-sized veranda. Em could see that the "logs" were actually just facings on a prefabricated wall, and the windows were plastic, painted brown and then grained to look like wood. The whole thing might have been a gigantic trailer disguised as a traditional dwelling. The inside was spacious and newly furnished. Em felt the air conditioning at once. He also noticed the stereo sound system and a well-stocked bar at one end of the living area.

"It's owned by a writer," Victor explained. "Comes here every two years to churn out his latest blockbuster. In between times he takes himself off to Bermuda and rents the place to anybody who wants to get away from it all. The Section arranged a calendar month, which should be more than long enough for what we have to do." He gave a slow grin. "One of the rooms has a water bed—you ever try one?"

Em shook his head, but his mind wasn't on the sleeping arrangements. He was still feeling uneasy, and now he realized why. It was just a small thing, really, something that had happened back in England when they were in the first safe house and Victor wouldn't let Em make a phone call in case the Knights traced him through his voiceprint. It had sounded reasonable enough at the time, if maybe just the tiniest bit science-fictiony, but then it had turned out later that Victor had a secure cell phone that couldn't be traced. Why hadn't he let Em use that right away? There was probably a very good reason. It was just that Em couldn't think of one and it niggled.

He wondered if he should ask Victor outright, thought it over, then decided against it. Was such a small thing worth worrying about? Especially since it was old history. Best to get on with the job at hand? "Okay," he told Victor brightly, "I call the water bed."

The water bed proved a bad choice. It felt cold despite the under-blanket, the motion made Em seasick, and he was constantly plagued by the thought of falling through and drowning. When he reemerged from the room, Victor was counting his yarrow stalks with his copy of the *I Ching* on the table beside him.

"What are you asking?"

Victor glanced up, but his hands continued to split and count the bundle. "Getting your father's proof isn't going to be as easy as I thought."

He was asking the *I Ching* about getting the proof? Sometimes Em thought Victor might be a bit unhinged. Aloud he asked, "Why not?"

"I thought it would just be a question of driving into the desert to the right coordinates, figuring out what he meant by the 'blind man's toe,' and maybe doing a bit of digging—my thought is that he most likely buried the documents. Biggest problem would be to make sure we weren't followed, hence taking this place and dropping out of sight for a few days."

Em nodded. "That's more or less what I thought too. So what's the problem?"

Victor released an explosive sigh. "The problem, my boy, is that I've just checked the area on a large-scale map. The coordinates your father gave are inside the Bederbeck fence."

"Oh," Em said.

"This isn't going to be like walking into the university to get the camera," Victor told him unnecessarily. "The guards are authorized to use lethal force."

"You mean they could *shoot* us?"

"This is Arizona, Em. Gold rush tradition."

"Shoot us just for *trespassing*? Suppose we're hikers who got lost or something and just wandered, like accidentally, onto their property?"

"We'd have to just wander over a ten-foot-high electrified fence with razor wire, but yes." Victor looked at him seriously. "The foundation has a lot of political clout around here, biggest employer for a hundred miles, contacts in high places. . . . They want to preserve their privacy. Couple of years ago they opened fire on a group of protesters who tried to break their perimeter security. Nobody killed, but they hospitalized two students and left one woman permanently disabled in a wheelchair. Judge said the foundation was within its rights to protect its own property. There was some fuss in the national press, but it soon died down. The local press didn't even report the story."

"Wow!" Em said.

"Wow, indeed," Victor remarked tiredly. "While you were taking your little snooze, I've been trying to figure out what to do. First thing, obviously, is that I go this alone. It's far too dangerous to consider taking you along."

"I wasn't taking a little . . ." Em began, then let it drop. He had more important things to worry about. "No," he said firmly.

"No, what?"

"No, you're not leaving me behind." Since he couldn't think of a single, sensible reason why not, he explained, "I'm not Charlotte, Victor. The message about the documents was for *me*." Which clearly wasn't going to carry much weight with Victor; but since there was no way, no *way*, he was going to miss out on finding the documents now that he'd come this far, he put his mind into racing gear and added, "I know what Dad meant by 'the blind man.'" It was a lie, but Victor wasn't going to know that, so he compounded it quickly: "It was a thing we had between us, a sort of a joke."

Victor stared at him. "Meaning what?"

"Oh no," Em said. "I'm not going to tell you that. Once you know, you'll leave me behind. Let's just say that when we get to the right place, I'll identify exactly where to look and tell you then. I'm going with you, Victor. You can't stop me."

"Listen, Em," Victor said soberly. "I don't think you appreciate how dangerous this mission is."

"You just told me how dangerous it is. I'm still coming."

Victor looked at him thoughtfully. "I'm not sure I believe you about 'the blind man.'"

Em shrugged. "Suit yourself. But are you willing to take the chance?"

Apparently Victor wasn't, because he said with an air of finality, "Okay, you come along. But only if you promise—*swear*—you'll do what I tell you. Stick close to me at all times. And if I tell you to get out of there, you get out of there."

"Okay," Em agreed. "So what's the plan?"

"That's what I've been trying to figure out. Finding the documents at night might be a lot trickier, but I don't see that we have any alternative. If we go in daylight, we'll be spotted by the cameras once we approach the fence. Even at night we'll have serious problems."

Em pulled up a chair and sat down at the table. "Why?"

"The cameras all have an infrared function."

Frowning, Em said, "If they have infrared cameras, we might as well go in daytime. We'll be spotted either way."

"I'm toying with the possibility of trying to take out some of the cameras. But how long will it take their security people to respond once a camera goes down? Or how, come to that? Do they assume it's a technical fault and send out a repair team? And they may send out an armed response unit just to be on the safe side. You see the problem?"

Em did. "Can't you fool infrared?" he asked.

"Infrared cameras detect heat radiation. From our bodies, in this case. Basically you *can* fool them in one of two ways. The simplest way is to mask the radiation from our bodies by setting a fire. The cameras can't separate out our body heat from the background of the much greater heat from the blaze. So long as you stay close to the fire, they can't see you. The high-tech way is to use a reflective suit that traps your body heat completely, makes you invisible to an infrared camera. Unfortunately, you can't wear a reflective suit very long, otherwise the buildup of heat inside will fry you. The more active you are, the less time you've got."

"Active like climbing the fence?"

"Actually," Victor said, "I wasn't thinking of climbing

the fence. Apart from the razor wire, triggering the electrical circuit will almost certainly let them know something is trying to climb over. I was thinking of digging our way under. The question is, can we dig under before the suits fry us?"

There was no answer to that, but Em thought about it for a moment anyway. "What about your other option: setting a fire? We wouldn't need the suits then."

A pained expression crossed Victor's features. "There are problems with that one as well. First of all, we have to start a fire without being seen by the cameras. Also, it's very dry in the desert at this time of year, so there's no guarantee a fire wouldn't get out of hand. Tell you the truth, I'd more or less ruled out the fire option."

"So we use the suits?"

Victor nodded. "I think so. We'll just have to move fast and hope we get lucky with the digging. At least getting out again should be easier once we've got hold of the documents." He flicked open the *I Ching* book.

"What were you asking the oracle?" Em inquired for the second time.

"Whether the omens were favorable for a successful mission," Victor muttered soberly. He turned several pages, then stopped.

Em felt a totally irrational surge of excitement. "What's it say?" He looked at Victor's expression and felt the excitement slide sideways into a sudden fog of fear. Something was wrong.

"Hexagram 29," Victor said slowly. "'The Abysmal.'"

He looked up at Em. "Repeated!"

"That's bad?" Em asked. Of course it was bad. When was something abysmal anything other than bad?

"That's dangerous," Victor said. "But we knew that before I asked. What really worries me is the moving line."

"Moving line?" Em echoed.

"Six at the top," Victor told him. He picked up the book and read aloud, "'Bound with cords and ropes, shut in between thorn-hedged prison walls: for three years one does not find the way. Misfortune.'"

A lot of the *I Ching* was obscure to Em, but not this reading. This reading was as clear as day. The oracle thought they were going to be caught and jailed for three years. "What are we going to do now?" he asked.

"Risk it," Victor said. "We have to get those documents. Let's just hope the *I Ching*'s got it wrong."

The infrared suits looked like silver body stockings with hoods and full-face masks that came with silvered fine-mesh grilles, allowing them to breathe and see. Em and Victor tried them on in the cabin with the curtains drawn.

"You look like something that just stepped out of a flying saucer," Victor remarked.

Em peered at him through his fine-mesh visor. "So do you." He could see quite clearly, but already the suit had begun to feel warm. Given that his only exertion had been putting it on and the cabin's air-conditioning kept the surrounding temperature to a comfortable level despite the outside heat, he wondered how long it would take before his body began to feel the real effects.

Victor obviously had much the same thought, for

he said, "Try jogging on the spot. I want to see how far we can get with these things." Without waiting for a response he began to jog himself. Em followed suit, a little more briskly. It took less than a minute before he found himself slick with a sweat that dripped to sting his eyes and leave his vision as impaired as if he'd begun to swim underwater.

Victor stopped jogging and pulled back his headpiece, gasping. His face was sweating as profusely as Em's and had turned a beet red. "Wow!" he said. "I thought we might have a bit more leeway than that!" He stared at Em, who was still jogging. "How close are you to cooked?"

"I'm okay," Em said without slacking pace. "Hot, but I think I could keep going a little longer." What he meant was a lot longer, but didn't want to sound boastful.

"You're fitter than I am," Victor said admiringly. "At least your body is adjusting to the heat buildup a great deal better. I think you may have to do most of the digging."

Em slowed, stopped, then pulled back his headpiece and wiped the sweat from his eyes with his sleeve. "That's okay," he said.

Victor was shaking his head thoughtfully. "Must be our age difference. This makes things a lot trickier. We'll have to wait until the last minute to put on the suits, conserve energy as much as possible, and just hope we can get under the fence before we fry. Meanwhile, we need to get in some practice in using the suits, maybe acclimatize to them a bit more before we attempt the actual mission."

"When *do* we attempt the actual mission?" Em asked him.

"About an hour's time," Victor said.

Before Em had arrived in America, his mental picture of the Arizona desert was something similar to the photographs he'd seen of the Sahara: vast, lifeless stretches of sand dunes reaching to a distant horizon beneath a merciless sun.

It hadn't been like that at all, of course. The parts of the Sonoran he'd seen were heavily vegetated, mainly with rough grass, shrub, and cactus, but still sporting a healthy scattering of spiky trees. It looked even less lifeless at night than it did during the day: the headlights of the truck kept picking up the glint of animal eyes in the undergrowth, some of them high enough from the ground to suggest creatures that could do you serious damage. As they bumped slowly along, Em couldn't quite shake the feeling that he was living in a Stephen King novel.

Victor had been over the plan with him several times in the cabin. He'd bought a mobile GPS system and converted their target latitude and longitude into GPS coordinates: N 31 17.224, W 110 54.151. Then they had charted a route that would keep them well clear of the foundation's boundary while taking them directly to what Victor kept referring to as "base camp": a hollow in the lee of a rocky outcrop where they could abandon the truck, don their infrared suits, and walk to the section of fence they planned to breach. Assuming that was successful, they could remove the suits and use the GPS to guide them to their final destination. It had all sounded great in theory, but now, under the desert stars, Em was feeling distinctly nervous. "Are we nearly there yet?" he asked Victor.

"That's the third time you've asked," Victor snapped at him impatiently. "You sound like a kid on a camping holiday."

"Sorry," Em said sourly. Then, because he couldn't avoid the issue any longer, he added, "I need to pee."

"Can't you hold on a bit?" Victor demanded. "We're only five minutes away—ten at the most."

"Too bumpy," Em told him. "I'd never last."

"Oh, for God's sake!" Victor snapped impatiently, and slammed on the brakes. "Try not to be too long—we're running late."

"That's better," Em said as he hauled himself back into the truck. He'd decided to stop worrying about Victor. The man had his own way—an odd way—of doing things, that was all.

The truck jerked forward as Victor slammed it into drive and floored the pedal. *He really was in a hurry,* Em thought. *Maybe he was just impatient.*

It seemed less than five minutes before Victor pulled the truck off the narrow desert track and stopped again. "Base camp," he muttered as he pushed open the driver's door. "Time to suit up."

They stood together for a moment in the hollow, listening to night sounds that somehow accentuated the silence. From this vantage point there was no sign of the fence at all, although Em knew it had to be close by. "Where do we go when we're ready?" he asked.

Victor was at the back of the truck unloading their equipment: shovels for digging, a small pickax in case they got unlucky and struck stone, nightscope goggles to help them see better in the darkness, their handheld GPS, and, of course, the infrared suits themselves. "Out of the hollow and over the rock," Victor said. "You can follow me. The fence is just on the other side."

"Do we have far to walk before we start to dig?"

Victor finished unloading. "Few yards once we're clear of the outcrop. Then we dig. It's a much longer walk after that to where your father buried the evidence, but we can take the suits off once we're clear of the fence, so it shouldn't be too bad. We can use the GPS then as well."

"Why not sooner?" Em asked. It occurred to him that the GPS would be useful right now to check their position.

"Screen lights up," Victor said. "It would be visible to the cameras."

"You want me to put my suit on now?"

Victor shook his head. "Nope. We climb until we're about to emerge from the outcrop. Then we strip off to our underwear and stand around like idiots until our bodies cool down. We get as chilly as we can stand, *then* put on the suits. After that we stroll over to the fence. And I mean *stroll*. Everything slow and easy so we generate as little heat as possible. Then the digging." He began to gather up his equipment. "You carry your own shovel and suit. I'll look after the GPS. Remember, no talking under any circumstances once we're clear of the rock. The cameras are all wired for sound, and you can be sure the mikes are very sensitive. Even if they can't see us, they can hear us: one word and they'll come running."

Something suddenly occurred to Em. "Won't they hear us digging?"

"They will. I was about to come to that. Our big danger time arrives when we reach the fence. If we try to dig under in the usual way, there's an excellent chance some guard at Bederbeck will hear the sounds, put two and two together, and figure out what they are. It's our job to make sure that doesn't happen, and the way we do it is to make the sound of digging come across as part of the natural night sounds."

"How do we do that?"

"What makes digging sound like digging is the rhythm," Victor said. "Shovel in . . . lift earth . . . empty earth beside you . . . shovel in . . . lift earth . . . empty earth beside you . . . People hear the sounds and figure out what's happening. What we do is push the shovel in as gently as possible, empty it as gently as possible, so we minimize the sounds." He hesitated, then added, "Hopefully."

"Right," Em said.

"I'll take out the first shovel of earth, then you, then me, and so forth. If I overheat I'll just stop and you carry on as long as you can. If I find I can go on again, I'll signal you like this—" He waved his right hand.

"Wait a minute," Em said suddenly. "I won't be able to see you."

Victor looked at him soberly. "How do you figure that?"

"The goggles work on infrared, don't they? With the suits we won't radiate infrared. We won't be able to see each other at all."

But Victor was shaking his head. "The goggles don't use infrared. They work by amplifying ambient light: starlight. It's new technology at this level, developed in Section."

"Okay."

Victor said, "You happy you know what you're doing?"

Em nodded. "Yes." He stopped himself from adding "Blissful" since he didn't think Victor would appreciate the humor.

Victor tossed him his shovel. "Okay," he said, "let's get the show on the road."

The nightscope goggles were a bit of a miracle. The second Em put them on, his whole environment lit up as brightly as it would have on a full-moon night. He could see Victor clearly, see the fence as they moved toward it. As they reached it, Victor pointed to a spot in the ground, presumably the area they were supposed to dig, then followed up by unslinging his shovel and carefully taking out the first scoop of earth. He was not entirely silent, but he managed to make so little sound that it might have been caused by a sigh of wind. Victor stepped back, waited a moment, then signaled to Em.

Em stepped forward and pushed his shovel gently into the earth. He'd been wondering how he was going to manage without making noise, but Victor's earlier comments turned out to be right: the earth beneath the fence was sandy and loose, so that he managed it easily enough. He deposited the earth quietly to one side and stepped back as Victor had done.

It was slow going. The trench they were digging so painstakingly soon exhibited a habit of filling itself in with miniature landslides of loose earth. At one point Em waved Victor back and tried experimentally to open a new trench nearer to the closest fence post, figuring the earth must be firmer there to support the post itself. He quickly discovered the post was sunk in concrete and went back to their original plan.

Frustratingly slow though it was, they began to see progress eventually. Finally the moment arrived when Em, slick with sweat, realized the trench was deep enough for him to wriggle through it. He was about to signal to Victor when Victor signaled to him and walked away toward the rocky outcrop, indicating that he wanted Em to follow. Once out of sight of the fence, Victor unzipped his infrasuit and pulled it down to his waist. "Bloody thing is frying me," he muttered. "You all right?"

Em nodded, but unzipped his own suit just the same. He was pouring perspiration and shaking from the effort of digging. The night air flowed across his body like a balm. "I could get under now."

"Yes, I know," Victor said breathlessly. "And that's exactly what you should do when you cool down." He shook his head. "This is proving far tougher than I thought. Change of plan. I want you to take the GPS. . . ." He hesitated. "You know how to work it, don't you?"

"Yes, I do."

"It's already set to TEXT ONLY, so you won't have to worry about making noise. I want you to take the GPS, get under the fence, and head for our coordinates. I'll dig deeper when I cool down and follow. It's going to take too long if you wait for me. The sooner we have the documents and get out of here the better."

"What do you want me to do when I reach the coordinates?" Em asked.

"You're the one who claims he knows all about 'the blind man,'" Victor snorted with just the barest hint of cynicism. "If you can find the proof, grab it. If not, I'll join you as quickly as I can."

Minutes later Em, safely suited again, pushed his shovel and the GPS underneath the fence, then lay flat on his stomach and wriggled after them. He emerged on the other side with a feeling of exhilaration. He'd scarcely let himself experience any emotion, but now the sheer sense of adventure almost overwhelmed him. Victor's cynicism was well-founded. Em knew nothing about the "blind man" in the message, but he was confident the answer to the riddle would be obvious once he reached the proper coordinates. His father would never have included something Em could not quickly figure out.

Em moved a distance from the fence before unzipping his infrared suit and switching on the GPS. Victor was still hidden behind the outcrop, presumably suitless, allowing his overheated body to cool down. But it made no difference; the GPS was already programmed with the coordinates. It was now showing a directional arrow and the written instruction: *Walk North 200 yards, then turn East.* Em allowed himself a satisfied smile and walked off.

Although it looked perfectly ordinary, the GPS proved to be a more sophisticated device than the ones he'd seen in England. He was far from any mapped roads now, but the device Victor had given him seemed to sense the wilderness terrain directly. The instruction "Walk North" took him over relatively even ground; but after two hundred yards, his progress was blocked by an enormous boulder. When he turned east, however, he only had to push between two bushes to find his way clear again, with a new message on the screen: *Walk 50 yards, then turn North.*

He was making his way around a clump of high-growing cacti when it occurred to him that Victor's promise to follow him made no sense. Without the GPS, Victor *couldn't* follow him. Em was now well out of sight of the place where they'd dug; and while the night goggles helped, there was no way Victor was going to track him.

Em frowned. Should he go back for Victor? But that

was wasting time; and as Victor had said, every minute they spent out here increased the chance of something going wrong. On balance he thought going on would be the best policy. According to the screen he was getting close to his destination now.

The last few yards were tough. Em pushed his way through some densely packed bushes, wincing at the thorns that scratched his chest, legs, and arms. Then he broke free. His destination was at the center of his screen. He was standing at the exact coordinates his father had given him.

Em looked around. He was in a clearing. He saw the "blind man" at once: a tall spur of rock that had weathered into a reasonable approximation of a face in profile, the eyes banded by striations like a blindfold. There was nothing to suggest a toe, but that might show up from a different perspective. At that instant Em didn't care. He was too startled by another feature of the clearing: a small, prefabricated hut to his right and beside it a parked RV. Muted lights were shining through the windows of both. Somebody was already here!

Em's mind raced. Company was the last thing he expected. Should he run? Should he back quietly into the bushes and hide to give himself a chance to survey the situation? Had something gone wrong, or was this something his father had arranged when he stole the documents from Bederbeck? Both Em and Victor had assumed the papers would be buried somewhere, stashed away in a hurry as his father escaped. But suppose it hadn't been like that? Suppose his father had had the opportunity of hiding the proof at leisure? Suppose he had actually arranged for the hut and the RV out here in the wilderness? It seemed unlikely, but—

There was a loud, metallic click, and the clearing flooded with light. Em screamed and dropped to his knees as the amplification technology in his night goggles blinded him, painfully and absolutely. On a reflex that cut in microseconds too late, he screwed his eyes shut and scrabbled to tear off the goggles.

There was a sound of running footsteps: more than one person. An American voice called out, "Something's happened; he's in trouble." Another voice, closer, almost beside him, asked solicitously, "You okay, Em? What's the matter?"

"Eyes," Em managed to gasp. They were stinging like mad, and even without the goggles he was blinded. But that didn't matter. What mattered was that they knew his name. Which meant they were expecting him; and whoever they were, they had to be from the Bederbeck Foundation—with the hut and RV on foundation land, nothing else made sense. Em was still watching fireworks in the darkness as strong hands helped him to his feet. But the greatest pain he felt had nothing to do with his eyes. He was both devastated and bewildered. He had been betrayed.

And there was only one person in the world who could have betrayed him.

41

They left the main desert highway and turned onto a well-maintained minor road with a prominent sign reading

BEDERBECK FOUNDATION

PRIVATE ROADWAY

NO ADMITTANCE WITHOUT PRIOR AUTHORIZATION

Em stared blankly as it flashed past. His eyes still stung and watered; but he could see again, and it was obvious there would be no permanent damage. He'd exchanged his infrared outfit for a T-shirt and jeans and was squeezed between two large men in the backseat of a luxury limo. Both wore tailored suits and tinted glasses. Neither showed any inclination to explain what was going on. Not that he needed an explanation. It was clear he was a prisoner of the Bederbeck Foundation, a front organization for his old friends the Knights of Themis. He wondered briefly how much they had paid Victor to turn him in.

Now that he knew what had been going on, there were things about Victor that were just as suspicious as the business with the security phone. He kept thinking about the way Victor had sent him to the airport on his own with the fake passport and visa. That *really* rang alarm bells. All very well for Victor to quote "security"; but all it really meant was that if the forgeries had been discovered, it was Em who was headed for jail with nobody to help him. He could imagine the reception a teenager would get if he started babbling about a government agency so secret nobody had ever heard of it. He didn't even know Victor's real name. Then there was the way Victor seemed able to get things done. A car was fine—anybody could call a friend and ask them to pick up a visitor—but a helicopter? A helicopter and pilot, and Em seemed to recall another man there as well. That was big-deal stuff, the sort of thing you wouldn't expect from a humble field agent. It all added up to one thing: Victor had never been what he seemed.

Their driver, an olive-skinned man with a heavy mustache, said something in Spanish, and the man to Em's right grunted. There were streetlights along the side of their road now and more lights clustered up ahead. As they drew closer, Em could see a manned barrier. The limo drew smoothly to a halt, and a uniformed guard strolled across carrying a clipboard in his left hand. Em noticed the holstered sidearm on his belt and wondered if it might be worth making a fuss: with a revolver, the guard would be more than a match for his captors. But he dropped the idea as quickly as it emerged. The guard had to be a Bederbeck employee just like the men in the car.

The tinted window whispered down, and the man on Em's right leaned out. "We have young Goverton," he said. "Check us through, then phone ahead."

The guard bent down to look into the car. He was a middle-aged, brown-eyed man who might have had Native American blood. He nodded slightly as he looked at Em, then glanced down at his clipboard. To Em's surprise there was a black-and-white photograph of Em attached to it. The background was out of focus, so he'd no idea where it had been taken; but the jacket seemed like the one he'd worn when he first met Victor.

The guard looked back up and gave him the benefit of a slow smile. "Welcome to Bederbeck, Mr. Goverton." To Em's captors he said, "Go ahead. And congratulations." The barrier rose as he walked back to the hut. As the limo pulled away, Em could see him lifting a telephone.

Em expected buildings; but when they passed through the barrier, the road led to a gateway in a high, mesh fence with warning signs about electrification. Em's view was limited, but he could see enough to spot an observation tower exactly like the ones they had in U.S.

prison movies. Creepier still, the four guards on this gate wore military uniforms and carried semiautomatic rifles. They moved crisply to surround the car, and one actually shone a flashlight in Em's face before waving them on. The gate opened of its own accord as they approached.

"Next stop is your champagne reception," Em's right-hand man remarked.

It looked more like a small town than conventional company buildings. As the limo drove slowly down a main street, Em could see towering office blocks interspersed with lower-slung research and laboratory facilities. Signposts on junctions guided the unfamiliar. Despite the lateness of the hour, there were pedestrians in suits and pedestrians wearing white coats. There was even—and this was the clincher to the small-town feel—an all-night café that seemed to be doing a roaring business. Victor had mentioned that the Bederbeck Foundation was the largest employer for miles around. It seemed that the foundation worked its employees on a twenty-four-hour shift rotation.

It also seemed his long journey was about to end. He glanced at the men flanking him and amended the thought: end *badly*.

Em closed his eyes, partly to relieve the stinging, but mainly to try to think. Now that the shock of his betrayal was wearing off, he was slowly coming to realize that his present situation made no sense. He tried to organize his thoughts in the hope of finding some flaw in his logic; but try as he might, there was none. The situation had unfolded in dramatic, but very simple, steps:

His father's research into Nostradamus had led him to discover a Knights of Themis plot. Professor Goverton had been murdered in order to keep his discovery quiet. But before he died, he'd hidden documentary proof of the plot, then passed its location on to Em. Since then the Knights had been hot on Em's heels to stop him from finding it.

Which was exactly where the whole business stopped making sense. Because it was obvious that the Bederbeck Foundation—hence its Themis masters—*already knew* where Em's father had hidden the proof. And had known it before Em and Victor worked out the secret message only days ago: they'd put up a hut on the site, for heaven's sake; they'd installed electricity and arc lights; they'd driven in an RV! Then they'd set their men watching, apparently for Em to turn up.

But *why*? Why not simply take back the proof and destroy it?

"You want that I drive to the main entrance?" came the voice of their driver.

"No," said the man on Em's right, who seemed to be the senior of the three. "The boss will want to see him at once. If we take him through the lobby, everybody in the building will be trying to catch a glimpse of him. We'll take him through the side door and use the service elevator. With luck we can make delivery before anybody realizes he's in the building."

The man on Em's left broke his long silence. "We

nearly blinded him with the arc lights. The boss won't like that."

"It was an accident," the man on the right growled. "Besides, he isn't blind—are you, Em?"

"No," Em muttered sourly. With his eyes still closed, he found himself reminded of the "blind man," the curiously shaped rock he'd spotted as he walked into the clearing. Could that be the clue to what was happening? Suppose the Knights discovered the area in which his father had hidden the proof but not the proof itself? Once the treacherous Victor told them that Em knew the meaning of the reference to the "blind man," the Knights would have redoubled their efforts to find him. They didn't know his claim was a bluff any more than Victor did.

The only problem with that theory was that the blind man rock was obvious. Anyone in the clearing would have spotted it at once. Working on their own property with all the time and money in the world, men from the foundation could have turned the entire site into an archaeological dig. They should have found the documents within days.

Em opened his eyes. The limo had entered a side street and was pulling up opposite a small door in one of the high buildings.

"This is where we get out," the man on his right told him.

This was where his captors might make a mistake, Em thought. He was no longer helpless. He could see as well as ever now. The three men all seemed relaxed, as if they expected no trouble from him, and he realized his accidental blinding must have lulled them into a false sense of security. All three looked reasonably fit; but they were considerably older than he was, and he was certain he could out-run any of them. Especially if surprise gave him a few yards head start.

The man on his right opened the limo door, slid out, then turned to hold it open for Em. The tinted glasses didn't allow Em to see his eyes, but his stance gave no hint of wariness. Em slid across the seat to follow him, moving casually—not too quickly, not too slowly. The man to his left opened the other door, climbed quickly out, and walked around the vehicle to join his companion. The driver remained behind the wheel, staring directly ahead. Em tensed. When he got both feet on the ground, he planned to take off like a rabbit. Once he lost the two goons, he still had to get through the security gates and somehow find his way out of the desert, back to the city; but he'd worry about all that later.

Em's feet landed on the pavement, and his two guards, working like robots, gripped his arms firmly, halting his planned getaway before it even began. In a moment he was frog-marched through the side door. A moment more and he was standing between the two men in an express elevator. He made one more try to find out what was going on. "Where are you taking me?" He didn't expect an answer and wasn't disappointed.

The elevator stopped on the twenty-third floor, and

the men marched him out without relaxing their guard for an instant. He had a brief impression of luxurious carpeting on the floor of a reception area, the startled expression on the face of a girl behind a desk.

"Is that him?" she asked, staring as if Em had grown a second head.

The man beside him merely grunted in a way that might have meant yes or might have meant no. Then there were swipe cards in security doors that shut off his last hopes of escape as they clicked shut. More carpeted corridors, then a brief halt before another door. One of his captors reached out to knock politely. After a long moment he knocked again.

"Gone off," said his companion.

"What do we do? The orders were to deliver him here."

"He's probably just been called to the conference suite. Do you have clearance to go in?" The man gestured toward the closed door.

"Level five," his companion nodded. "Should do it. But I'm not sure we—"

"Won't thank us for leaving him out here. You know the regs. See if your card works."

Em watched the man step forward and tentatively try his swipe card in the door lock. It flashed green at once.

The man gave a small grunt of satisfaction and turned to Em. "Inside," he said tersely. "Boss will be with you in a minute."

Em stepped through the doorway. He was expecting an office, but instead he was in a luxurious penthouse suite with abstract art on the walls, plush modern sofas, thick pile carpet, and a wall-mounted television screen twice as large as any Em had ever seen before. Off the living area was a small study with a polished desk, behind which was a whole bank of personal computers on their own countertop. Several of the screens were tuned to CCTV cameras throughout the building; or possibly some other building.

As the door closed, Em noticed that a swipe card was needed to get out of the office as well as get into it, meaning he was still effectively a prisoner. He wondered who the boss was who was coming to see him. His guess was Bederbeck Foundation's head of security or some other foundation executive. But a niggling, scary little voice in the back of his head kept asking if it might be the boss of the entire foundation.

Em realized his train of thought was going nowhere and took a cautious step farther into the room. The place reeked of money. Two of the abstract paintings on the wall looked like early Picassos, and Em would have bet anything that they were originals. He found himself wondering if the suite didn't belong to the CEO of the foundation but rather to the head of the Knights himself.

To take his mind off his increasing nervousness, he walked to the floor-to-ceiling curtains on one wall and drew them aside. As he suspected, the wall behind was entirely glass. Em looked out. The impression of a small town in the desert came through as strongly as ever. The sky to the east was lightening with the approach of dawn, and banks of streetlights were already beginning to wink out. Somehow it made Em feel even more afraid, as if the night had been a fiction but sunrise must bring his day of reckoning. He glanced straight down and experienced a wave of vertigo that drove him away from the window. Instead, he moved through to the study area and walked over to the computer screens. One had an internet connection and was displaying the familiar Google search page. On impulse Em typed in "Bederbeck Foundation." As he hit ENTER, he heard the sound of the office door opening behind him.

Em swung round, heart pounding, then stopped in sudden, absolute paralysis.

"Hello, Em," said the man in the doorway.

Em squeezed his eyes shut and opened them again before he believed what he was seeing. But even then he could not, did not actually believe it. His heartbeat rose until it almost filled the room. Waves of sudden darkness threatened to engulf him. His knees felt weak; but somehow he managed to speak, somehow he managed to gasp out one word. "Dad?"

It was like being ill with a fever. His heart was a jack-hammer. He felt weak and shivering. But worst of all, nothing was real anymore. His world had the shifting quality of a dream, and there seemed to be snakes moving at the edges of his vision. "You're dead," Em said in a voice that echoed and reverberated through the empty recesses of his skull. "You died last month." He thought of using the word *murdered*.

"I'm not dead," said Edward Goverton. His voice was as it should be and infinitely familiar. It did not quaver or shake or *wooo* the way ghosts were supposed to. Em didn't believe in ghosts anyway. How could you see a ghost if you didn't believe in it?

"You *were* dead," Em insisted. "You were cold." He remembered the cold. The body had felt like meat.

His father took him gently by the arm and led him to one of the upholstered sofas, encouraged him with subtle pressures to sit down. His father sat beside him, and Em could feel the cushion move. Cushions didn't move when ghosts sat down. "I'm sorry," his father said. "I should have prepared you for this."

"You were cold and not breathing. I felt your wrist. There was no pulse." It was true. After he'd called for Mum, he'd gone all grown-up and efficient and tried to find a heartbeat. He'd held Dad's wrist the way nurses did on TV and used his fingertips to feel. There was no pulse at all.

"I'm sorry," his father said again in his nasal, slightly reedy professorial voice, and sounded genuinely sorry, although Em wasn't certain for what. "I deceived you. But let me explain, and you'll realize it was necessary. Terrible, but necessary."

"Explain," Em echoed vaguely. For some reason the word *terrible* didn't seem to have any meaning.

His father took it as an instruction to action. "Everything was arranged to make you think I was dead."

"I did think you were dead," Em told him. Behind the strangeness and all the other emotions, he caught a glimpse of anger. How dare Dad do this to him? How dare Dad pretend he was dead?

"An injection lowered my body temperature and respiration. The lack of pulse was an old stage magic trick. A billiard ball in the armpit. If you squeeze it, your pulse weakens, then disappears altogether. Crude but effective."

His father was talking about stage magic tricks as if they were discussing the entertainment at a party. It was too bizarre for words. "Why?" Em asked almost desperately. "Why did you want me to think you were dead?"

"They were closing in on me. Actually, they were very, very close to discovering everything," his father said. He had to mean the Knights of Themis. Em had most of that story already: the secret prophecy . . . the discovery of the plot that put his father in so much danger. "The symptoms of my illness were caused by poison."

"I thought your *death* was caused by poison. That's what Mum thought too."

His father dropped into a familiar lecture mode, his voice crisp and sharp. "You need to listen carefully, Em. This is a complicated story."

"I'm listening, Dad," Em said. Strangely, the lecture voice helped. It was like the old days when his dad decided to tell him something important. The familiarity made Em feel better.

"I thought they might be getting close, but I wasn't sure how much they knew. I certainly didn't anticipate an attempt on my life. They were very, very subtle. The toxin was very subtle. I assumed I'd just picked up a bug. Fortunately Alex—Dr. Hollis—was more suspicious and ran tests."

"Dr. Hollis helped section Mum!" Em told him, suddenly outraged.

"For her own protection," his father said patiently.

"We didn't think they'd attack her—why should they?—but we couldn't take any chances. With her safe, we were free to act without having to worry."

Safe? Em thought. In a Knights of Themis clinic? But his father probably didn't realize how far the arm of the Knights reached, even after they'd poisoned him. He wouldn't have realized it *was* a Themis clinic. Em opened his mouth to tell him, but his father was talking again: "Once we'd confirmed that they'd poisoned me, it was obvious we needed to come up with a plan—and urgently. Clearly I couldn't continue as I had before. Actually, I needed to get out of the country and into hiding before they made another attempt on my life. I—"

"Why didn't you just *tell* me?"

"We couldn't risk it," his father said soberly.

Seated on the sofa with his arms folded across his chest, his knees tight together, Em found that he was feeling sick but buried the sensation. "You say 'we'—who else . . . ?"

"Well, Dr. Hollis knew, of course. He had to sign the death certificate. And Tom. Tom was in on it."

"Tom Peterson?" Em gasped. "He didn't say anything to me!" He found himself wondering if Charlotte knew, but decided at once that she couldn't have. She'd never have kept anything that important from him.

Edward Goverton shook his head. "Well, he couldn't, could he? Basically the plan was that I had to die—appear to die anyway—and let those bastards think they'd succeeded in killing me. Then when I went into hiding, they wouldn't come looking. It was vital to make this believable. I couldn't tell your mother, and I couldn't tell you. One small slipup by either of you and the plan would be ruined. But if you believed I was dead, you couldn't slip up, could you? It was really the only way of being safe."

"Mum isn't safe."

"There's no need to worry," his father said without explanation. "Your mother knows what happened now, and she's on her way to join us. I made the arrangements as soon as I knew you were in Arizona."

"How's she getting here?" Em asked. There were more important things he needed to know—like how Dad had got her released from the clinic—but his mouth wouldn't do what it was told when it came to questions.

"Private jet."

Private *jet*? His father could scarcely afford a bicycle. Maybe when he died he claimed his life insurance. Em suppressed an urge to giggle, then realized he was becoming hysterical. He made a massive effort to pull himself together. The world around him seemed to solidify a little. He concentrated hard, trying to focus. Eventually he said, "Your message to me . . . about the prophecy and . . ." He shrugged helplessly. If his father was still alive and had proof of the Themis plot, why send Em on a wild-goose chase to find it? There were parts of the story that weren't making sense.

For the first time his father smiled, albeit grimly. "That was the clever part. Obviously once I was secure and had things properly set up, I wanted your mother and you to join me. But frankly, Em, I also wanted to strike back. The problem was, dealing with an enemy like that, you have to flush them out into the open. That's why I dangled the bait of the Themis vaccination plan. That's also why I involved you. This part of the plan had to be as believable as my death. Obviously I would never have entrusted something like this to anyone outside the family. Which only left you, young as you are." His father's smile broadened. "And as you can see, it worked to perfection."

Except it hadn't. As far as Em could see, it hadn't worked at all. They were both locked in a Bederbeck Foundation building, and the Bederbeck Foundation was a front for the Knights. Heck, the Bederbeck Foundation was manufacturing the very vaccine his father was trying to expose.

As he tried to piece together the more confusing elements of his father's story, Em was abruptly struck by a blinding revelation. Maybe Dad didn't *know* that the foundation and the Knights of Themis were one and the same. It was the only thing that made sense. Em had no idea how his father had managed to end up here. Obviously there was more to the story than he'd told yet; and just as obviously something had happened to fool him completely. Although Em still couldn't figure out the details, he found himself suspecting, with a sinking heart, that the Knights had played his father like a fish. "Dad," he said urgently, "we have to get out of here!"

His father looked at him blankly. "Why?"

"They'll kill you. They'll have to. Nothing's changed about your secret prophecy discovery, except now they know you're still alive." They would probably kill him as well, Em thought, since he also knew about the vaccination plot.

The blank look changed to one of confusion. "They don't know I'm still alive. How could they? We've taken all necessary precautions; and thanks to you, we have their best man under lock and key."

"Who's *we*, Dad: the Bederbeck Foundation?" Em demanded. He leaned toward his father with an air of urgency. "Dad, the Bederbeck Foundation is a front for the Knights of Themis. *They're both the same thing!*"

Professor Goverton blinked. "Yes, of course," he said. "You *know*?"

"Of course I know. What do you think I've just been talking about?"

"The Knights of Themis!" Em exclaimed. "You've been talking about the Knights of Themis and how they tried to kill you and how you set them up using me and—"

"Em," His father interrupted gently. "I'm afraid you've misunderstood the situation completely. It was *Section 7* who's been hunting me. I thought you must have realized that."

This time it was Em's turn to look blank. "Why would Section 7 want to kill you?"

"Because I am Grand Master of the Knights of Themis," his father told him.

43

His dad called the place a canteen, but it looked more like a five-star restaurant to Em. He picked up the breakfast menu with a feeling of disbelief. *Eggs Benedict . . . eggs Mornay . . . beluga caviar . . . French charcuterie . . . venison sausage . . .* plus a mind-blowing list of more familiar food, including American favorites such as waffles with maple syrup.

Despite everything, Em discovered he was ravenously hungry and put in an order for bacon, eggs, sausages, black and white pudding, fried mushrooms, grilled tomato, potato cake, baked beans, and a pot of coffee. His father stared at him with an expression of amazement, shook his head slightly, then told the waiter he would have fresh fruit salad followed by Darjeeling tea and brown toast.

The food appeared with miraculous speed. Em

speared one of his sausages and asked, "What's going on, Dad?"

His father nodded. "You deserve to know the truth, Em. But I'm afraid it's a little complicated."

"You said that before," Em informed him. "If it makes things simpler, Victor told me about the Knights." He thought he might as well get it out in the open. He was still reeling from his dad's confession.

"I suppose he told you we were a supersecret, power-mad organization set on dominating the world and enslaving everybody in it?"

That was about the size of it, all right. "More or less," Em admitted. He bit the end off his sausage and discovered it was delicious, but was having difficulty concentrating on his food.

His father shook his head sadly. "Did you believe him?"

"More or less," Em repeated. But it occurred to him that he'd never questioned any element of Victor's story, never asked for proof, never tried to check it out. Now that he knew Dad was a member of the Knights of Themis— heck, a fairly high-up member, to judge from his title—it also occurred to him that he might have been less trusting. Nothing Dad was involved in could be all that sinister. "I mean, I did when he told me. Not now, of course. I mean, not . . . if you're in it." It was embarrassing, but he couldn't quite make the words sound confident.

His father smiled. "Our organization isn't quite like that."

"Okay," Em said, "what is it then?" It came out a little more belligerently than he intended, but he was feeling guilty about accepting everything Victor said so readily.

"Historically, it was a group founded in ancient Greece. But that isn't Themis as it exists today."

Em hastily swallowed a mouthful of egg. The Greek business tallied with what he'd already been told. It was his father's second comment that rang a different bell. "It isn't?"

"The original Knights were eventually broken up. But some Themis ideas lived on, and eventually the movement was reconstituted by a group of intelligent men as a Masonic-style organization in the Middle Ages. Its most important principle was—and is—the notion that our leaders aren't doing a very good job."

Em had never taken much of an interest in the Middle Ages, but he doubted there were many people who'd argue with that today. He was always hearing about how politicians ruined the country financially, then fiddled with their expenses while telling everybody else to tighten their belts. It wasn't much better in America, where their politicians got everybody into wars nobody wanted and legalized torture by calling it a different name. And that was before you got to the really nasty countries: dictatorships such as Burma and North Korea. But Victor had blamed that all on the Knights themselves, claiming they were basically antidemocratic. Suddenly Em decided to put his father to the test. "At least we have democracy," he said.

"I'm afraid some of us aren't as keen on democracy as we might be," his father said without a moment's hesitation. "What's called democracy today is a far cry from the original democracy of ancient Greece, and even that had its failings."

Em wasn't so much interested in ancient history as his father's take on democracy today. But his father had that look he sometimes got, and Em knew he was going to get the complete lecture anyway.

"When the Greek authorities wanted to do anything important—like change a law or go to war—they had to put it to a general vote," his father said. "The voters turned up at the forum and said yea or nay. If you didn't get a majority, you couldn't go ahead with your plan. That was something close to *real* democracy: the people decided all the important issues; and if you couldn't be bothered to turn up at the forum to vote, you couldn't very well complain about the outcome afterward."

"What's so different about today's democracy?" Em asked, intrigued despite himself. Everybody went on endlessly about democracy and the Free World, and he'd always more or less accepted that this was what he was living in. The way he accepted what Victor had told him about the Knights. Without thinking.

His father shrugged lightly. "In our Western system, we don't generally vote on any particular issue. We vote to elect leaders who decide all the issues for their term of office while we have no more say in the matter. That's how wars start. We vote in old men who send young men to their deaths because our old men get annoyed with other old men or want to extend their power. And even on the very few occasions when we do have a direct vote on some issue—a referendum, for example—the general public can be manipulated so easily by political lies and promises that the response is almost always entirely predictable."

Em recognized the light in his father's eye and realized he was in for a major political speech if he didn't head him off at the pass. "Yes, but what's all this got to do with the Knights of Themis?"

"The original Knights were intelligent men who looked at the messes their leaders were making throughout Europe and decided they could do better. Unfortunately, intelligence and power are not the same thing, so Themis really got under way as an intellectual movement, not a revolutionary one. But that changed. Around the turn of the last century a group of American intellectuals, all of them secret Knights of Themis, decided not only that current political systems were no longer serving humanity, but that something should be done about it. Their main concern was America itself, of course; but they quickly realized two things. One was that the rot was apparent in just about every other country of the world. The other was that the world was becoming more integrated, so that any reform could not be confined to America alone.

"These were concerned men, Em. They wanted a better world, a more equal world, a more peaceful world where national conflicts no longer slaughtered millions, where common problems were no longer ignored because of narrow political interests. But they knew intelligent analysis would never be enough. So they began to recruit powerful people to their cause. They concentrated first on the very wealthy: bankers, oil and rail magnates, industrialists—all individuals in positions of great power unencumbered by any need to answer to voters or lobbyists. Later they expanded their reach to senior civil servants, selected politicians, judges, newspaper and other media owners. The result was Themis as it exists today. As an organization, we are not hungry for power—most of our members already wield more than enough power to satisfy any rational man. Nor are we hungry for money. Collectively, we can call on resources greater than those of many sovereign nations. What we are is a wholly benevolent organization dedicated to the welfare of the human race."

Em looked at his father's familiar features. What he said had to be true. It fitted in with everything he knew about his father: the thoughtful, gentle, concerned professor so popular with both his colleagues and his students. All the same, Em heard his own voice ask brusquely, "What about the vaccination business?" Now that he realized his father was involved with the Knights of Themis, he knew the vaccination story couldn't possibly be true. He had already tucked it away as another of Victor's lies. But the fact remained that Victor had only *interpreted* the story: it was Em's own father who had created it as part of the coded message that brought Em here. There were still things his father needed to explain.

If his father was in any way perturbed by the question, he did not show it. "I think before we go into that I'd better tell you a little about Section 7. Have you heard the term before?"

Em nodded as he buttered the last piece of toast. "Victor said he was one of their agents."

"I'm surprised he mentioned it by name. Victor isn't just one of their agents, and Section 7 is arguably the most secret, most sinister, most dangerous, most *evil* organization on the planet."

Em glanced at his father in surprise. The old man wasn't usually given to exaggeration. "It's just part of the British Secret Service, isn't it?" He wasn't sure Victor had actually said that, but it was certainly the impression Em had been left with.

His father raised one eyebrow. "Is that what he told you?" He shook his head with an expression of disgust. "No, it's not just part of the British Secret Service, although Britain did have a hand in setting it up. The agency itself was set up in late 1946 as a joint venture between America, Britain, Australia, New Zealand, France, and, oddly enough, Finland. British India was briefly in as well, but withdrew after independence the following year. The code name for the agency was Watchman, but since it was the seventh Anglo-American agency to be set up at the end of World War II, those involved took to referring to it as Section 7."

"Sounds respectable enough to me," Em remarked.

"It was, until 1955. That was the year the Soviets formed the Warsaw Pact. By then the agency had stumbled onto the Knights and, frankly, became obsessed with our activities. By the middle fifties the obsession had turned to paranoia. Section 7 concluded that we were actually the ones behind the Warsaw Pact, that we had somehow manipulated the Soviets. Complete nonsense, of course. Even the American government didn't buy it. Apparently exchanges got a little heated. President Eisenhower consulted with his counterparts in Britain and the other countries involved, and made the decision to disband the agency. But when they failed to persuade Eisenhower to change his mind, the agency went rogue. They dropped out of sight—they were experts in concealment—ceased to report to the administration, and embarked on criminal activities to replace their official funding."

Em had finally stopped eating and was staring at his father with undivided attention. It was difficult to picture Victor as a member of a rogue, criminal organization, but then it had never occurred to him that Victor had lied so consistently about the Knights. He licked his lips. "What sort of criminal activities?"

"Human trafficking, mainly."

"Jeez!" Em breathed. He'd read about that. East European girls were smuggled into France or Britain on the promise of well-paid jobs. But once separated from friends and family, they were forced into prostitution. It looked as if he'd completely misjudged Victor. The man was mixed up in some very nasty business.

"Since 1955—more than fifty years—Section 7 has tried to destroy the Knights of Themis. It is their single most important goal, and they have pursued it with almost unimaginable ruthlessness. The Knights have been forced to respond by becoming more and more secretive, particularly in terms of our membership. Unfortunately, this policy has proven less than successful. In recent years Section 7 had a change of leadership. The new man introduced a policy of directly targeting members of our ruling council. Several have been assassinated. He was getting close to discovering who I was. Once he did, I would be next for the chop." He paused, sighed, then went on. "I decided we had to do something about it for my own protection."

Em swallowed. "Like what? Assassinate them back?"

"Really, Em, you seem to have been reading far too many trashy thrillers. Besides, we're not assassins, whatever you've been told. But we did decide to fight fire with fire. We thought that if we could capture and hold the new Section 7 leader, we might guarantee my safety and the safety of our people at least for a time. The only problem was discovering his identity." His expression softened. "These agents work in the shadows, and we had no idea who the new man was. We had to bring him into the light of day—and quickly. I'm pleased to say that I was the one who came up with a plan—ingenious, if I say so myself—to flush him out."

It was weird to think of his father involved in stuff that wouldn't have been out of place in a James Bond movie. But no weirder than the simple fact that the father he thought dead was talking to him now.

"It was my interest in Nostradamus that gave me the idea," his father went on. "When I finally tracked down the wording of the secret prophecy, one interpretation that occurred to me was that it could predict a pandemic of some sort and that the 'slender lance' reference might refer to vaccination. But it was the 'yoke of slavery' that really set bells ringing. I knew that one of Section 7's great myths was that we of the Knights planned to enslave humanity rather than help them. It struck me then that we might use their very paranoia against them."

"How?" Em asked.

"My plan was dangerous," his father told him, perhaps a little proudly. "But given that, I was certain it would work."

"Well, don't keep me in suspense, Dad. What was the plan?"

His father smiled again. "I let it be known, very discreetly, in certain circles that my interest in Nostradamus had led me to uncover a dastardly Themis plot to wipe out a generation of children by means of a toxic vaccination program. I knew that word of my supposed discovery would reach Section 7 eventually; and for something like this, our psychological profiles suggested the new leader would take personal charge of the investigation—he had apparently been a very successful field officer before his promotion. When I faked my own death, I drew him deeper into my plan and distracted him from investigating me too closely— he had to remain focused on the details of the supposed plot. In short, I led him here."

Em stared at him. "So the whole story of a Themis plot . . . ?" He already knew the answer, but he wanted to hear his father say it.

"Was fiction," his father said.

"And the new leader of Section 7, the one who ordered your people assassinated . . . ?"

"Was your old friend Victor. I'm sorry, Em; I know you trusted him. But you mustn't feel bad about that. He is an expert in the art of deception."

"What have you done with him?" Em asked stonily.

"Our security people are holding him here for questioning."

And after that? Em wanted to ask. But something stopped him.

44

The guided tour of the Bederbeck facility was bizarre. Em's earlier impression of a small town was strongly reinforced; but now he saw it almost as a small town from the future, with science-fiction touches such as segments of motor-driven walkways leading to the major buildings and robotic voices responding to swipe card security. The office towers weren't particularly high by American standards, but high enough to British eyes. Everything looked eerily clean, as if it had only just been built. There were gigantic storage tanks attached to the lower-slung warren of laboratories and manufacturing plants. (Em assumed they were for fuel until his father explained that many pharmaceuticals were based on petrochemicals nowadays.) But what really got to Em was the reaction to his father and himself.

Although they used electric-driven pods from time to time, most of the tour was on foot, accompanied by an entourage his father hadn't felt the need to explain. Em worked out that one was a secretary, another a personal assistant. A young man in a neat linen suit might be some sort of communications officer—all he seemed to do was talk on a cell phone and whisper messages into Dad's ear. Two others could only be security. They were pressed from the same mold as the characters who had brought Em in: beefy men in shades and suits.

"This is our research division," his father said as they entered another busy building; and once again Em couldn't help but notice the reaction. His father wasn't treated like a UK visitor. His father was treated like God. Or at least like the company president. Staff members rushed to greet him, fussed to help him. He seemed to be able to go anywhere he wanted, demand to see anyone he wished. Yet even the idea of a big boss didn't quite explain it. Many members of the staff looked at him with expressions that bordered on awe; and not just junior staff either. Em noticed the odd reaction sometimes extended to himself, presumably because he was his father's son, although in his case the expressions showed curiosity rather than respect.

The tour ended at a low-slung residential building set well away from the remainder of the facility behind a screen of trees. Em took in the manicured lawns and swimming pool at a single glance. "Wow!"

"Home sweet home," his father said, clearly pleased

by his reaction. "Bit better than we had in England, but no harm in that. Okay, Em, this is where we're living for the duration of our stay, and this is where I leave you for the moment—some things I need to see to." He handed Em a plastic swipe card with a delicate eye-in-pyramid hologram embossed in one corner. "The doors are all self-locking, but this will let you in. It'll also let you in anywhere you want to go in the rest of the foundation, although, obviously I'd want you to avoid the high-security danger areas; there are a few of them in the facility, but they're all clearly marked. It also doubles as a cash card. You can use it to pay for meals or anything else you need to buy here. Try not to bankrupt me on your first day if you can possibly avoid it."

They walked slowly together toward the front door. Em noticed that the entourage hung back, as if entering holy ground, although they were probably just tactfully giving his father and himself a little private time.

"You didn't get any sleep last night," his father said. "You must be exhausted. I'd suggest you get your head down for a few hours now. You'll find everything you need in your room: change of clothes, pajamas . . ." He smiled suddenly. "You'll know your room because it has your name on the door. I'll join you for dinner."

Tired though he was, Em still had a hundred questions, but his father was already walking away. Em made his way to the door and swiped his new card through the security system. "Welcome home, Edward Michael," said a robotic voice; and the door swung open.

The place was *incredible.* Especially compared to what he was used to back in England. He quickly discovered that the whole house was computerized. Spoken commands worked lights and curtains, a massive flat-screen television in the living room, a stereo system, internet-linked computer screens in what he took to be an office, and when he reached his bedroom, every drawer in the room and his wardrobe doors. The really cool thing was that his commands were acknowledged *by name. Lights on, Edward Michael . . . Drawer open, Edward Michael.* When he finally found the operating manual on a coffee table in a lounge, the introduction explained that the system was keyed to the personal swipe cards of the occupants. While he carried his card, the house was his. If he left it behind, nothing worked at all. In fact, he wouldn't even manage to get in. He flicked through the remainder of the manual and noticed with real satisfaction that it was possible to change the "Edward Michael" salutation, although you needed a special card reader attached to your computer to do it. He made a mental note to ask his father about that later.

His father's advice about getting some sleep made a lot of sense, but Em was too excited to take it. He explored a kitchen that looked like the control center at NASA. He dipped his toes into the pool and promised himself a swim. He stood outside the door of his parents' bedroom for a moment—both their names were on the plaque—then opened it with a vague sensation of guilt. To his surprise the room had a Spartan feel, as if nobody had moved in. Which his mother hadn't, of course, since she hadn't reached the States yet: maybe his father was waiting for her to set up things the way she wanted. He'd never really cared much about his surroundings.

Em returned to his own room and threw himself fully clothed onto the bed. What was happening was incredible. All of it. His father was alive. His mother was flying in. They were all living in this astonishing—

Em woke with a start to the sound of voices. For a moment he lay, wondering where on earth he was, then remembered the fantastic events of the day. He swung his feet onto the floor. His bedroom door was open, and the voices were floating in from the direction of the living room. When he went to investigate, he found the living room a hive of activity. His father was shouting orders at two harassed Mexican workers who were struggling to move in a new sofa. Behind him, Em could see his father's best friend, Tom Peterson, looking unaccountably nervous. And beside Tom, incredibly, was Charlotte. There was an odd warning expression on her face as she caught his eye and mouthed something he couldn't quite make out. But the overall meaning was clear enough: *say nothing—I'll explain later.*

"Hello, Charlotte. Hello, Tom," Em muttered numbly. Tom looked as if he wanted to say something, but he stopped.

"They're joining us for dinner," his father said

cheerfully. "Isn't that nice?"

It was more than an hour before he got the chance to speak with Charlotte privately. By then Tom and Em's father had disappeared together, muttering something about a meeting. Charlotte had left the house a little earlier, but he found her beside the pool. She'd changed into a two-piece swimsuit.

"What the hell are you doing here?" Em demanded. "What's your father doing here?"

To his surprise, she quickly placed one finger to her lips, shook her head, and whispered, "Not here." She was searching in the pocket of a fleecy robe that was flung over the back of her lounger. She threw him what seemed to be a warning glance as she pulled out a small notebook and scrawled something on it with a tiny pen. She tore the page out and handed it to him, then threw the robe across her shoulders and stood up.

Em stared at the note.

Microphones. Shut up. Walk with me.

Em opened his mouth to say something, then looked at her, decided she was serious, and closed it again. She pushed her feet into open sandals and marched off without a word, fastening her robe as she did so. He followed obediently.

They ended up in the belt of trees that screened the house. It was only yards thick; but once in the shade, it felt like entering a wood. Charlotte stopped and pulled him toward her and lowered her voice. "They have microphones throughout the house and directional microphones that can pick up anything said around the pool. Daddy told me. I don't think they can hear us here."

"Who can't hear us?"

"The security people. Your father. Anybody."

Em's head was in turmoil and had been since he'd first set eyes on her. When Victor had said Tom was coming to collect her, Em had assumed he would take her back to England. The question was, how much did Charlotte know about the Knights? The *real* question was, how long had Charlotte known it?

"Did you know my father was alive?" Em blurted. He'd been experiencing a turbulent mix of feelings since everyone arrived. First his father's miraculous reappearance after Em had watched his coffin being lowered into his grave. Then the news that he was an official of the dreaded Knights of Themis, swiftly followed by the realization that the Knights weren't so dreaded after all. Now this. He had to know where Charlotte fit in.

"Not until we arrived in Arizona," Charlotte said urgently. "I swear it. I thought we were going home. Daddy only told me where we were actually headed just before we boarded the plane."

"Did he tell you about the Knights of Themis?"

"Not at first. He was absolutely furious about my kidnapping, and especially the use of drugs—apparently your father didn't tell him—but he was afraid too. You don't betray an organization like Themis lightly . . . and to be fair, I suppose he was worried about putting me in danger if he told me their secrets. But the Knights had already used me, drugged me, even when I knew nothing; and I suppose that convinced him that I'd be safer knowing what was going on than staying in the dark. So he started to tell me a little during the flight; and by the time we were landing, I'd managed to get it all out of him, or the important bits anyway—but by then there was no way I could get in touch with you. My dad's a member of the Knights, of course. Your father and he have been in the organization for years. They joined at the same time, but your father has a higher rank now. My dad never agreed with your father's plan about Death Flu, and my kidnapping was the last straw. He wanted to confront your father about that, but at the same time he wanted to prepare me in case things got really nasty. When I heard what was going on, I was terrified that you might be in danger."

Em suddenly realized to his horror that she was close to tears. He wondered if he should hug her or something to comfort her. He reached out and touched one shoulder awkwardly. "It's okay," he muttered, even though he didn't know what *it* was or whether it was really okay.

"Who were the men who were following you?" Charlotte asked him. "My dad said they weren't from the Knights."

"Victor claimed they were," Em said, "but then they turned out to be from Section 7." He hesitated. "It's terribly complicated."

"Did your father tell you that?"

"That it's terribly complicated? No, I worked it out for myself."

Charlotte shook her head vigorously, in no mood for jokes. "About Section 7."

"Yes," Em said. "Yes, he did. Victor's actually the head of it."

"What about the vaccination plot?"

"That's all fiction—it was just a scam to bring Victor out into the open. They faked it like—" He'd been about to say "Like my father's death" but felt embarrassed for some reason. He wondered why Charlotte had insisted on their talking among the trees. Even if there *were* microphones all over the place—and he'd already seen how tight security was in the Bederbeck Foundation, so that was possible—they were *friendly* microphones. Besides, they weren't talking about anything they shouldn't. "They faked it," he concluded.

Charlotte was still facing him, looking up soberly into his face.

"Your father lied to you," she told him urgently. "The vaccine's not a scam! They really are going to kill millions of children."

E m stared at her. He knew the vaccine story was fiction, of course, but the sheer intensity of her words still managed to chill him. One look at her expression told him that she believed what she said, and believed it implicitly. "What makes you think that?" he asked carefully. All the same, careful or not, it came out more coolly than he'd intended. His father had told him the story was pure make-believe. *Your father lied to you.* Charlotte's words echoed in his mind.

Charlotte sounded equally careful, but not nearly so cool, and her first words sounded as if she'd just read his mind. "I know your father told you the vaccine plot was just a story. My father told me something very different."

"Yes, but Tom might have misunderstood—right? I mean, he could be wrong about the plan. Or maybe he wasn't telling you the truth." *Of course* he was telling her the truth. Why wouldn't he tell his daughter the truth.

"You don't want to believe me, do you?" she said. He thought he heard resignation in her voice but decided at once it was actually determination. Charlotte looked around her as if watching for anyone who might be creeping up on them. "Listen," she said. "I'm nervous standing here." She reached out and took his hand. "Let's walk for a bit."

They began to walk together, a slow walk that circled the edge of the grounds. Looking one way Em could catch glimpses of his new home through the screening trees. Looking the other, he could see the sweep of the Bederbeck Foundation: a little town in the desert. "Can we still talk?" he asked her.

Charlotte nodded. "There are cameras along the perimeter, but no mikes."

"How do you know all this stuff about the security systems?" Em asked her. "I suppose Tom told you. But how does *he* know all this stuff? You've only just got here."

Charlotte glanced at him. "He's been here before," she said dismissively, then added, "I've been worried sick about you since Daddy told me what was really going on."

Em liked the "worried sick" bit. "What exactly did he tell you?" If he found that out, he might discover why she was so certain of the vaccination story.

"I *told* you!" Charlotte exclaimed almost angrily. "About the Knights and him being a member and your father being the big cheese and all that sort of background stuff, but the important—"

"My father being the *what*?" Em exclaimed.

"Didn't you know? You must have known. What do you think all this is about?" She waved one hand vaguely toward the house with its pool glinting in the sunlight. "Even the president of the Bederbeck Foundation doesn't have a place like this, and it's only for your father's use when he *visits*. They keep it for him specially." She looked into his face as if searching for evidence that he might be kidding with her. "They pretend it's because he's chairman of the board, but it's actually because he's Grand Master of Themis."

"Aren't there lots of them? Grand Masters, I mean?"

"There *are* lots of them, or not *lots* lots, I suppose; but at least one in every country where the Knights operate. But your father is the Grand Masters' Grand Master. He runs the whole show."

Em stared at her openmouthed. How could his father have kept *that* hidden?

"He's a very clever man," Charlotte said as if reading his thoughts. "How do you think the Knights operate? It's all secret, secret, secret. I suppose you could call his job in the university a front, but it's not like that really. It's more like being in the Masons, only far more secret. It's having two lives. In one life you're a professor, and you live like a university professor, and you really *are* a university professor. In the other life you're a member of the Knights, and you work to bring forward Themis plans. But you don't tell your family or anybody else about the Themis life. You don't tell your wife or your son . . ." She scowled a little. ". . . or your daughter. One of the reasons Mum divorced Dad was that he was away so much on Knights of Themis business. She didn't know about the Knights, of course. She thought he was having an affair."

Em seized on it. "But they *have* told us," he protested. "Tom's told you, and Dad told me, and Mum knows now, so he must have told her." That was the really weird one. Tell Mum something, give her a drink, and it was like putting it on the BBC. Maybe that's why Dad was in such a hurry to fly her to Bederbeck, where he could keep an eye on her.

"That's because everything's about to change!" Charlotte said excitedly. "The big Themis plan is scheduled to go into action. Once that happens, they'll all come out in the open—all the Knights—and they'll start to take over."

Em wasn't getting his head around this at all. He frowned. "You're not still talking about this business with the vaccination program, are you? Honestly, it was only a story to—"

"Of course I'm still talking about the vaccination business!" Charlotte snapped. "But that's only the start. Once they kill off the children, they plan to spread the plague farther, across certain ethnic groups using another genetically engineered virus. Then they leak misinformation about who started the plague so there are more wars—not a world war, but a whole series of nasty ethnic wars: Muslim against Jew, black against white. . . . It doesn't matter who you are; there's always somebody who's the enemy."

Em shook his head. "That makes no sense. That would just be chaos!"

Charlotte rounded on him. "Chaos is what the Knights want. So they can step in and take over. That's why they've started to come out of hiding. I'm not saying they're going to announce their existence on the television news tomorrow; but they'll happily allow controlled leaks so the public gets used to the idea that there's a powerful, well-organized, well-disciplined elite waiting in the wings. Just the sort of organization people would turn to in a time of chaos. Once they're ready to take over, what remains of the world population will welcome them with open arms."

Em's frown had deepened so much it seemed to be etched permanently onto his forehead. "This isn't happening, Charlotte. It just isn't *true*."

Charlotte stopped walking and turned to look at him. He was astonished at the look of fury on her face. "Don't patronize me, Em. Don't you *dare* patronize me." She shook her head. "You think it isn't true? Why? Because your father told you so?"

"Yes!" Em exclaimed desperately.

"Your father is a liar. Everything he told you is a lie, or at best a half-truth. Do you know how I know this?"

After a moment Em said softly, "No."

"Because my father is a liar too! He lied to Mum and me for years, just like your father lied to your mum and you for years. My dad only stopped lying when the Knights went too far and drugged me. Even then he was terrified. Em, these things don't have to be *either . . . or.* What your father told you about using the vaccination plan to flush out Victor is probably true. It's certainly what my father told me. Section 7 has been a thorn in the side of the Knights for years, and the man you call Victor is their agency head. He was getting very close to discovering your father's identity as Knights Grand Master. A man like Victor would be a real loss to the Section if the Knights got him. Which they have now. But your father lied to you when he told you the vaccination plan was a fake. Every laboratory in the Bederbeck Foundation is working round the clock to manufacture the toxic vaccine."

"You can't be sure about that," Em said desperately. Even if Charlotte was telling the truth, he didn't want to hear it.

"Oh, yes, I can," Charlotte told him. "What Dad told me was so awful I didn't want to believe it either. And even though he said he disagreed with your father's plan, I wasn't happy that he'd done nothing about it. So after we landed and before we came out here, I went searching among his things."

"You what?"

"Oh, don't sound so shocked. You'd have done the same thing."

"No I wouldn't!"

"Yes, you would. So would anybody. Your father admits to being in a secret organization, then tells you he disagrees with its policies but didn't do a thing about them? Of course you'd want to find out everything."

"I suppose so," Em said, even though he supposed nothing of the sort. But he wanted her to keep talking.

She must have picked up the hesitation in his voice, for she said crossly, "I didn't find anything in his cases, if that's what you're worrying about. I didn't find loot from his last armed robbery or corpses from some human sacrifice. Then I broke into his computer."

"Oh my God!" Em exclaimed.

"Enough with the judgment face. Don't you want to know how I did it?"

Em shook his head vigorously. "No." He wasn't sure he wanted to know what she'd found out either. But he was sure now that she *had* found out something. You could tell from her expression.

But Charlotte was determined to tell him anyway. "He had it password protected—the whole PC. I tried everything I could think of. Grandma's maiden name . . . his birthday . . . his *dog's* birthday . . . You'll never guess what it was."

Em didn't want to guess. "What was it?" he asked woodenly.

"Mum's first and middle names: Alice Marilyn.

Who'd have thought it after she divorced him? Anyway, once I was into his computer, I found the emails."

"The emails?" Em echoed.

"From your dad to my dad, except I didn't know it was your dad then: they were just signed G.M. for Grand Master. Themis business. Dad had a whole folder of them. They were encrypted, but that was just for sending them across the internet. Dad had the encryption key; and since he didn't want to go through the trouble of decrypting each one separately, he'd set his computer to decrypt them automatically. So I was able read them. Dad can be pretty stupid about things like that sometimes. Anyway, that's when I found out you were being used as bait for this whole Section 7 thing. I couldn't believe it when I read about the vaccination plan—"

Em made one last attempt: "The *fake* vaccination plan." But it was as much as he could do to keep the question mark out of his voice.

"It's not fake," said Charlotte simply. "It wasn't just in the emails about Section 7; the whole plan was outlined in other emails. It was one of the things that worried my dad so much. He was completely against it, but not completely enough to betray the Knights. He satisfied himself with protesting about it, and they happily ignored him."

The perimeter fence meandered so much that they had almost lost sight of the house now. But they were still walking on well-watered lawn, well watered and well manicured—a token of how costly maintaining the temporary home of Em's High Knight of Themis father was. After a long, thoughtful pause, Em shook his head. "You're sure my father was involved?" It sounded stupid even as he said it. If he believed Charlotte, his father was the instigator of the entire plan. If he believed Charlotte, his father was a monster.

Charlotte caught on at once. "They're going to kill millions and millions of young people like us, millions and millions of *children* even younger, with some ghastly, miserable disease," she insisted. "You have to listen to what I'm telling you, Em!"

The edifice Em had been building in his head suddenly collapsed. His mind, as it sometimes did, was working at high speed, making connections, examining things said, recognizing his own weaknesses. He knew he'd often been in denial, stubbornly believed what he wanted to believe. The question was, had he gone into denial now? There were things she said that he knew to be true. Their fathers were liars. They had lied about their secret lives, lied about Em's father's death. Was it possible, as Charlotte claimed, that they were lying about the vaccination program as well? Em couldn't believe it. Em *didn't* believe it. All the same . . . "All right," he said.

"All right *what*?" Charlotte demanded.

"All right, I hear you," Em said. "I'm not sure of anything yet. But there's somebody else who knows the truth, and I'm prepared to try to get it out of him."

She looked at him almost suspiciously. "Who's that?"

"Victor," Em told her.

E m brought it up so casually that it must have seemed
of no importance to him whatsoever. "Did you get
anything interesting out of him?"

Strangely enough, his father knew right away who he
meant. "Victor?"

"Yes," Em confirmed. "He just came into my head for
some reason." It never did to underestimate his father's
intelligence; but when he was distracted, as he was now,
you could often slip things past him. Em had managed
that trick lots of times in the days when his father was
just a humble university professor.

Professor Goverton glanced up from the papers on
his desk. "Security is questioning him. The process may
take some time."

"Yes, I know," Em said, trying to sound cheerful,

even though it was the last thing he felt. It was, he'd decided, all a question of appearing his old annoying self, pretending everything was the way it used to be when he'd interrupted University Dad preparing his next lecture. That way he could put his doubts on hold. And he did have doubts—doubts about everything Charlotte said, doubts about what his father had told him, doubts about Victor. But at least if he could see Victor one more time, something might be said to resolve some of the doubts; and if it was, he could take action. He was already prepared to take action. "I just wondered if they'd got anything out of him. About Section 7 or whatever."

"Not much—it's early days," his father grunted. His eyes flickered back toward the papers.

At one time Em would have taken the answer at face value. Now he found himself considering it more carefully, wondering if his father was lying. Not that it mattered: the question was no more than an opening gambit. But an analysis of the answer—dear God, he was beginning to *sound* like his father—was revealing in its own right. It showed, for example, that Victor was still at the foundation. *And still alive,* a small voice whispered in Em's head. The thought would have been inconceivable only a month ago. He could no more have considered his father a murderer than walked naked on the moon. But that father, ironically, was dead now. "Won't you have to hand him over to the police or something?" Em asked innocently.

"Hardly," his father told him distractedly, turning his full attention back to his papers—a familiar gesture of dismissal.

This, Em knew from past experience, was the time to pounce. "Maybe I could get something out of him."

"Mmm?" his father murmured.

"We got on well," Em said. "I mean, genuinely. I think he sort of liked me." The trick was not to push it too far. So long as his father split his attention, he was vulnerable. Em smiled, stretched, and pushed back his chair. "I thought if I went to see him, brought him a little gift or something, got chatting . . . he might let something slip. I mean, you could give me a list of things you want to find out, and I'd try to work them into the conversation. Subtly."

His father looked up again. The focus in his eyes told Em that this was the crunch. Professor Goverton, Grand Master of the Knights of Themis, was no longer distracted. The question was, would he buy Em's suggestion? "You know," his father said thoughtfully, "that might be an idea—nothing else is producing results." He shook his head suddenly. "Not the list of things we want to know—he'd spot what you were after at once; just a relaxed, friendly chat. And you're young. Men always underestimate young people. He might well relax his guard. Congratulations, Em; that is a very good idea indeed if you're willing to carry it through."

He wrote something on a small sheet of letterhead, folded it in half, and pushed it across the desk. "That's your authorization. Do you know where our security division is?"

Em shook his head. "No." He kept his face studiously blank, but behind it he was buzzing with excitement.

"My secretary will direct you," his father said dismissively. "Ask for Kardos—that's K-A-R-D-O-S, Stefan Kardos; he's the Bederbeck security director—and show him the note. He'll arrange it from there. You'll get as much time as you need with Victor, so don't rush. The longer you take, the more likely he is to relax and make a slip." He held Em's eye. "I want you to report back directly to me. You understand that? Not to Kardos, even if he asks you questions. To me."

Em fought desperately to keep his face impassive at the mention of the name Kardos. What if the man did work for his father? He had only Victor's word for it that he was a trained killer, and Victor had proved to be as much a liar as everybody else in Em's life now. "I understand, Dad." He hesitated long enough to push Kardos out of his mind, then asked, "How much does Victor know? About you? I mean, about me? You know what I mean—does he know what happened?"

"Nothing," his father said. "Security has told him nothing. It's their job to ask questions, not to answer them." He shrugged. "You're a smart boy; you decide how much—or little—to tell him."

"Good." Em nodded. He picked up the folded paper, slid it into his jacket pocket, and headed for the door. As he closed it behind him, he noted that his unsuspecting father had gone back to the papers on his desk.

Em walked through the revolving door of the security building, took in the situation in the lobby, and kept walking until it spilled him outside again. Not for the first time, his heart was thumping like a jackhammer. The man talking to the receptionist was all too familiar. It was the man who carried a sidearm to his father's funeral, the man on the train to Paris, the man at the café table with the coffee in his lap, the man Victor claimed was a killer. The receptionist listened to him politely. The receptionist called him Mr. Kardos.

Em did not break stride until he was back in the diner with Charlotte. His mind was made up now.

"Do you know if the foundation has a bookshop?" he asked before she could say anything.

"There's one behind the reception building—I noticed it coming in." She attempted a small, puzzled smile.

"Does it have a good philosophy section?"

Charlotte's smile turned to a frown. "How should I know?" Her frown deepened. "What do you want with a good philosophy section?"

Em looked down at her soberly. He felt wired, yet strangely at ease. At least his basic conflict was resolved now. Charlotte had gone a long way toward shaking his confidence in his father's story. What had just happened completed the job. During one of their cozy little chats, his father had assured him that he'd been followed by someone from Section 7. Kardos was living proof that this was simply a lie. And if his father was lying about one thing, the likelihood was that he was lying about everything. Which meant that Em knew how to act now. "Just something I forgot," he told Charlotte. "I wanted to bring Victor a little present. I've just thought of a book that might do very nicely."

Stefan Kardos gave no hint of having ever seen Em before. Em for his part kept his face expressionless during the initial introductions and handed over his authorization without explanation or comment. Kardos scanned the sheet of paper, mumbled "Excuse me," and thumbed a button on his cell phone. With the phone to his ear, he stared blankly at Em, listened for a moment, then cut the connection. "He says you're to go ahead. Denise will show you where." He hesitated. "What's in the package?"

"Present for Victor."

"Mind if I take a look?"

"Not at all."

Kardos ripped the paper without a further by-your-leave. A puzzled expression crossed his features as he contemplated the gift inside. "Do a lot of reading, does he?"

"I think he'll enjoy this one," Em told him deadpan.

Kardos flicked open the book, then shook it to dislodge anything that might have been slipped between the pages. Nothing had. He opened the inside front cover. "What are these?"

"Chinese coins." There were three of them taped to

a card stuck inside the book.

Kardos stared at them for a long, sour moment. "Now they're even exporting money." He closed the book with a snap and handed it back to Em. "Okay," he said.

They had Victor in a cell. Denise opened the door with the familiar swipe card, then stood back to allow Em to enter. "Aren't you afraid he might try to make a break for it?" Em asked her curiously. For such a supposedly dangerous man as Victor, the security seemed lax, although there *had* been several locked doors to pass through before they reached this one.

"I'm armed and authorized," Denise told him. She was a pretty girl and neatly dressed, and looked to be in her twenties.

"Authorized to what?"

"Use lethal force," she told him without a flicker of expression. "Knock when you want to come out; I'll be right here."

The cell was small and windowless, lit by a fluorescent strip in the ceiling. Victor was sitting on a bunk bed set against one wall. He was wearing an open-necked shirt, and the bruises on his chest were clearly visible. He glanced up as Em came in. "This is a pleasant surprise."

Em waited for the door to close behind him, then looked around for somewhere to sit and eventually found an upright wooden chair that he moved beside the bed. "I suppose this place is bugged?"

"You can rely on it."

"Cameras or mikes?"

"Both, I expect. You would know that better than me."

Em ignored the jibe: Victor was bound to be suspicious. "Actually, I don't know any better than you, but I expect you're right." There was a purple bruise high up on Victor's left cheek that looked both fresher and more painful than the bruising on his body. His questioning must have taken a violent turn. Em looked away quickly. "I brought you a present." He held out the book.

Victor's expression underwent a change as he took it. Something close to a smile crawled across his lips. "A new translation of the *I Ching*! Well, well, well. They took mine away."

"Might be a blessing in disguise," Em murmured. He made the effort to catch Victor's eyes and hold them. "I think this one may be better."

Victor stared back at him, face now expressionless. It was impossible to tell whether he got the message. Eventually he said, "Perhaps it will. But not many things I want to know in here. Except how I can get out. Don't suppose you can help me on that?"

Perhaps the I Ching *can help you there,* Em thought, but was too cautious to speak the words aloud. Instead, he said, "I couldn't find an edition that included yarrow stalks."

"Very few do," Victor told him.

"This one has three coins taped to the inside cover. I looked at the Introduction, and I think you can use them."

Victor nodded. "The Coin Oracle can be very useful,"

he said. "Perhaps not as good as the yarrow stalks, but easier to use and a lot faster." He was holding the book but looking at Em. "It's very popular in China because of the time it saves."

"I definitely think you should use it," Em said with as much emphasis as he dared.

But Victor only tossed the book casually onto the bed. "I'm not sure I care much what you think," he said bluntly. "Until I find out why I'm locked in here while you're free as air and wearing new clothes."

"That's a difficult one, all right," Em agreed. He realized all of a sudden that he hadn't thought this visit through. It was obvious that Victor would want to know what was happening, and Em wasn't at all sure how much he should tell him. Victor was bound to realize he'd been trapped by the Knights, perhaps even assumed Em was a prisoner as well, until as he said, Em turned up in new clothes, friendly with the jailers.

Em hesitated. His instinct was to tell Victor everything, to try to reestablish trust. But that could be dangerous, considering the fact that their conversation was almost certainly being recorded. Besides, how could Victor trust Em if Em told him he was the son of the Themis chief? He decided to compromise. "The Knights trapped us," he said soberly. "But I expect you guessed that already."

"The possibility did occur to me. Especially after that clown Kardos gave me this—" He indicated the bruise on his face. "I'd like to meet the bastard who was giving him his orders."

That bastard would probably be my father, Em thought. But his father's complicated resurrection was the last thing he wanted to go into. "They know you're head of Section 7," he said instead.

Victor didn't seem the slightest bit fazed. "I assumed that must be what they thought."

"What have you been doing?" Em asked. "Sticking to name, rank, and serial number?"

Victor nodded. "Something like that."

Em was fast running out of things to say without getting himself into muddy waters. "How are they treating you?" he asked a little desperately. There were people listening, people watching, people almost certainly thinking that, as an interrogator, Em was a complete idiot. He consoled himself with the knowledge that his father would probably be taken in. His father had advised him to put Victor at his ease.

Victor looked at him in surprise, then said, "Apart from the beatings, rather well. The food's good."

"You're being sarcastic."

"Clever boy," Victor nodded. "I always said you had a brain in your head." He shifted his position slightly, drawing one knee up onto the bunk bed. "I notice you didn't answer my question."

"They gave me the clothes," Em said.

"That's only half the answer," Victor said. "And not even the important half." His expression had changed, taking on a threatening aspect. "How come you're free to come and go when I'm only free to get beaten up?"

"They didn't realize I was helping you," Em said. It sounded feeble as he said it, but it was the only half-decent lie he could think of—one he could easily explain to his father if he had to simply by claiming he was only trying to gain Victor's confidence. He caught Victor's eye again and held it. "They don't realize I'm trying to help you now." Victor was bound to ask how, and Em didn't know what to say to that. He'd been digging a hole for himself since he came into this place and seemed incapable of preventing himself from digging it deeper. This was what happened when you didn't prepare.

But Victor didn't ask him how. Instead he said, "By advising me to cooperate with them, I suppose?"

Em grabbed the lifeline. "Something like that." He decided to cut his losses and stood up. Victor either had the message by now or he hadn't. No further amount of waffling from Em was going to change that. He turned toward the door and heard his own voice say "I'll see if I can get my father to stop the beatings." Em froze.

After a moment Em turned around. Victor was staring at him. Em waited for him to say something, then when he didn't, walked to the door and knocked briskly. He was sweating a little when Denise opened it.

"How did it go?" Charlotte asked him.

"I think I cocked it up," Em said. He considered for a moment, then added, "Royally."

47

Em was even more convinced he'd cocked it up when the following day passed without incident, as did the day after that. Even the debriefing with his father proved a nervous anticlimax. Clearly Professor Goverton hadn't expected much from Em's meeting with Victor for he did little more than shrug when Em reported he'd got nothing of use from their prisoner.

On the evening of the third day, Em went to bed in a fog of frustration, uncertainty, and fear. Once Victor escaped Em would hear about it. He was bound to. His father would certainly tell him something like that, maybe even question Em again about their meeting. But Victor should have escaped by now. Unless, of course, he hadn't found Em's swipe card. Em's imagination kept replaying the dismissive way in which Victor had thrown the *I Ching* onto his bunk. He might not have bothered to pick up the book again. Or, if he *did* pick it up, he might not have found his escape key hidden underneath the card on which the three Chinese coins were mounted. Or, worse still, he might have found the card, tried to use it, and been caught again. The more Em thought about it, the more things he could imagine that might have gone wrong. He lay awake for more than an hour imagining them before sinking into a fitful, dreamless sleep.

Em woke, heart pounding. His bed was unfamiliar, the room in pitch darkness. For a moment he didn't know where he was. What he did know was that there was somebody with him.

He tried to control the rasp of his breathing. There was a lamp on a bedside table—he was sure of it. He started to reach for it, then remembered: everything in this place was computer controlled, voice controlled. To make the lamp work, he had to say "Lights on."

What Em did say was "Who's there?" It came out as a croak. There was not a glimmer of light in the room. The windows were made from some sort of reactive glass. When he climbed into bed, they automatically turned themselves opaque. He couldn't remember the command to turn them transparent again.

A rough hand clamped over his mouth. A hoarse voice snapped, "Quiet!" Then: "Where the hell are all the light switches?"

Em pried the hand away from his mouth. "Victor?" he whispered.

"You wouldn't believe how difficult this place is to break into," Victor whispered back. "Bloody alarm systems all over the shop. Last thing I need is to cope with the foundation's private police." He withdrew his hand completely. "How do you turn on lights?"

"Lights on," Em said, remembered the modifier, and added, "Level one." His bedside lamp illuminated with a gentle glow. For eyes adapted to the velvet darkness, it lit up the whole room. Victor was dressed as Em remembered him in the cell, with one difference. Somehow he'd found a balaclava to cover his face.

Victor pushed up the mask. His features looked tense, and for some reason his scar seemed much more prominent than usual. "I need you to talk to your father," he said without preliminary. "There's not much time."

"Father?" Em echoed stupidly. All the same, he slid out from beneath the covers and reached for the clothes he'd left on the floor when he came to bed.

"We've mined the petrochemical tanks," Victor told him grimly.

Em woke up fast. "Who has?"

"The Section. We air-dropped a crack team. The Knights are just days away from distributing the vaccine."

"When did you break out?" Em asked, tugging on a sock.

"About an hour after you left me—thanks for the card, incidentally. Clever to hide it under the coins; you must have known I'd use them."

"I wasn't sure you'd found it. My father didn't tell me

you'd escaped." It occurred to Em that his father must already have known at the time when Em reported back to him. It also occurred to him that Victor might still not know his father's position in Themis.

But Victor acted as if he *did* know. "I'm afraid your father has never told you everything. All the same, I wouldn't want him . . ." Victor stopped.

"Wouldn't want him what?"

"Dead," Victor muttered. "We just wanted to stop the vaccine."

Em laced his shoe. "What's going on, Victor?"

"Once we mined the tanks, we sent your father a warning so he could order an evacuation. The charges are staggered to produce a rolling explosion—maybe even a firestorm. The plan isn't just to destroy the current vaccine stocks, but to demolish most of the facility so they can't produce more—at least not quickly. If there are people still on the premises, hundreds, maybe thousands of them will die. But your father didn't issue the evacuation order."

Em stared at him, trying to make sense of what he was hearing. Eventually he said, "He didn't?"

"Told us to defuse the charges, otherwise we'd have any deaths of foundation employees on our conscience. Made the point that most of them would be entirely innocent victims." Victor shook his head. "I'd forgotten how ruthless the Knights can be."

"Did you?"

"Did I what? Defuse the charges?" Victor shook his

head again. "*Nobody* can defuse those charges—they're tamperproof. They'll explode at once if anybody tries to defuse them. And when one goes, the others follow automatically." He looked faintly apologetic. "It was the only way we could be absolutely sure of destroying the vaccine—and the facilities to make more."

"So people are bound to be killed when the explosions happen? Especially those close to the tanks?"

"Yes."

"Including my father?"

"Your father is in his office in the center of the facility, waiting to hear from us. There's a storage tank next to the adjoining laboratory. It's unlikely he will survive."

"Does he know that?"

"We've made it absolutely clear to him," Victor said soberly.

"But he doesn't believe you?"

"He believes us, all right. The man is a fanatic. He's perfectly prepared to die for his Themis principles."

Em was getting the full picture now, and the last remnant of sleep had cleared from his mind. "Wait a minute. If the charges are tamperproof, he must *know* you can't defuse them now. So why's he trying to hold out?"

"He doesn't believe us," Victor said. "At least, he probably believes we've set safeguards on the charges, so he's unlikely to risk having his own people defuse them; but he doesn't believe we can't do the job ourselves.

That's what he's gambling lives on; and he's going to lose." He hesitated, although only barely, before adding, "Unless you can persuade him otherwise."

And there it was, laid out before him. Victor was making him responsible for any lives lost in the Bederbeck Foundation. How many were employed? Ten thousand? Twenty thousand? The facility was a small town in the desert: the figures must be somewhere in that range. Given those numbers, the death toll could be enormous. It was a responsibility Em didn't want to take on. "How much time do we have?"

Victor glanced at his watch. "About three quarters of an hour."

"Oh, for God's sake, Victor!" Em exploded. "What are we hanging about here for?"

48

"You'd better have this back," Victor said.

They were standing at the side-street entrance to the building where Em had first been taken to meet his father. Through the glass door he could see that the reception area was closed, with only limited lighting. Most of the rest of the building was in gloom as well, with the exception of a few well-lit offices, presumably in charge of late-working Bederbeck executives. One of them, so far as Em could judge from street level, was the office his father used. Em could imagine him up there now, soberly waiting for Section 7 to make its next move.

Em glanced at the swipe card, then took it wordlessly.

"Can you find your way up to him?" Victor asked.

"You're not coming with me?"

Victor shook his head. "He hates me—he hates the

whole of Section 7, and now he knows who runs it. You'll have a far better chance of persuading him if you're on your own. Now, can you find your way up?"

"I think so," Em said. He hesitated. "Unless somebody stops me."

"There'll be no security," Victor told him confidently. "He *wants* to talk to us."

So it was *us* now—Em had joined Section 7, at least in Victor's head. Em wondered how he felt about that and decided it was okay. He was far less certain how he felt about his father. He glanced around him. The streets were largely deserted, the buildings largely darkened. But all around him were thousands of people, asleep for the most part, who would soon be in peril of their lives. Unless Em could make his father see sense. He was not overconfident.

"Em . . . ?" Victor said quietly.

Em turned back to him, wondering what was coming now. "Yes."

"You know that you don't really have three quarters of an hour, don't you?"

Em eyed him cautiously. "I don't?"

"If your father *does* give the word, it's going to take at least half an hour to be sure of getting everybody to safety."

Em did the math. "You're saying I've only got *fifteen minutes* to persuade my dad?"

Victor jiggled one hand, palm down. "In or around that." He hesitated. "The thing is . . ." He hesitated again.

"The thing is, when I say it will take at least half an hour to get everybody to safety, that includes you."

"You're saying if I don't persuade my father inside fifteen minutes, I'm dead?"

"I'm saying if you haven't persuaded your father inside fifteen minutes, you walk. Fifteen minutes, Em, not a second more. Then run. You get out of the building; we'll make sure you're out of range when the balloon goes up. Our first priority."

"What about my father?"

Victor looked at him grimly. "You're not responsible for your father," he said.

After a moment Em said, "Better get on with it then." He used his swipe card to open the main door.

The door to his father's penthouse suite was wide-open, as was the door to the study area inside. The study was lit by a single reading lamp. Em's father was standing at the far side of his desk, silhouetted against the light, staring through the window at the street outside. He looked a lonely figure.

"You have to give the order to evacuate, Dad," Em said without preamble.

His father turned slowly. There was no surprise on his face or in his voice as he said, "So you've gone over to Section 7, Em. Or were you with them all the time?"

This was the last thing Em wanted to get into. "Dad, we don't have time. You need to issue the evacuation order *now*, otherwise people are going to *die*!"

His father moved away from the window. For the first time Em noticed a microphone on his desk attached to a control console and wondered if this might be the facility intercom. "I don't think so," his father said. "I think your friend Victor is bluffing. He doesn't want those deaths on his conscience any more than I do."

"He doesn't want millions of deaths from your vaccine either!" Em blurted. A part of him still didn't believe his own father could have planned something so monstrous. There had been too many lies for Em to hold to the old certainties anymore.

"Ah," his father said thoughtfully.

"Ah?" Em echoed fiercely. "Is that all you can say: *Ah?*"

"I wasn't sure how much you knew, how much you believed," his father said calmly.

"I didn't believe any of it at first," Em told him. "How could I? Wiping out a whole generation of young people is something you expect from Dr. Evil in a comic book, not from your own father!" The denial would come now. Of course it would come now.

But the denial did not come. "Em," his father said gently, "would you rather sacrifice a few million souls or see the entire human race wiped out?"

Em stared at him. Eventually he said, "The entire human race isn't going to be wiped out."

His father moved behind the desk and sat down. Suddenly he looked very tired. "Oh, yes, it is," he said. "With an absolute certainty, we are as doomed as the dinosaurs. And soon. Unless someone does something about it."

Em's mind went back to something Victor had told him about the Themis plan. "Are we talking about global warming?"

"Of course we're talking about global warming. For all the denials and the twisting of statistics, there remains one incontrovertible fact: the climate of our planet has been warming since the beginning of the industrial revolution. If the trend continues, it will eventually wipe out all life on Earth—with the possible exception of a few particularly hardy bacteria. Nobody argues about that. The only real controversy is about the cause: is it due to a warming of the sun or to the production of greenhouse gases in the atmosphere by human activities? But that's a false controversy, because even if the warming *is* ultimately related to a cycle of the sun, we are still hurrying the process along through the production of greenhouse gases. Our own scientists have calculated that we are less than two decades away from the tipping point." He knuckled his eyes. "Do you know anything about the planet Venus?"

Em stared at him in bewilderment. What had Venus got to do with anything? "Not much."

"Venus is roughly the same size as Earth; it was once called our sister planet, and perfectly respectable scientists speculated that it might harbor life. Then in the 1960s, space probes showed it had a surface temperature high enough to melt lead. Know the reason?" Professor

Goverton did not wait for Em to answer. His face flared into an expression of high intensity. "A runaway greenhouse effect. All the heat reaching Venus from the sun is trapped by its atmosphere." He leaned forward. "And that's what we're racing toward on Earth *right now* with our greenhouse gas emissions. If we don't stop it, the human race and just about every other life-form on the planet will be wiped out."

"But we *are* stopping it!" Em protested. "With better cars and new laws and carbon emissions and stuff." He was a bit vague on the details, but every time you picked up a newspaper, there were articles about international protocols and limits on industry and something about carbon emission trading that he didn't really understand.

His father snorted. "Tokenism," he snapped. "Too little, too late. Frankly, what an invidual can do will not make one jot of difference. Only large-scale action is going to touch this problem, but there isn't a government on the planet that would dare to take the steps actually necessary to make a difference—they'd be out of office in a week if they did. Everybody talks about saving the planet, but how many people do you know who have given up their cars and their consumer goods—all the pretty gadgets that are polluting the planet in their operation or their manufacture? This is the problem with our so-called democracies. They have to pander all the time to the will of the people, as if the will of the people were something noble, or even sensible. Can't you see that experience has shown time and time again that the *will of the people* is just another way of saying *mass stupidity*?" Once again he didn't wait for an answer. Instead he asked another question. "Em, what do you think is actually causing global warming?"

Em blinked. "What you just said. Greenhouse gas emissions."

"That's only a symptom. The actual cause is the population explosion. There are too many people on the planet—far too many. Em, you and I produce a liter of methane from our backsides every day. So, on average, does everyone on the planet. That's 6,866,000,000 people. Methane is a greenhouse gas. We're pumping nearly seven billion liters of it into the atmosphere *every day* just by digesting our food! Two trillion five hundred and fifty-five billion liters a year."

"But—" Em protested, without quite knowing what he was going to protest about.

As it happened, his father gave him no chance. "World population is increasing exponentially. Eventually it will reach unsustainable levels. The result will be worldwide famine and misery. Believe me, Em, humanity doesn't have a whole host of problems, as most people believe. It has one single problem from which all else follows: overpopulation." He stood up. "Democracy will never, can never, tackle that problem. You're too young to remember when China introduced a single-child policy to curb its own population. The whole Western world was up in arms, accusing them of infringing on individual liberties. As if individual liberty didn't simply amount to

'Me first and to hell with everybody else.' The Knights are the only people on the planet with the power and the will to do anything about these problems!"

"But you don't have to *kill* people!" Em exploded. "You don't have to *murder* a whole generation."

"What solution would you propose?" his father asked quietly.

Em stared at him blankly. Solving the world's problems wasn't something he had time for right now. Em glanced at his watch. To his horror, he discovered he'd already spent twenty minutes in this office—five longer than the deadline Victor had given him. Em forced himself to stay calm. He'd already decided that if he couldn't talk his father around about evacuation, his next move had to be to persuade his dad to leave the building with him, thus saving both of their lives. But that was a last resort. Before then he had to make one last try.

He saw the flash, like a nearby lightning strike, then, a heartbeat later, the window blew violently inward, carrying a shower of burning debris. Em's father, who was nearest, was lifted off his feet and flung directly across the desk like a sack of potatoes. His head met the leg of a wooden chair with a resounding crack. Em was struck in the chest by a giant fist and careened backward, gasping for breath, to strike the half-open door.

His legs failed him, and he slid to the floor with a single thought cascading through his mind. *Too late ... too late ... too late ... too late ...*

After that he must have passed out briefly, for he opened his eyes to confusion and smoke against a background of flickering flames in both the office and the penthouse suite. The fire had not taken full hold yet, but it was too far gone for him to put it out on his own. Through the window he could see that the neighboring building was on fire as well; and the storage tank between them had disappeared, leaving a bomb crater in its wake. It seemed that one of Section 7's charges had gone off, exploding the petrochemical tank; but so far there was no indication of the rolling explosions Victor had forecast, nor the firestorm.

Em caught a lungful of smoke and began to cough violently. He dragged a handkerchief from his trouser pocket and held it to his mouth. It helped, but not a lot. He looked around with streaming eyes and discovered the body of his father huddled near the desk.

Em pushed himself painfully to his feet. The smoke was thicker the farther he got from the floor, and his coughing worsened. The thought occurred to him that smoke could kill you—hadn't he read somewhere that more people in fires died from smoke inhalation than were burned to death?—but what option did he have? That was his father there, his father who'd believed there were too many people in the world. Now there was one less, because there was blood oozing from his father's head, and he wasn't breathing.

You made a mistake about his death last time, a small voice whispered in Em's head.

He staggered across the floor and knelt beside the body. Carefully he placed two fingers on the side of his father's neck (the old billiard ball trick wouldn't stop a pulse there) and felt the heartbeat at once, weak but regular. Em shook him, and his father groaned.

"Got to get you out of here," Em murmured. There was the *woomph* sound of a small explosion behind him, and he glanced back to discover that a sofa in the penthouse was now burning fiercely. It would not be long before the whole suite was engulfed. He shook his father again. "Can you hear me?" he shouted urgently into his ear.

His father groaned again, louder this time, then said quite distinctly, "Hit my head."

"Can you get up, Dad?"

"What for?"

Em almost smiled. "The place is—" He stopped abruptly. He'd been about to say "The place is on fire" when another thought struck him. Instead he said, "You have to order the evacuation, Dad. The bombs have started going off."

His father lay where he was. His eyes were open but glazed. In the main living area of the penthouse, soft furnishings had caught fire and were blazing fiercely. Em was painfully aware that if they were to get out, they would have to pass through this area. At the moment it was possible, but given the rate the fire was spreading, it would not be possible for long. He turned back and slid his arm underneath his father's shoulder. "Stand up,

Dad. You have to stand up."

His father made an effort, drawing one extended foot beneath his body and pushing down with both arms. Em tugged on his shoulder, marveling at how heavy he felt for such a slightly built man. "Come on," Em urged. "You can do it, Dad!"

Professor Goverton clasped the edge of his desk and made a gargantuan effort. Em shoved fiercely, and together they got his father to his feet. "The microphone," Em gasped. Another waft of smoke filled his lungs, and he dissolved into a further fit of coughing. When he recovered, he asked, "Can you use the microphone?"

His father was trembling, but at least so far he seemed to be immune to the effects of the smoke. He swallowed and said distinctly, "Yes."

"You have to order an evacuation," Em urged him. "The explosions—" He began to cough again and this time could not stop. After a moment he bent double and managed to clear his lungs. "Do it now," he gasped. Maybe it was the smoke, but a horrible feeling had crept over him that he was leaving it too late: by insisting that his father take time to order the evacuation, he was condemning them both to death. The building was well and truly alight now. There was every chance that if they left it even a minute longer, the flames would cut off their escape.

But what option did Em have? The other charges were bound to go off any second now. The people had to be warned. "Come on, Dad; do it for me. You know it's the right thing. You *must* know it's the right thing!"

Something changed in his father's face. He leaned over the desk and reached for the microphone. Em wanted to believe his father did know it was the right thing but had no real idea what was going on in his mind.

But his father *did* know what he was doing. He pressed a button on the control panel, then typed in some numbers, presumably an access code. "Tell them to get out fast!" Em urged unnecessarily. He glanced behind him to discover that a wall of flame had almost cut off the doorway.

"Evacuation Code Five Eight," his father said into the microphone. He coughed smoke, but only for a moment, then said, "Authorization IGM 1." Then he slumped forward across the desk, sending the mike crashing to the floor with a sweep of one arm.

"Is that it?" Em leaped forward. It could be an emergency evacuation code, but his father hadn't mentioned fire or explosions or danger, and Em couldn't be sure. Except that being sure hardly mattered now, because his father was unconscious again, and Em knew he had seconds left at most to get them out of here. He pulled his father's free arm around his shoulder and tugged him upright. "Come on, Dad. We have to get out of here!"

Professor Goverton was not a big man. But he was swimming in and out of consciousness so that Em had to half drag him away from the desk and toward the door. The fire was blocking their way completely now, but Em did not hesitate, could not hesitate. His father's head was hanging down. Em used his free arm to cover his own eyes and dragged them both directly through the wall of flame. The gamble paid off, and they emerged on the other side with nothing worse than a smell of singed hair. But the respite was momentary. He could see at once that almost the entire penthouse was engulfed now. Heavy smoke obscured the far wall, but he thought he remembered where the door was. Whether he could find a clear path to it was another matter. His father seemed to have passed out again and turned into a dead weight. Em wasn't at all sure he could carry him much farther.

He managed half a dozen steps before his father came to again. "Bloody Section!" he screamed, and jerked himself out of Em's grip.

"Dad!" Em shouted. "Wrong way! The door's—"

There was a resounding *crack* above their heads. His father tripped and fell, sprawling heavily on the carpeted floor. "Dad!" Em screamed again, and launched himself toward him. There was a rushing sound and an avalanche of sparks and flame as the roof collapsed. Something caught Em with incredible violence across the side of his face.

Then the fire went out and there was only darkness.

49

The darkness lasted an eternity, but a time came at last when Em slowly swam upward. "What happened?" he asked. His voice sounded far away; and he had no idea where he was, except that there was no smoke, no flames. He was on his back, and his overall impression was of whiteness. It occurred to him that he might be looking at a ceiling.

"You're safe now," said a familiar voice.

"Mmmm," Em said. He knew he was safe, needed no reassurance; but he could not place the voice, which was annoying. He remembered fire and smoke as if he'd been in a burning building. He remembered an important microphone, but not why it was important. The side of his head ached badly, and he was unable to open one eye.

Victor's face swam into view. Then Charlotte's, then

Em's mother's. They were standing together by the side of his bed. At the sight of them, a cascade of memories came crashing back. "How did I get out?" he asked quietly.

"I dragged you," Victor said. "Had to break down the door to get in."

So Victor had braved the fire to rescue him. "How's Dad?"

There was one of those long, silent pauses that told you everything you needed to know. That, and the frozen looks on their faces. All the same, he had to hear it. He could have aimed his question at his mother, or Charlotte, but he chose to ask Victor. "Will you tell me?"

"He didn't make it," Victor said finally.

"Dead?" Em asked, just to be certain.

"Yes," Victor said, then paused before adding, "he ordered the evacuation."

"I know." That bit Em remembered clearly.

Nobody seemed particularly anxious to talk. After a while Em said, "Where am I?"

"Clinic in Nogales," Victor told him. "It's very well equipped. Section made the arrangements."

He must have been unconscious for at least an hour to allow them time to get him to Nogales. He reached up cautiously to touch his aching face and found it had been bandaged. "How long have I been here?"

"Eleven days."

"Eleven days?!" Em struggled to sit up.

"You're not supposed to move, darling," his mother

said anxiously, speaking for the first time.

"You've been in a coma," Victor told him. "The doctors induced it because there was some brain swelling. I'm sorry about your father. I had to choose between you and him, but I think it was too late for him anyway."

They couldn't have delayed a funeral, not in this heat. "Then Dad's . . . ?"

The others left that to Victor as well. "Gone."

Again, Em thought, and was seized by a ghastly urge to giggle. Instead, he licked dry lips and tasted antiseptic on the bandage at one side of his mouth. To Victor he said, "I want to know what happened. Did you set your charges off early?"

Victor shook his head. "It was an accident. A faulty timer. We could never have foreseen it."

"So Dad needn't have died?" Even as he said it, Em thought about his father's refusal to evacuate the compound. Maybe Em hadn't persuaded him that it was the right thing to do. Maybe he'd only agreed when he thought it was too late. Before Victor could answer his question, he asked another. "Was the compound evacuated?"

"Mostly," Victor said.

"What about your other charges?"

"They exploded as planned. Vaccine stocks and manufacturing facilities were destroyed."

Em voiced something that had been on his mind for a while. "The Knights will only rebuild. They'll do it all again."

Victor shook his head. "Perhaps not. There was internal disagreement about your father's policies—more than we realized. Now that he's gone . . ." He shrugged. "But if they do try again—mass murder or any other nasty scheme—we'll be ready."

Em sank back in the bed and closed his eyes. "At least next time I won't be involved." He felt a warm touch and opened his eyes again to find that Charlotte was standing beside the bed and had taken his hand. She smiled down at him, and there was something in her eyes that seemed . . . mischievous, as if she was harboring a secret.

Victor coughed. "Well, you never know where life may lead you," he said mysteriously.

They'd been plotting something, Em thought suddenly, and wondered if it had to do with Section 7. He closed his eyes again as his own words floated back to him: *At least next time I won't be involved.*

Maybe he'd spoken just a bit too soon.

DATE DUE